"Harlow is a delight. . . . There's something a bit magical about this series. Ms. Bourbon has taken a premise, characters, and a setting that may not have worked with anyone else at the keyboard, and created a fab-tastic series." —Once Upon a Romance

"A fun book, with the wide assortment of characters filling the page." —Fresh Fiction

"The perfect blend of dressmaking and intrigue."
—Sew Daily

Pleating for Mercy

"Enchanting! Prepare to be spellbound from page one by this well-written and deftly plotted cozy. It's charming, clever, and completely captivating! Fantasy, fashion, and foul play—all sewn together by a wise and witty heroine you'll instantly want as a best friend. Loved it!"
—Hank Phillippi Ryan, Agatha, Anthony and Macavity award–winning author

"Melissa Bourbon's new series will keep you on pins and needles."
—Mary Kennedy, author of the Talk Radio Mysteries

"Cozy couture! Harlow Jane Cassidy is a tailor-made amateur sleuth. Bourbon stitches together a seamless mystery, adorned with magic, whimsy, and small-town Texas charm."
—Wendy Lyn Watson, author of the Mystery à la Mode series

Also by Melissa Bourbon

A Killing Notion

A MAGICAL DRESSMAKING MYSTERY

Melissa Bourbon

AN OBSIDIAN MYSTERY

OBSIDIAN
Published by the Penguin Group
Penguin Group (USA) LLC, 375 Hudson Street,
New York, New York 10014

USA | Canada | UK | Ireland | Australia | New Zealand | India | South Africa | China
penguin.com
A Penguin Random House Company

First published by Obsidian, an imprint of New American Library,
a division of Penguin Group (USA) LLC

First Printing, April 2014

ISBN 978-0-451-41720-6

Printed in the United States of America
10 9 8 7 6 5 4 3 2 1

PUBLISHER'S NOTE
This is a work of fiction. Names, characters, places, and incidents either are the
product of the author's imagination or are used fictitiously, and any resemblance
to actual persons, living or dead, business establishments, events, or locales is
entirely coincidental.
   The recipes contained in this book are to be followed exactly as written. The
publisher is not responsible for your specific health or allergy needs that may
require medical supervision. The publisher is not responsible for any adverse
reactions to the recipes contained in this book.

This book is dedicated to Debbie Johnson Stafford,
because sometimes friends become family,
and that's you, Coco. ;)

Cassidy Family Tree

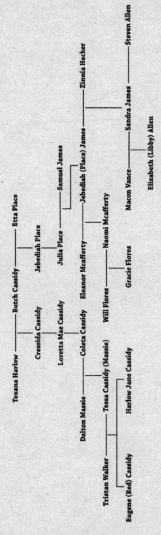

Chapter 1

Go big or go home. That had to be the philosophy of the people who spearheaded the Texas homecoming mum tradition. Big flowers made of ribbon, with trinkets and more ribbon, and even the occasional cowbell, to be worn by girls across Texas during homecoming week, were a sign of status in most Lone Star State schools. The grander, the better. There was no other logical explanation, and at this particular moment, I wanted those homecoming boosters strung up by their toes.

"Everything's bigger in Texas," I said aloud to the three people in my shop. Earl Grey, my little teacup pig, snorted before going back to rooting his way into a mound of fabric scraps I'd yet to bag up.

Mrs. Zinnia James stood framed beneath the French doors that separated the front room of Buttons & Bows, my custom dressmaking shop, from my workroom. Danica Edwards stood on the fitting platform I'd pulled out next to the cutting table, a length of black tulle draped over one shoulder. She was fairly new to Bliss, and she'd signed up to be part of the Helping Hands community outreach program, so along with a mum, I was also making her homecoming dress.

And so far, the visions I normally saw of people in outfits that would help them realize their wishes and dreams weren't materializing. A black dress, even though it was a flirty, intricately silver-beaded embroidery number with a waist belt and a sheer illusion neckline and tulle underlay, felt far too serious for a seventeen-year-old. I'd have to go back to the drawing board for her.

My grandmother, Coleta Cassidy, stood next to the open window in the workroom, cooing at Thelma Louise, the grand dam of her goat herd. Her Cassidy charm as a goat whisperer served her well. Every woman in my family had a magical gift, thanks to the wish my great-great-great-grandfather Butch Cassidy, had made in an Argentinian fountain. Nana communicated with her goats. My mother had a powerful green thumb. And my gift had to do with dressmaking.

"All this . . ." Mrs. James waved one arm around at the mum paraphernalia, the right side of her top lip curling up. "It's just absurd."

She'd sprayed and teased her silver hair to within an inch of its life in a very Texas do. As she shook her head, not a strand of her hair even budged. I had to grin. She'd always had a heavy hand with her makeup and an affinity for Botox and fillers, but still, her papery skin revealed a map of blue veins.

She was the wife of Senator Jebediah James, which made her the quintessential Texas blue blood, and she'd fight her age until her dying breath. With both barrels blazing, I'd heard her say on more than one occasion.

Still, even with all her effort, the evidence of her years was there. Her skin pulled tautly over the hardscape of her cheeks and jawbones, but the indentation of fine lines curved around both sides of her mouth and her eyes.

She looked like a slightly odd, cloned version of herself, and I sometimes thought that if I squinted my eyes, I'd get a glimpse of the real Zinnia James. But then I'd blink and she'd have that frozen-in-time look she wore like a mask. It had been more than a year since I'd been back in Bliss, but I still hadn't grown completely used to the mannequin look of my biggest fan, Mrs. James.

"It wasn't always like this," she remarked.

"No?" I peered at the mounds of ribbon heaped on the cutting table in the center of the room. I'd amassed yard upon yard upon yard of red, black, and white grosgrain, satin, organza, wire-edged, double ruffled, and ultrathin curly ribbon, all in the name of the homecoming mum. Some of the ribbon was emblazoned with the words BLISS BRONCOS, CHEERLEADING, RODEO, FOOTBALL, and other extracurricular activities our high school offered to their student body.

"Good heavens, no, not in our day," Mrs. James said. "Isn't that right, Coleta?"

My grandmother tugged her cap down as she shook her head, the two dancing goats that formed the logo of her Sundance Kids dairy farm doing a jig as she forced it back into place over her wavy hair. "Got that right." She pointed at me as if it were my fault and she was setting me straight. "Your granddaddy gave me a *real* chrysanthemum."

I flung the back of my hand to my forehead, letting

my mouth gape and my eyes widen. "What? No ribbons? No bows? No trinkets?" I said in my best Scarlett O'Hara drawl as I pointed to the pile of plastic adornments Bliss's teens wanted hanging from their mums.

Thelma Louise wrenched her lower jaw to one side, baring her teeth at me. Apparently she didn't like my sarcasm.

Nana lowered her chin. Neither did she. "That's right, ladybug." She waved her arm around. "None of this non-sense."

"A few ribbons," Mrs. James said.

"A few," Nana agreed. "You can't hardly count the three strands of ribbons we had back then to the million and one these girls wear today. Good Lord, I've heard people say they pay up to five hundred dollars for a mum. Five hundred dollars! That would buy a whole lot of grits and grain for my goats."

"And they were pinned to the bodice like a corsage," Mrs. James added, shaking her head. "Not like the mammoth mums today that need harnesses."

Danica stood on the fitting platform, riveted by the discussion. Nana leaned against the windowsill, crossing one white-socked foot over the other. "There aren't even any silk chrysanthemums on them anymore. Why they bother calling it a mum is a mystery."

Mrs. James and my grandmother had grown up together in Bliss, and had spent forty-some-odd years in a feud that had only recently ended. Now they were thick as thieves, their distaste over the state of the homecoming mum apparently fueling their camaraderie. "Why in heaven's name are you making them, anyway, Harlow?"

It was a good question, and one I'd wrestled with. The

bottom line was, I wasn't going to *stop* the madness, so I'd decided that I might as well join it. "The girls want them. They're going to buy them. If I don't make them, they'll get them from the mega craft store or the local florist. So why not me? With all the bad press the *Bliss Tribune* has laid at my doorstep after the *D Magazine* fiasco, I figured this might help turn things around."

"Murder does have a way of putting a damper on business, I imagine," Mrs. James said.

I spread my arms wide. "Which is why I've been doing a million and one Buttons and Bows do-it-yourself mum parties. It's like Pampered Chef home parties, only with crafts."

They all three stared at me. "So let me get this straight," Nana said, her eyes sweeping the array of mum materials in the workroom. "You've been hauling all this stuff to people's homes and helping them make their own mums?"

I pushed my glasses back into place, nodding. "That's exactly right. I made some of the foundations ahead of time with the backings and the ribbon flowers over these polyurethane bases I have—they'll support twenty or thirty pounds—"

Danica gasped, clasping her chest with both hands. The tulle dropped from her shoulder to the floor. "Is that how much they weigh?"

"Some are even more, and if you want the crown jewel—a double mum that sandwiches the body, front and back. I bought these dog harnesses to support the weight."

She hopped down to retrieve her lost tulle, tossing it over her shoulder. "That's crazy," she said, gliding back into place. "My mom never—" She stopped short, swallowing the grief that instantly seemed to bubble up. She hadn't talked much about her mom, and whenever she mentioned her in passing, the hole inside her seemed to open wider.

"It is crazy," I said. I hadn't even attended the homecoming dance, let alone had a mum, so to hear the words "double mum" and "harness" coming from my mouth felt foreign and absurd. But business was business, Texas was Texas, and the craziness of the tradition notwithstanding, the crafting part of the project was fun.

Mrs. James patted me on the shoulder. "My dear, you never cease to amaze. You get tossed a bushel of lemons; you turn around and make lemon bars. Buttons and Bows will be just fine, you'll see."

Danica shifted around nervously. "But you . . . you're making this for free," she finally said, gesturing toward the morose black tulle.

Mrs. James moved her attention from me to Danica. "My darling," she said, "Helping Hands is my special project. We have volunteers and the foundation pays for some services. Harlow's just fine.

"So while I don't adore the enormity of the mum, I do think every young woman should have a beautiful dress to wear to the homecoming dance. And if a girl wants a mum, she should have one."

"I don't have to have the mum—"

"Of course you're having a mum," I said. "We're going to make it together as a group. Don't you worry about a thing. Just think of yourself as Cinderella, and we're your fairy godmothers."

Mrs. James handed Danica an oversized notecard. "I need you to fill this out with your address, any dietary preferences, and such."

Danica arched a brow in question.

"It's for the Helping Hands brunch the day of the dance."

Danica obliged, carefully writing the information and handing the card back to Mrs. James, and then stepping back onto the fitting platform.

Mrs. James tucked the card into her purse. "Thank you, darlin'. And thank you for letting me put a little more light in your life."

Danica smiled shyly, gazing down at the platform and brushing back her black hair to reveal earbuds tucked in her ears. So she was like every other teenager, listening to her music twenty-four seven. I wondered what her natural hair color was. A lighter brown, judging from how pale her skin was, but she died it raven black, emphasizing her fair complexion. "I don't know how to thank you."

Mrs. James gave her hand a squeeze. "You just have fun at the dance and look gorgeous. That's all the thanks I need."

"And don't turn into a pumpkin," Nana added with a chortle.

Mrs. James and Nana ambled into the kitchen, leaving Danica and me alone with our dress design. I looked long and hard at her, from her straight black hair to her wide shoulders and hips, to the trim indentation of her waist. Rather than stick thin, she was curvy in a way that reminded me of Jessica Rabbit, but so far, whenever I'd seen her, both here and at Villa Farina, the bakery where she worked part-time, her body was hidden under baggy tops and jackets.

"The black's not going to work," I said, tapping my finger against my lips. I was also making a dress for another Helping Hands girl, Leslie Downs. Hers, I already had clear in my mind. It had been easy: I'd looked at her and seen the exact dress, just like that.

It was a sapphire blue floor-sweeping semisheer tiered overlay with an explosion of confetti-colored sequin fabric as the main skirt and bodice. The strapless bandeau neckline, an A-line silhouette, a high-low hem, coming to the fingertips in front and sweeping the floor in back, would all set off her ebony skin beautifully. An updo for her hair, high-heeled black sandals, and she'd be a standout at the dance.

But Danica . . . She was a different story, and with her design, I was less confident. I'd had a vision of the short, flirty black dress I'd been planning, but it wasn't quite right. Everything around me faded away as I looked at her. Her blue eyes and pale skin reminded me of Emma Stone, but her black hair, heavy black boots, and patterned black stockings paired with a lacy black skirt gave her a hard look. Mostly, though, there was an underlying sadness to her. Completely understandable, given the fact that she'd been in foster care and now, at nearly eighteen, was finishing high school and would be living on her own soon. Not the way most teenagers envisioned their lives turning out.

I pulled the tulle away from her and wound it up in a haphazard ball. "Danica, I want to play a little game with you."

She took out her earbuds, turned off her music, and tucked it all away in her pocket, lifting her gaze and looking at me through her long, spidery eyelashes. "Okay?" she said, more like a question than acquiescence. "What kind of game?"

"Word association."

She pulled her lips in thoughtfully until they disappeared. "Okay," she said again. "Why?"

"I can't quite get a picture in my head of the right dress." Apparently my charm was failing me, but I couldn't tell her that. "This will help me get to know you better. I'll sketch tonight, and show you some ideas tomorrow. I want your input on this."

She batted her eyelashes, whisking away the thin layer of moisture glazing her eyes. I wished I knew her background. Had her relationship with her parents been okay, or strained? What about her foster family? Had they wanted her? Shown her love?

More than ever, I wanted to give Danica a Cinderella night at the dance.

"Let's give it a try," I said.

She nodded as I fired off my first word. "Homecoming."

"Parade," she said. No hesitation. So she liked the festivities.

"Monday."

"Day off."

"Saturday."

"Car shows."

"Sunday."

"Church."

So far, so good. Her answers didn't give me any insight to her psyche, but she was talking, so I was hopeful.

"Car."

"My dad," she said quietly. She wasn't with her dad anymore, but that's all I really knew. Now didn't feel like the right time to push for more information, so I moved on.

"High school."

"Torture."

I left that one alone. "Mums."

"Status."

Danica's perspective on school reflected her situation, namely that she was alone in the world. The next set of words that came to my mind were family, home, and vacation. Having her respond to them could give me more insight to her, but on the other hand, thinking about what she didn't have could drive her deeper into herself. I waffled back and forth, but finally made up my mind. If I had cancer or my husband—if I had a husband—had cheated, I wouldn't want my friends or the people I ran into to cower and pretend like my reality didn't exist. My grandmother, Loretta Mae—and all the Cassidy women, for that matter—had taught me to face adversity head-on. No pussyfooting around.

I decided Danica deserved the same honesty.

"Family," I said, but I held my breath.

Her lip twitched almost imperceptibly and she closed her eyes in a slow, sad blink. "The people you choose," she said softly, and once again, my heart went out to her.

She'd lost her family, so from here on out, the people she peppered her life with would be those she hand-picked.

As I patted her arm and rattled off the next word—home—the front door opened, the strand of bells hanging from the inside of the front door jingling.

"Deceitful—" Danica said, stopping short when she saw Gracie Flores and her boyfriend, Shane Montgomery, tumble in, laughing. Gracie and Shane couldn't have heard what she'd said, nor would they know what she'd been talking about, but still, she looked as if she'd been caught sneaking cookies at midnight.

Gracie and Shane stopped just inside the door, Gracie's eyes growing wide and excited as she took in the trims and mum accessories. A shimmering trail of diffused light circled inside the house like the tail of a shooting star. It was the ghost of Meemaw, my grandmother Loretta Mae. Gracie's mouth drew into an O, her gaze following the glittery stream, but no one else seemed to pick up on Meemaw's presence.

She knocked the back of her hand against Shane's arm, grinning up at him. "It's like an enchanted land," she said.

He raised his eyebrows and I got the impression that Buttons & Bows was nothing like any enchanted land he'd want to spend time in, but then he nodded and pulled her forward. "This is, like, the total opposite of Bubba's."

Shane's family owned Bubba's Auto Repair, and Shane worked there part time. I'd taken Buttercup, my old Ford pickup truck, there for service plenty of times. *Growing up with a dad who works on cars means I work on cars*, he'd told Gracie. She'd added that he made good money. "Enough so we can go out on real dates."

Two teenagers couldn't ask for more than that.

Danica stepped down from the fitting platform as Gracie and Shane came into the workroom. "Hey," Gracie said.

Danica dropped her gaze shyly, but threw up her hand in a quick wave. "Should I come back tomorrow?" she asked me.

"Perfect, yes. Thanks for playing along. I'll work up some sketches, and you can tell me what you like and what you don't."

"I've never had a dress like this, Ms. Cassidy. My dad died and my mother, she couldn't afford it —"

She paused, her voice heavy with sorrow. This was the most she'd said about her parents. It wasn't much, but it was a start. "I'm happy to do it, darlin'," I said, ushering her toward the front door.

The fact that I'd used a Southern endearment wasn't lost on me. The more time I spent back home in Bliss, the more my Southern roots took hold of me again. Sure, I was a Texan first and foremost, but like most of the folks I knew, unless they were from the border, I also felt Southern. Downhome accents and shared idioms could do that for people.

By the time I'd been twenty-four and living in New York, I'd all but ditched my accent, but it wasn't long before I'd had a big realization. You could take the girl out of the small town, but you couldn't ever take the small town out of the girl.

Now I was thirty-three, back home in Bliss, and before long, I'd sound just like my mama, dropping every G and saying *might could* and *right quick*.

"See you at the bakery," Mrs. James called, coming out from the kitchen.

Danica draped a Bliss High letterman jacket over her arm, smiled, and waved to her. "Yes, ma'am. Skinny hazelnut latte —"

"And an Italian cream puff." Mrs. James touched her mouth as if she could taste the sweet cream on her lips.

"Good grief," Nana said, following her. "Pastries will clog your arteries. But a good smearing of persimmon chèvre on a thin slice of French bread? That's a treat worth havin'."

The bells on the door tinkled again as I shut it behind Danica. A minute later, her car revved and she was gone.

I went back to the workroom to get ready for Leslie's consultation, which I knew would go more smoothly than Danica's had. I pulled out the sapphire jacquard and the confetti-sequined fabric for the underskirt, setting it on the worktable. I already had my sketches for her dress, so I was good to go.

Gracie bopped up and down on her toes, looking like a child at her first rodeo who was trying desperately—and unsuccessfully—to stay cool and calm. She snuck a glance at Shane, who looked a bit stricken by the array of colorful ribbon assortments, small stuffed bears in cheerleading outfits, and cowbells.

But to his credit, he seemed to sense her excitement and put a grin on his face. "Go big or go home," he said. My exact sentiment just a little while ago.

It was all the encouragement Gracie needed. She went from toe-bopping to full-on bouncing, moving around the worktable and picking up different adornments. "I don't want a teddy bear," she said after a minute, referring to the center focal piece of the mum.

"Not even a bear holding a pair of sewing scissors?" he asked.

Wow, I was impressed. He knew Gracie and her passion for sewing—and respected it. That was pretty major for a fifteen-year-old girl and her sixteen-year-old new boyfriend.

But the moment was lost on Gracie. She just shook her head and said, "No. Something besides a teddy bear, for sure." Miniature bears were traditional, and while Gracie wanted a mum, I knew she was going to do it her own way. I could see her wanting squares of colorful fabric, an honest-to-goodness pair of Ginghers, or a rolled-up measuring tape.

He ran his hand through his hair, making it stand on end. The dark blond color set off his tanned skin. Gracie, on the other hand, had a beautiful olive complexion, courtesy of her father, Will. Shane and Gracie fit together, both sun-kissed and fresh-faced, clearly smitten, without a care in the world. "I guess we'll figure it out," he said.

"I'll make it," I volunteered. "You don't have to worry about a thing."

"Oh, but I want to help," Gracie said. "Can I?"

"Absolutely. Darlin', you and I are going to have a mum-making party," I said, just as Leslie, my second Helping Hands student, and another girl, came in the front door of the shop.

Leslie's brown doe eyes opened wide. "Where you, like, get together and everybody makes their mums?"

"Awesome," the second girl said.

"Everyone," Leslie said, gesturing to her friend, "this is Carrie. She's pretty new to Bliss. Carrie, this is everyone."

Carrie smiled, a faint dimple marking her cheek, and waved. She immediately headed across the room to look at the prêt-à-porter.

"Do you have one yet?" I asked Leslie.

She shook her head.

"Then you can come and help make yours." The more, the merrier. "You, too, if you like," I said to Carrie.

"I have mine," she said. "But thanks."

But Leslie's eyes grew even wider. "I get a mum?" Her gaze slid to Shane for the briefest second. "But I don't have a boyfriend," she said, her voice dropping.

"You don't need a boyfriend to wear a mum," Gracie said. "You just need a mum."

Leslie looked at Gracie, then at Shane, as if she were trying to decide if this were true. "It's the twenty-first century," I said. "You can give yourself a mum if you want to."

Leslie relaxed, but her shoulders lifted and her chest rose and fell with her excitement. "Then I want the biggest mum at Bliss High! I want to show those girls who . . . who—"

She broke off, once again looking at Gracie and Shane, her attention focusing on Shane for an extra few seconds.

"Those girls who what?" I asked.

She rooted her feet to the ground and raised her chin slightly. "I want the shy girls and the geeky girls and the girls like me to believe in themselves," she said. "I want them to hear what you just said. That this is the twenty-first century and we can give ourselves mums."

I smiled at her, part of me wanting to applaud her confidence. She and Danica both came from foster homes, but they seemed to handle things so differently. Danica was quiet. Removed. Almost injured. But Leslie was bent on proving that she was as good as everyone else. If proving that was what she wanted, the dress I was going to make her would help her get there.

This was the second time I'd met Leslie, and when I closed my eyes, I still saw her in the sapphire confetti dress. The vibrant colors matched her vibrant personality. Carrie was in the love seat studying my lookbook, which was perfect. It gave us time to work.

"Come here, Leslie. I want to show you the sketches I came up with." I flipped open my sketchbook, turning to the pages where I'd drawn variations of the dress I envisioned for her.

She looked at the sketches, glanced in the freestanding oval mirror in the corner, and a slow smile lit her chocolate brown face, a rosy glow dusting her cheeks. "I love it!"

I hadn't realized I'd been holding air in my lungs, but now I breathed out, relieved. There was always a moment of apprehension when whomever I was designing for saw my ideas for the first time. What I visualized and what they thought they wanted didn't always mesh. But in this instance, Leslie saw my vision. And she liked it.

Shane's cell phone rang as I showed Leslie the fabric choices I'd come up with. He stepped back into the front room to answer it. Ten seconds later, the sound of his guttural cry sent a chill down my spine.

Gracie ran to the front, stopping short when she saw Shane's face. His cheeks had gone ruddy, his eyes glassy. His jaw pulsed, hollowing out his cheeks and giving him a drawn, angry look.

"What's wrong?" she asked, holding back as if she were afraid he might explode.

He shoved his phone back into his back pocket, looking shell-shocked. "This can't be happening," he said. He wheeled around, pacing the room, weaving in and out of the paisley love seat, couch, and red settee. His hand tore through his hair, pulling angrily at it until it stood straight up.

Gracie took a step backward, her lips trembling.

I squeezed her hand as I scooted past her. Leslie came up next to her, looking more curious than anything else. Mrs. James and Nana had wandered out from the kitchen, and Carrie sat forward on the love seat.

"Shane?" I said sternly, trying to break through to him. "What happened?"

He abruptly stopped his pacing, digging all ten of his fingers through his hair. "There was a car accident," he said. His chin quivered and he struggled to get the rest of the words out. "My dad . . . my dad was in an accident. He's . . . he's dead."

Chapter 2

"Poor Shane," I said, handing Will Flores another dish to dry. We'd spent our dinner talking about the car accident, Gracie's boyfriend, and how Shane would handle having lost his father.

"It's a tragedy," he said, and from the tone of his voice, I knew part of him was wondering how Gracie would manage if something ever happened to him.

We processed for a few more minutes, and then Will did a complete about-face on our topic of conversation. First, he moved to the archway between the dining area and the kitchen of 2112 Mockingbird Lane, his arms folded over his chest, a cream-colored straw cowboy hat on his head. He looked like a cross between Toby Keith with his bandanna-biker look, and Tim McGraw, goateed and lean. Only with a deep olive complexion. "When things have settled down, let's do a weekend getaway, Cassidy. You. Me. The hill country."

I stared at him. "What?"

"The place is called Biscuit Hill. A bed-and-breakfast. You're going to love it."

I pushed aside my sorrow for Shane as much as I was able to and asked the first thing that came to my mind. "Do they have homemade scones?" After all, no bed-and-breakfast would be complete without sweet biscuits, British style.

"I'm sure they do."

"With Devon cream? If you're going to have scones, you have to have clotted cream to go with them. Or lemon curd. Lemon curd could work, too."

He stifled a grin. "I'll call and make a special request for lemon curd and cl—?"

"Clotted cream," I repeated.

He pushed off the wall and ambled over to the sink where I'd been rinsing our dinner dishes.

"Supper was good," he said, taking up the dish towel and drying my hands.

"Secret recipe," I said. We'd grown easy with each other since I'd moved back home to Bliss and Meemaw had done her matchmaking from beyond the grave. Dinner together a few times a week, a shared teacup pig that Will and Gracie had given me for Christmas, and even comfortable silence when I was working on a project and Will was drawing sketches to restore an historic building in Bliss on my sofa all got me thinking more and more how we belonged together.

"Biscuit Hill sounds lovely. But being alone with you for the weekend," I said with a wink, "sounds even better."

He tossed the dish towel on the counter beside me,

and then he placed his arms on either side of me, moving in close and lowering his lips to mine. I started to wrap my arms around his neck, but stopped as the bells in the front room jingled, announcing someone's arrival.

"Dad! Harlow!" Gracie's voice bellowed, echoing in through the rooms as if she were shouting into a megaphone.

"In the kitchen," Will said, pulling away from me and dropping his arms to his sides. The warmth that had seeped in between us chilled. It was more than just the space created when Will stepped back. Meemaw, I knew, was reacting to something.

The second I saw Gracie's face, I knew she was the reason for the chilled, tense air. Will and I moved forward at the same time. "What's wrong?" I asked as Will clutched her shoulders and said, "What happened, are you okay?"

She half nodded, half shook her head. "It's Shane," she said, breaking down into a sob.

Will's spine stiffened and he went into what I was beginning to recognize as full protective mode. "If he hurt you—"

"Daddy, no. He didn't. He wouldn't!"

"What is it, Gracie?" I asked. Her anxiety flooded the room, weighing down the air and pressing down on us.

"The sheriff said they think someone tampered with Mr. Montgomery's car, and . . . and . . . and they think maybe it was Shane." Her voice rose an octave, nearing hysteria. "Just because he works at Bubba's, they say he'd know how. They think he might could have *caused* the accident that killed his dad. Like he might have tried to kill him!"

Will and I both stared at Gracie. Death wasn't a mystery to either one of us. We'd each seen our share, and helped solve a mystery or two right here in Bliss. But Gracie's young boyfriend being accused of murdering his father? That was too close to home.

"Harlow," she said, dragging the back of her hand under her nose. "You have to help him."

I opened my mouth to speak, but Will rolled his eyes and jumped in with a quick, "Whoa, Harlow may like poking her nose where it doesn't belong, but I'm sure the sheriff has it well under control." He held his hands out to her, palm first, the message clear. Simmer down and knock that thought right out of her head.

Her mouth dropped open and her head jutted forward. "But they don't, not if they think Shane had anything to do with it. Daddy, he couldn't possibly kill anybody. He just couldn't!"

Will's jaw pulsed and his eyes narrowed. He looked like a panther ready to strike, and I was grateful Shane wasn't anywhere near Buttons & Bows, because he'd get the brunt of that attack. "I hope not," he muttered.

"Innocent until proven guilty," I said to him under my breath, stepping closer and putting my hand on his arm to simmer him down.

"He's innocent," Gracie said again, but this time, instead of looking at her dad, she looked at me. Tears pooled in her eyes and her lower lip quivered again. She was barely holding it together.

"I'm sure he is, darlin'," I said, taking her hand. "The sheriff"—who just also happened to be my new stepdaddy—"is a fair man. He's got to look at all sides of a situation before he can know what happened."

"What about his son? The deputy. You don't like him much, Harlow. What if he thinks Shane's guilty?"

"I like Gavin McClaine just fine," I said. More, even, since he was carrying on a real, albeit long-distance, relationship with my good friend Orphie Cates. The deputy sheriff had grown up with a chip on his shoulder, but love at first sight with Orphie had dug away at it. His attitude could still stick in my craw, but not quite as often as before. "But more important than that, he's good at his job. He and Hoss both believe in justice. They're not going to do anything that would falsely imprison an innocent person."

I hadn't really thought about it so succinctly before, but now that the words had left my mouth, I knew it was true. The McClaine men were good, God-fearing, honest people, and both of them would fight for the truth.

Gracie didn't look like she believed me, though. I gave her hand another squeeze. "Let them do their jobs," I said. "You just be a friend to Shane right now. He's going to need that more than anything."

"So you can't help him?"

I sighed, pulling her into a hug. "Darlin', I'll keep my ears open, okay? If Shane's innocent—"

"If? He *is* innocent!"

She tried to pull away, but I held her like I would have held my own daughter, rubbing her back. "Then the sheriff'll figure that out and find out what really happened to Shane's dad. You have to let it be."

"Let it be." She repeated it like a mantra, her breath calming. Her heartbeat settled down to a more steady rhythm and I let her go. She stepped back, her eyes red-rimmed, but dry. "He's innocent," she said, her voice calm and full of conviction.

"I'm sure he is," I said, but from the pulsing of Will's jaw and the tightness of his eyes, I wasn't so sure Will agreed.

Chapter 3

At least half the population of Bliss was in attendance at Christopher Montgomery's funeral. It had been a closed casket, which was disturbing since that most likely meant his remains weren't in good condition. I'd looked for an enlarged photo of Mr. Montgomery on an easel or a framed image on the table with the guest book, but there hadn't been one. "It was a request in his will," someone had said. "He wanted everyone to remember him in their own way, not from some snapshot or staged image."

The turnout was either a testament to the impact he'd had on so many people's lives . . . or it was proof that the people in our small town couldn't resist the pull of morbid curiosity. Word had circulated pretty quickly about Shane being a suspect in his father's death.

I wandered through the crowded living room, absorbing snippets of conversation, most in hushed, secretive tones.

"Such a shame. If only he didn't travel so much be-

tween here and Granbury, maybe it would have turned out differently."

"That poor Teagen, bless her heart. She's going to grow up without a father."

"Reba must be beside herself about Shane."

"How could he have done it?"

"You have to have a mountain of hatred to kill your father."

That was the truth, but Lord almighty, it seemed the people were ready to string Shane up before he was ever charged, let alone convicted.

Will sidled up to me, placing his hand on my lower back, as the newly widowed Reba Montgomery came up to us. "I want to thank you for coming, Harlow. Will." She clasped a hanky in one hand, dabbing at her eyes as the tears pooled. She was the spitting image of Reba McEntire, wavy locks of feathered red hair, crystal blue eyes framed with black eyeliner, shimmering dangly earrings, and a generous bust usually accented by a halter-style top. I'd heard her tell the story of her naming plenty of times. Her mama took one look at the shock of red hair she'd been born with and named her Reba right on the spot.

But right now her face was drawn, her cheekbones more hollow than normal, and her usual radiant smile was absent. The death of her husband had taken its toll on her, but in my mind's eye, I couldn't see her in anything but the smart, fitted suit she currently wore. To a lot of Southern women, as Miranda Lambert so aptly phrased it in "Mama's Broken Heart," it didn't matter how you felt, it only mattered how you looked. Miss Reba, as everyone called her, in all her ginger glory, took that sentiment to heart. She put her best into looking like a lady, and not even her own broken heart over her dead husband could change that.

"We're awfully sorry for your loss," I said, feeling like the sentiment was way too formal and didn't really convey how awfully sorry we really were. She wrung her hands, poor thing, trying to keep a brave face. She could only mask so much.

"I still can't believe it. Sometimes I think I'll wake up and find this is all a horrible nightmare."

I didn't know how to respond to that. Everything I thought of to say sounded cliché and vacant in my head. Being next to her, squeezing her hand was all I could do, and it seemed to bolster her.

"Us meeting was fate," she said, "and I don't even believe in fate. Or at least I didn't." She shook her head, her hair tumbling around her tired face. "The moment I laid eyes on him, I knew, and when he spoke, you know, I would have married him on the spot."

I had only met Chris Montgomery a few times, but I had to agree with Miss Reba that there'd been something about him, a quality that made people like him on the spot. He looked like George Clooney and had the charisma to boot.

"How did you meet?" I asked, sensing that she needed to talk about it.

She gave a melancholy smile. "He and Eddy Blake— his partner at Bubba's—had just started their store here in Bliss. The minute I walked in and saw him, I knew he was the one. He was a real spitfire. He serviced my car personally, and instead of charging me, he asked me out." She laughed halfheartedly, swiping at the tears falling from her eyes. "We went to the Porterhouse on Vine and had surf and turf, and then do you know what we did?"

"What?" I asked.

"He took me to Dairy Queen. Dairy Queen, can you believe that? But that just sealed the deal for me. I thought, if this guy can be comfortable at Dairy Queen *and* Porterhouse on Vine, he's some kind of man." Her voice hitched. "It became our tradition. We always went there on our anniversary. To Dairy Queen. Sort of a joke, you know?"

Will's hand against my lower back gave me strength to fight the tears welling in my eyes. Miss Reba had loved her husband, and I couldn't imagine her loss.

After a moment, she squared her shoulders. "I've heard people talkin', you know. About Shane," she added after Will and I looked at each other, and then back at her. "The sheriff came by even."

Oh Lord. Talking to the deputy sheriff about this subject was one thing, but hearing Reba's grief compounded by the rumors that her son had been involved? That was jumping from the frying pan into the fire. "No one believes it, Miss Reba," I said.

She turned abruptly to face the buffet table, grabbed a white ceramic plate, and began piling it up with food. A fried drumstick. A scoop of macaroni and cheese. A hunk of chicken-fried steak. Soupy baked beans. And a helping of peach cobbler. She had the big eye, or she just wasn't paying attention.

I snuck another raised-eyebrow look at Will, but before he could reply with his own facial gestures, Reba swung back toward me and thrust the overloaded plate at me. I took hold of it without thinking, but she didn't release her own grip. Instead, she tugged on it, pulling me closer, the sauce from the beans drenching the other food. "You have to help us, Harlow," she said, her voice cracking again.

I startled, letting go. "What?"

She stumbled back a step before catching herself, and then dropped her voice even lower. "You've done it before. Shane didn't do what people are saying. You have to help him, Harlow."

Criminy, why was I suddenly the go-to person in Bliss for private detective work? Will's hand snaked around my waist—his protective mode. At this rate, he was going to have me locked up to keep me out of it. "Miss Reba," he said. "You're upset. I'm sure Harlow understands, but you have to let the sheriff do his job."

But Miss Reba didn't want to hear that the sheriff had things under control. Her eyelids fluttered spastically before falling to half-mast. "He's my son," she said with a low hiss. "My *son*. They'll be accusing my daughter next, as if either one of them could have killed their father." She looked me in the eyes. "It doesn't make a lick of sense, Harlow. Shane didn't have anything to do with this."

"Mama," a girl said, sliding in to the space next to Miss Reba. Their ginger hair and the clear ice blue of their eyes were identical. She handed a black cell phone to her mother. "It's Mr. Blake's."

She stared at it for half a second before blinking and coming back to herself. "Thank you, love. Harlow, Will," she said to us. "My daughter, Teagen. Teagen, this is Mr. Flores. And this," she said, lifting her arm toward me, "is Harlow Cassidy, the dressmaker."

Harlow Cassidy, the dressmaker. The four words went together more often than not, these days. I was the only Harlow Cassidy, as far as I knew, so the clarification that I was the dressmaker seemed unnecessary. But not to the people of Bliss.

The girl looked a few years younger than Gracie, so I pegged her at around thirteen. She was heavy in the thighs and still had an adolescent softness around her middle.

"Buttons and Bows, right?" she asked me. I nodded, noticing how the red rims around her eyes emphasized the clear blue of her irises. She put on a brave face, though, just like her mother.

"Mama said we could come by your shop to look at your clothes," she said.

"You're welcome anytime, Teagen," I said, a sudden vision of her in low-rise jeans, a graphic tee, and a modified, embellished Army jacket. Puzzling, since none of these clothes were anything I designed. I'd thought my power was more specific, homing in on how the clothes I made helped a person's wishes and dreams come true. Apparently not.

I looked at Teagen again, the image of the same outfit popping into my mind for the second time. Definitely store-bought. But the jacket . . . it was embellished with strips of fabric, beads, and other adornments. I hadn't done a lot of that type of thing, but maybe . . . ?

"Did you see Mr. Blake?" Miss Reba asked Teagen. "My husband's business partner," she said as an aside to us.

"No. I just found the phone by Daddy's side of the bed."

Miss Reba looked alarmed, her eyes opening wide. "What were you doing in the bedroom? Teagen, you can't—"

"I miss him!" She swiped at the tears spilling from her eyes. "I thought I'd feel closer to him there."

Will squeezed my hand. I looked at him and he tilted his head, the message clear. We were intruding, so we should step away. My heart ached for Teagen, Shane, and Miss Reba, but Will was right. This was their private moment, Teagen's pain palpable, and we needed to leave them to their sorrow.

We inched away, but Miss Reba's chin lifted and her voice rang clear. "I really should find Mr. Blake."

She looked over her shoulder, searching the mourners.

I took that as a dismissal and started to walk away in earnest, but Miss Reba's hand shot out, her coral fingernails clawing the bishop sleeve of my blouse. "Harlow, I've heard about you," she said, her voice coming out in a hiss.

I gulped. "I'm sorry, Miss Reba, but what do mean?"

Instead of answering, she swung her gaze to Will. "Your girl, she cares about Shane."

"She does," Will said, looking none too happy about his baby girl caring for a kid some people thought capable of killing his father.

Miss Reba flicked her gaze back and forth between us. "She said you could help, Harlow. That you've figured out the truth before."

"Yes, but, Miss Reba, but that's different—"

"How is it different? Someone died and you helped find out who the killer was." She clasped her hands around mine and squeezed. "I want you to help Shane. Gracie said you could do it."

A low growl came from Will. He'd told Gracie not to get involved, and that he didn't want me involved, but she hadn't listened, and she'd convinced Miss Reba that I could help.

A hush came over the room and I spun to see Shane walking toward us, his head hung, shoulders hunched. The quiet turned to a low whisper. Inside, my blood pulsed. It seemed that people had already decided Shane was guilty. Maybe he was, but what if he wasn't? He'd lost his father, and until he'd been proven guilty, he was a victim here.

"He called me from the car, you know," Miss Reba said. "Told me to wait up for him, that he was taking care of something in Granbury, but that he'd be back and he wanted to talk." A sob caught in her throat, but she swallowed it, closing her eyes for a beat while she gathered her emotions up and tucked them away. "I told him I'd wait up for him, but he never came home, Harlow."

"I'll help," I said, the words coming before I could stop them—or even think about what helping would involve.

"Cassidy," Will said into my ear, a warning in his voice. "Don't get involved."

But Loretta Mae's voice was in my other ear saying, "Do what's right, darlin', and you'll have no regrets."

Shane walked right through the front room, not looking at his sister or his mother. He ignored the whispers and a moment later, he was out the door, the screen door banging closed behind him. No more laughter. No light in his eyes. No dreams of homecoming as he'd had a few days ago.

"I'll help," I said again, and this time I meant it one hundred percent.

"Is it true?" I asked, cornering Gavin McClaine a short while later. He wore his typical tan uniform, a sharp crease from a good iron running up the legs of his pants. Gavin was a stickler for keeping a shipshape uniform.

The deputy sheriff lifted his chin slightly as he scratched his scalp. "I reckon you want me to read your mind, is that right, Harlow? Because otherwise, I don't know what in tarnation you're talking about."

Will sauntered up next to me, two clear plastic cups in his hands. He gave me one and I took a sip of the ice-cold lemonade. September in Bliss meant the temperature still hovered just under the triple-digit mark. Another month and the humidity would be gone and cooler weather would settle in on the town, but for now, I fanned myself with one of the floral napkins Miss Reba had set out on the buffet table.

"I'm talking about the rumors going far and wide about Shane—" I broke off and peered around, making sure no one could overhear us as I'd just overheard them earlier. Lowering my voice, I continued. "I'm talking about the rumors that Shane had something to do with his father's death."

Gavin let a slow smile spread from cheek to cheek. "Harlow, did your stepdaddy deputize you when I was up in Missouri visiting Orphie?"

I bristled. "You know he didn't."

His smile grew even wider. "So then, I'm at a loss as

to why you're grillin' me about the Montgomery boy when that would be top secret police business."

"Top secret. *Pft.*" I glanced up at Will who, after a year now, had figured out the love-hate friendship Gavin and I danced around. We went way back to elementary school together, and now that we were both in our thirties, we'd come to a sort of peace with one another. The fact that his daddy had recently married my mother made us stepsiblings, something I had a hard time wrapping my brain around.

"She's worried about Gracie, that's all," Will said, "and she wants to make sure you're not going to lock Shane away without looking at the whole picture."

Gavin's smile was gone. He and Will were eye to eye, and while I knew that in a one-on-one challenge, Will would come out on top, Gavin looked mighty intense at the moment. "She's pokin' her nose into police business," Gavin said, speaking as if I weren't right there in front of him.

I jammed my hands on my hips. "Because I'm looking out for Gracie and Shane, and I don't want anyone accused of something they didn't do." And because Gracie and Miss Reba had both asked me, and I couldn't very well deny either one of them.

He swung his head to stare me down, looking more intense than I was used to seeing him. I'd gotten his dander up. "And you think I do?"

I could see why he was upset, but my self-appointed job was to protect Gracie. "Of course not, but I'm telling you, Shane's innocent."

"Because you said so, it must be true," he said, sarcasm dripping from the words.

"That's right." I had a sixth sense—my charm—but

that didn't help me determine if a person was innocent
or guilty. I had to listen to my gut, though, and it was
saying Shane didn't hurt his own father.

"You're a dressmaker, not a detective," he said, making it sound almost as if dressmaker was a dirty word.
"You leave the investigatin' to me, and I'll leave the
homecoming mums and dresses to you, sound good?"

I glared at him, my feathers officially ruffled. "No, that
does not sound good," I said, sounding more like a riled
up Meemaw than like my normal, even-keeled self.
"Gracie is one hundred percent positive that Shane
didn't have anything to do with what happened to his
dad, and I believe her, which means I believe him."

"Police work is based on more than a Cassidy gut in-
stinct," he shot back.

Will, bless his heart, had stood by watching and listening, not daring to leave me alone with Gavin, but not
wanting to get wrapped up in the middle of our argument, either. But Gavin was rubbing him wrong, too, because he piped up with, "Shane didn't have anything to
do with this, McClaine, and I'll tell you what. Harlow and
I will prove it to you."

Gavin seethed, the veins in his temples pulsing. "Oh
no, you won't," he snapped. "This is police business, and
you will both stay clear out of it."

His response warranted a good, solid stomping of my
foot followed by a resounding, "You're not the boss of
me!" But I was raised to have good manners, and that
type of outburst, even if it was deserved and felt down to
the marrow of a woman's bones, wasn't acceptable. "I
can't help it if people talk to me, Gavin," I said sweetly.

As if on cue, Reba Montgomery called my name from the buffet table. "Harlow, come on over here for another second, would you?"

And so I did—with a backward glance, Will by my side, and Gavin left to stare at our backsides.

Chapter 4

"You start by adding ribbon loops all the way around the edge of the cardboard base," I said, holding up the sample mum I'd created so the group of girls could see.

"So they're like the petals of the mum?" Danica asked.

"Exactly." I picked up a two-and-a-half-inch length of the red ribbon from the pile I'd precut, folded it with a little twist, and stapled it onto the cardboard.

Danica and Leslie, the two girls I was making homecoming dresses for, as well as Gracie and her best friend, Holly Kincaid, sat around the dining table, a circular piece of white cardboard in front of each of them. They each had a stapler and scissors, and piled in the center of the table were the black, white, and red ribbon pieces. Cutting them had been mindless work the night before, which I'd relished. I'd spent the time mulling over Chris Montgomery's death and how in tarnation I was going to help figure out what had happened.

So far, I hadn't come up with a plan. The sheriff and

deputy were running their own investigation, and I didn't have any information they didn't already know.

The four girls concentrated on ringing their mum backings with the ribbon loops. Danica was slow and precise, sucking in her lower lip, clamping her teeth down each time she stapled a red ribbon along the outer edge. She switched to black and created a second ring. She was slow and meticulous, and I could tell she was imagining just what her mum would look like when she was finished with it.

Leslie, on the other hand, worked quickly, picking up a length of ribbon, twisting, stapling, then doing another one—boom, boom, boom—alternating colors. Red, white, black, red, white, black. At the pace she was going, she would have two or more mums done, none of them looking like the other, by the time the others finished their first.

Holly worked at a steadier pace. She used black first, then white, with just a few red pieces for accent. The contrast and pop of color was vibrant. I turned to Gracie, and what I saw made me suck in a breath. Her loops were different sizes, some twisted at the top, others not, and there was no rhyme or reason to her color choices. No pattern.

I sat in the open chair next to her, putting my hand on her knee. "It's going to be okay, Gracie," I whispered so only she could hear.

Her eyes glazed with tears, her lower lip quivering. "I don't know why I'm making this," she said, her voice sounding as tortured as she looked. "He says I shouldn't go to homecoming with an accused murderer. He's not going to take me."

My heart broke for her. Just a few days ago, Shane Montgomery had been swinging Gracie around and hugging on her like any good sixteen-year-old boyfriend. Yesterday, after the funeral, he'd looked despondent. And now it seemed he'd moved on to anger, shutting out at least one of the people who cared about him. The thing I didn't know was if it was guilt or helplessness talking.

"We all know he didn't do it," Danica said, stretching her arm across the table.

Gracie hesitated before reaching for it. She managed a nod, but her eyes still teared.

This would never do. I couldn't let Gracie wallow, feeling powerless. A subtle movement of the curtains caught my eyes. Meemaw. And just like that, I knew what I had to do. Gracie would go to homecoming. She'd wear her mum. And she'd be on Shane's arm.

I slapped my open palm on the table. Holly, Danica, Leslie, and Gracie all jumped in their seats.

"We're not going to sit here and do nothing. We'll figure out what happened, Gracie." I'd already told Miss Reba I'd help, but there was no reason Gracie couldn't lend a hand. After all, she knew Shane.

Gracie managed a smile. "I knew you'd help, Harlow."

"We, Gracie. We'll do it together. Now let's think." I waved my hand as if I were casting a spell. "Come on, girls, y'all, too. Mr. Montgomery's car crashed on Saturday morning, right?"

Gracie, Danica, and Holly all nodded. Only Leslie seemed unsure of when the accident had actually happened. "Right," Gracie said. "He was on the country road between Granbury and here."

"Coming or going?"

She shrugged. "Going, I think. He was always driving out there to check on his second auto shop or something."

"Did you hear how the crash happened?" Danica asked.

Leslie's chin shot up. She put her mum down, dropping the strands of ribbon gripped in her hand. "I heard the brakes were cut, and that he lost control and drove into oncoming traffic."

Danica gaped at her. "So, what, the sheriff thinks Shane tampered with the brake lines? That happens in the movies, but don't you think that's a dumb way to try to kill somebody?"

"Right!" Gracie bobbed her head in a vigorous nod. "Because you'd either cut the line, or whatever, all together, right? And then you'd know right away there were no brakes. Or you'd cut a little bit—can you do that? And it would drain slowly, but you'd probably have enough sense to figure out that something was wrong, wouldn't you?"

Danica nodded. "I'd think so. And Shane would know that, wouldn't he?"

"Yes," Gracie said. "Since his dad owns—owned Bubba's. He knows everything about cars."

Holly frowned. "Maybe it wasn't the brakes," she said. "I heard some people talking about it in town. Steering maybe? Or transmission?" She shrugged. "I'm not sure."

That was more than I'd gotten out of Gavin McClaine. It wasn't a lead, but it was something to look into. What, exactly, went wrong with Chris Montgomery's car? Now I just had to figure out a reason to go have a chat with the people who worked at Bubba's.

I went back to directing the girls on their mums. After the loops around the base were complete, we moved on to the streamers, which would be stapled to the bottom third of the cardboard circle and would cascade down like a multicolored waterfall.

"You can use as much of that ribbon as you like," I said, pointing to the mound I'd piled into a rectangular basket sitting in the corner of the dining room. "You have to decide how long you want the strands to hang." I'd seen them stop at the thighs, but I'd also seen them hanging down almost to the floor. It was all about personal preference.

They each stood, grabbed a handful of ribbon from the basket, and gauged how long they wanted it to be by holding the base to their chests and letting the ribbon fall.

Danica went for the shorter strands, Leslie for the longest, and Holly chose a clump that fell in between. Once again, Gracie seemed stuck.

"Maybe I should make Shane's mum first? If I make it, he'll have to come to the dance, right?"

The Cassidys had hidden their charms for generations, but on some instinctive level, people knew Cassidy women were different from everybody else. We all had charms, and Gracie had Cassidy blood in her, courtesy of Butch's illicit affair with Etta Place. She couldn't make things come true the way I could; instead, she saw images from the fabric of old garments, and sometimes it shook her to the core. Slowly, though, she was getting a handle on it. "If you want to, that's fine, but it might not work."

"But it might."

I conceded. "Yes, it might."

The boys' mums were much smaller and had short ribbon strands. They were attached to a garter and the guys wore them on their upper arms. Most didn't care about how many embellishments there were or the length of the mum as a whole. No, the mum mystique was for the girls, and the guys went along for the ride.

But Gracie dove into making Shane's mum with both feet. The concentration she hadn't possessed when working on her own mum was there in spades for Shane's. In ten minutes, she had the short ribbons looped and stapled around the smaller base used for the boys. She moved right into attaching the longer strands, using the rough measurement from her shoulder to her elbow to determine how long to keep the ribbon.

She finished at the same time Leslie, Danica, and Holly wrapped up the last of their long strands.

"Time to add the embellishments," I said, pulling out another basket, this one filled with miniature teddy bears, plastic football, volleyball, soccer, and cheerleading charms. I'd walked up and down the aisles at a local craft store, gathering up an array of goodies girls could attach to their mums. Digging through the basket was like diving for treasure.

Leslie didn't have to search long. She chose a strand of miniature gold bells, one giant cowbell, a wide strand of red ribbon with BLISS HIGH SCHOOL printed down the front, and a handful of other silver and gold decorations. "The more bling, the better," she announced, wasting no time in tying and attaching the items to the strands of ribbon.

Holly eyed it skeptically. "It's going to be massively heavy."

"Then Ms. Cassidy can make a harness," Leslie said, "because nobody's going to have a better mum than me."

"Or a better dress," Danica added.

"You're going to be the belles of the ball," Holly said. "I wish Harlow was making my dress."

Leslie attached another plastic charm to her mum. "Why isn't she?" She looked at me. "Why aren't you?"

Holly grabbed the stapler, frowning. "My mother says she's inspired by Harlow and she wants to make mine."

I stifled a smile. The impression I'd had of Miriam Kincaid during high school was that of a privileged girl who didn't have to do much of anything for herself. My opinion had changed when my good friend Josie had fallen in love with Miriam's brother, Nate, and their family had fallen apart amidst a sordid mystery full of debauchery and secrecy.

Miriam, I'd learned, had a penchant for crafting her own jewelry, had opened up a bookshop on the square, and now, it seemed, she'd taken up sewing. I was afraid she'd find that sewing wasn't as easy as it looked, and creating the right garment for a person was even more challenging.

Leslie swung her head to look at Gracie. "What about you? Is Harlow making your homecoming dress?"

Gracie shook her head, but kept her gaze down. "I'm making my own."

Leslie and Danica stared at her, their mouths gaping. "By yourself?" Leslie asked.

After Gracie nodded, Danica said, "Is it fancy?"

Gracie looked up. A veil of shyness had slipped over her. She wasn't confident in her dressmaking skills yet, although she was a natural and gifted beyond what I'd been at her age.

"It's . . . different," she said. I'd helped her with the design, but the way she spoke now made me wonder if she liked it or not, and if I'd led her astray.

"It's beautiful," I said, hoping my words would circle around her and bolster her confidence.

She nodded, almost to herself. "It is. It's a cream-colored dress with spaghetti straps on top, and all these rosettes on the skirt in pink, rose, and red crinkled chiffon."

And void of anyone else's history.

In that way, she was just now starting to control her charm. She'd realized that making clothing from new fabric was a clean slate for her.

The girls plied her with more questions about the dress as they continued to add adornments to their ribbons. They talked about how Danica had ended up in Bliss after her mother passed away, how Leslie lived with her grandmother, and how Holly was an auntie to her uncle Nate and aunt Josie's baby. Shane and the death of Chris Montgomery didn't come up again, but despite the lightness that had come into the room, the likely murder of Shane's father never left my mind.

Chapter 5

"Buttercup is due for her inspection," I said to the mechanic on duty at Bubba's. He looked to be in his mid-thirties, a hint of gray slowly working its way into the stubble of his beard and sideburns, his skin bronzed, but craggy. His blue oil-stained coveralls hung loosely, the company's name emblazoned on a patch on the left side of his chest.

He wiped his greasy hands on a blue rag, cocking an eyebrow. "Buttercup? That what Loretta Mae called her?"

"You knew Loretta Mae?" I shouldn't have been surprised. Meemaw had known everyone in Bliss, and everyone had known her.

"'Course. Everyone knew the old girl. Sure didn't know she called her truck Buttercup, though. Most folks use Bessie, or somethin' like that, ya know?"

We both turned to look at the ancient Ford with the rounded fenders and domed cab. "She's the color of a buttercup, though, don't you think?"

"I reckon she is at that," he said.

"I'm Harlow." I lifted my hand in a little wave instead of shaking his grease-streaked hand. "Loretta Mae is my . . . was my great-grandmother," I added, but of course he already knew that.

"You're the spittin' image," he said.

"Aw, thank you." I threw my shoulders back, proud, and grinned. Every Cassidy woman had a tuft of blond hair sprouting from the left temple, and we all had hazel eyes, leaning toward green, with gold flecks. There was a striking resemblance between us, leaving no doubt we were related.

I smiled sweetly, knowing, as Meemaw always said, that you catch more flies with honey. "I didn't get your name."

He grinned, revealing slightly crooked, yellowed teeth. "Otis," he said; then he gestured to the sign hanging from the roofline. "But you can call me Bubba. Everybody does."

Everybody called everybody Bubba in Texas, but Otis had a name patch with the name emblazoned on it and he worked at a shop with the same name. Not everyone could say that.

"You know how it is. Every tenth hombre's called Bubba round these parts. Given name's Otis, but I's the last of seven kids and all anybody's ever called me is Bubba. 'Cept my wife, 'course. Anyhow, I cain't unstick it."

"Working here is a good fit, then," I said.

"Yup. Need an inspection, you say? Sticker says you got another month."

He had good eyesight, and he was observant. Maybe he was that observant about everything, and he'd know something about Shane that could help clear him. "I like to be ahead on things," I said. "You know, in case I run out of time later on, it'll already be done. Loretta Mae taught me that."

Pay bills when they arrive, put things away where they belong, and plan ahead so you won't ever be caught unprepared. Those were three of the many rules she'd lived by, and she'd passed those rules on to me.

"She was a good woman. Smarter than most."

He shifted his weight, looking antsy to get back to work. It was now or never.

"Such a shame about Mr. Montgomery," I said, my gaze downcast.

He stilled. "Sure is. He was real well liked, ya know? Everybody's friend. Weren't afraid to get his hands dirty."

"Did you know him for a long time?"

"Oh, sure. He hired me to work the Granbury Bubba's when it first opened what, goin' on nineteen years now? That was before either of us got saddled down with wives." His lips curved into a tepid smile. "He found love. Mine, well it was a shotgun weddin' and all that, but Sally's a good woman, all the same."

Sounded like the makings of a passionate relationship, I thought dryly, but I kept quiet and let him continue.

"Eddy offered me the job here at the Bliss shop and it was perfect back then. Sally 'n' me, we separated for a while, ya know."

"Eddy Blake from the Granbury shop?"

"Eh?"

"You said Eddy offered you the job here."

"Right. Got me outta Granbury when me 'n' Sally was

havin' troubles. But then Chris came along, 'n' I stayed here. Sally 'n' me finally bit the bullet and moved the family to Bliss just a few months ago."

"So you came here and Chris worked at Granbury with Eddy so you could have some space from Sally?"

He nodded. "Yup. That's about it. Chris saw her every now 'n' again. She'd bring her car to Bubba's over there. He had a run of seeing her every week for eight weeks in a row. I told him I could take his place again, you know? But he said he didn't mind Sally, and he liked driving back 'n' forth between the shops."

"I guess it's not too far," I said. "And they're all country roads."

"Thirty-five miles, exactly. We stay open late a few nights a week. He'd stay over at the shop those nights."

"With Mr. Blake?"

Bubba shifted on his feet. "Come again?"

I thought back to Teagen Montgomery finding her father's business partner's phone after the funeral, but maybe I'd misunderstood. "Eddy Blake runs the Granbury shop and Chris Montgomery ran this one, right?"

He blinked, real slow. "Right. Eddy don't come round here much. Granbury's a busier shop. Chris slept in a little room off the office whenever he stayed the night over there. Home away from home," he used to say. "Didn't like being on the roads real late. I wouldn't neither. Awful glad we're livin' in Bliss now. Easier to see the kids, ya know?"

He pulled out his worn, curved leather wallet and slipped out an equally worn and curved picture of two teenagers. The girl had a dimple in her smile and shoulder-length dark hair. The boy had the same dimple, but his hair was more of a dishwater blond. "Best things me 'n' Sally ever did," he said before tucking the picture away again for safekeeping.

It wasn't a ringing endorsement of love, but there was a sweetness to it, nonetheless. Whatever else they'd done together, Sally and Otis were still making it through on the same side of their marriage and they loved their kids.

I figured now was as good a time as any to dive in and just ask about Shane. "Otis, I heard someone say that maybe the brake lines were cut in Mr. Montgomery's car. Or something. Is that what you think happened?"

He scoffed. "You've been watchin' too much bad TV. Tampering with the brakes of someone's car, especially a mechanic's car, is the dumbest way to kill someone."

"I heard the deputy sheriff say they were looking at the car, though. And I heard some people saying that his son, Shane, might have—"

"That's what I been hearin'." His temples pulsed and his skin had taken on a red hue.

"Do you think he could have done it?" I asked, afraid of the answer for the first time.

Blue veins popped just under the surface of his skin, but he just shrugged. "Hell if I know."

"What do you think happened?"

His gaze darted left and right before settling back on me. "Gavin McClaine came by." He moved a little closer and lowered his voice a tad, as if there other people milling around and they might overhear. "Said their inspection showed steering linkage sabotage."

My eyelids fluttered and I stared at him. He might as well have been talking about catalytic converters and transmissions. It would be akin to me talking pleating and ruching and scalloped hemlines. Bubba would feel my bewilderment.

"Steering link what?"

"Steering linkage sabotage. If someone sheared through the linkage—messed with the steering—the driver would lose control."

"He wouldn't have felt it coming?"

Bubba shook his head, frowning. "Nope. It'd be sudden. Total loss of control and way more likely to cause an accident than messing with the brakes. Anyway, way I hear it, he was forced off the road. Steering went, he was chased down, and then he crashed."

Forced off the road. That was something I hadn't known. It still seemed like an imprecise way to kill somebody, but if someone knew Chris Montgomery had been driving to Granbury—or back to Bliss—they could have lain in wait, following from a safe distance until the steering started to go.

But the question was why? Why would anyone do that?

If Gavin was right and someone had tampered with the steering linkage, or whatever, that someone would have had to know the inner workings of a car. Unfortunately, that drew a straight line to Shane.

Bubba wiped his hands with his oily rag, antsy as he moved his weight from one heavy black-booted foot to the other. Had his eyes grown small and beady . . . or was that my imagination?

My goal was to prove that Shane wasn't involved in his dad's death, but the realization hit me that whoever had sabotaged Christopher Montgomery's car might well be an employee at one of the two Bubba's Auto Repair shops.

My heartbeat ratcheted up in my chest and I took an uneven step backward.

It could even be the Bubba standing in front of me.

"It'll take about twenty minutes, give or take."

I blinked, chasing away the flurry of nerves in my stomach. Sociopaths excepted, murderers always had a motive that made perfect sense to them. Even if Bubba here had tampered with Mr. Montgomery's car, he had nothing against me. And he had fond memories of Meemaw, so I was 99.9 percent sure I was safe.

I handed over my keys, placing them in his upward-facing palm. "Perfect, thanks."

As he clomped toward Buttercup, he turned and called over his shoulder, "There's coffee inside."

The sidewalk up to the building was emblazoned with a large stamped outline of the state of Texas. I smiled to myself at Texan pride. I couldn't think of another state that had so much love for itself.

I stepped into the lobby, the bought air instantly sending a chill all the way to my bones. I'd dressed for the ninety-degree late-summer weather, not thinking Bubba's would be more like an igloo than a sauna. I stifled a shiver and rubbed the goose bumps from my arms as I took in the details of the shop.

The lobby was merely a grimy sitting room with aluminum-framed chairs, an oak-and-glass coffee table that had seen better days, and a stack of mostly men's magazines. Anyone interested in cars, sports, and fishing had their pick of reading material.

I didn't know what I was looking for, but I seized the opportunity to snoop. Keeping one eye on Bubba through the glass window, I peeked behind the counter. The computer was in sleep mode. I tapped the mouse, bringing the screen to life. Bubba's logo of a cartoon mechanic holding a stethoscope to the hood of a car appeared, along with a password box. I left it to fall asleep again, and turned to look at the wall. A few thank-you notes addressed to Bubba's hung on an inexpensive bulletin board. Next to it was the framed business license for Bubba's with Eddy Blake as the proprietor. Odd, since they'd owned it together, but maybe Chris's partnership was more the silent kind.

Next to the license was a metal Texas star, the quintessential symbol of love for the Lone Star State. I spun around looking at the shop, but nothing struck me. No handy slip of paper lay on the counter or floor with a name and motive scribbled on it, squarely pointing the finger at the killer. Not that I expected there to be, but it would have been nice.

I sat in one of the cloth-seated chairs, opened my bag, and withdrew my sketchbook. In fashion school, I'd learned to find inspiration all around me. From the steel beams and cranes at a building construction site. From people bustling on the street. From the trees at the city park.

But Bubba's wasn't doing it for me. The Cassidy women had taught me to surround myself with things I love—and I'd taken that to heart. My yellow farmhouse and Buttons & Bows were filled with fabrics, color, trims, Meemaw's old dishes, an old milk bottle chandelier, and retro appliances. All things that made my heart swell with comfort, history, and memories.

But no matter how I tried, no visions circled in my head from Bubba's Auto Repair Shop. I flipped through the first half of the book, bypassing the faces and bodies and pastel designs I'd painstakingly drawn, until I got to a blank page. I dove right in without thinking, sketching the lobby, more as a distraction than anything else.

My pencil flew over the page and before long, I had the entire lobby finished and shaded. I stood, peering through the glass window in the door separating the waiting area from the garage. Bubba crouched beside Buttercup, holding the hose from the air compressor to one tire. After a moment, he moved to the next. I leaned against the counter, cradled the sketchbook on my forearm, and drew the garage next, adding a rough outline of Buttercup, the empty car bay at the opposite end of the garage, the tools scattered across a workbench in the back. Socket wrenches, air guns, ratchets, screwdrivers. Tools to a mechanic were like notions to a seamstress, which made me realize that Bubba and other mechanics were artists in their own way. They problem-solved, created, fine-tuned, and loved cars in the way that I used thread and a sewing machine, an iron, and other notions to design, create, and execute the perfect garments.

I flipped the page, an image of a dress with hard lines and edges, a sharp bodice, and pencil skirt forming in my mind. The sketch came quickly, the lines long and precise. Bubba's had inspired me after all. But before I could add any details, the door from the garage opened. Bubba walked behind the counter, brought the computer to life, and in seconds, had printed out an invoice for Buttercup's state inspection.

"Thanks, Otis," I said, handing over my credit card. "It was nice to meet you."

"Yes, ma'am," he said with a nod. "Glad to see you takin' care of Loretta Mae's truck."

"Buttercup," I said with a smile.

I felt his eyes on me as I walked to the door. Stopping, I turned back to him. "Tell Shane I said hey."

"Shane ain't been 'round since the accident," he said. "Before, even."

For a split second, I had a glimmer of hope that that would somehow prove his innocence. But it vanished with a pop. Anyone who knew how to tamper with a car would do it covertly, and certainly not for everyone to see right at an auto repair shop. "Of course not. I imagine being here would remind him too much of his dad."

Otis arched a bushy eyebrow at me. "I think you got it all wrong, Ms. Cassidy."

I arched an eyebrow right back at him. "How so, Bubba?"

"I'd bet my own life that Shane did it. He had the know-how. He woulda had the opportunity. And with the way he fought with his old man, he might coulda snapped."

Chapter 6

I'd gone to Bubba's hoping to find something that would help Shane. Instead I'd come away with Bubba's parting statement weighing heavily on my mind. *The way he fought with his old man, he might coulda snapped.*

Three staccato blasts from a horn sounded behind me. I jerked out of my thoughts, glancing at the stoplight — still red — and then in the rearview mirror. Will's truck was directly behind me at the light. He raised his hand in a wave, then pointed to the side of the road.

I pulled into the first parking lot I ran across. He rolled to a stop behind me, exiting his truck and ambling up to my door as if he'd pulled me over for a traffic violation.

"Fancy meeting you here, darlin'," he said, leaning down to the open window, one side of his mouth lifting in a small grin.

I smiled right back. "Mr. Flores, are you followin' me?"

"I'll follow you wherever you wanna go."

"What if I told you I was heading to Granbury," I said,

batting my eyes coquettishly. "Would you still follow me?"

He tugged on the bill of his Longhorns ball cap, considering me. "I'd ask you what you were after in Granbury."

"Ah, so you have conditions on your attention," I said.

His grin widened. "Nope, no conditions, just curiosity."

"Then it doesn't matter what I'm after in Granbury," I said. He knew I was looking into Mr. Montgomery's death, but I had a niggling feeling he wasn't fully on board with the idea.

"It only matters so I can decide if I should follow you"—he stood up and pointed his keys at his truck. It beeped twice in quick succession. He came around to Buttercup's passenger side and got in—"or if I should just drive with you. But I figure you're up to something. . . ."

I swung my body to face him, stifling my smile. "What makes you think I'm up to something?"

"If you weren't, you'd be back at your shop sewing something."

I started to object, but closed my mouth instead. He was right.

"Cassidy, you're an open book. You're heading to Granbury to see what you can dig up at Montgomery's auto shop—am I right?"

My shoulders slumped. "That obvious, huh?"

He leaned toward me, his smile still in place. "Only to me," and he kissed me, slow and tender. It was the kind of kiss Elvis would have sung a ballad about.

"So you're coming with me?" I asked, my voice muffled against his mouth.

He smiled, his lips curling against mine. "So happens

I have some free time, so I guess I will." He sat back as I started Buttercup, threw her into gear, and headed west.

It took forty minutes to get to Granbury on the one-lane country back roads. At one point an enormous truck bore down on me, laying on his horn until I was able to pull onto the dirt shoulder and let him pass. A short time later, a teenage driver passed a car coming the other direction, nearly plowing into me head-on. By the time we got to Granbury, my hands were shaking and my heart was in my throat. I could see Chris Montgomery wanting to stay off the roads and spend the night when he'd been really tired. Even if he wasn't really tired. Texas back roads could be treacherous.

We took a few minutes to drive around the historic town square with its Old West picturesque shop facades and restaurants, and the courthouse smack in the center. It was just like Bliss, only bigger and a little bit grander. More tourists came to Granbury than to Bliss, and with good reason. The square oozed character, and from the looks of things, they hosted town celebrations more than they didn't.

"The Bliss Historical Society wants us to become a mini Granbury," Will said. He'd taken out his cell phone and was snapping pictures out the passenger window. "I came down here a few months back to look at the playhouse and the outdoor amphitheater."

"Is Bliss getting a playhouse and amphitheater?" We didn't have a movie theater, so somewhere local to see plays would be fun.

Will shrugged. "Anything's possible. Just takes money."

Like anything else. I had taken on the homecoming

mums to earn a little extra money just to make ends meet, and I was constantly thinking of what else I could do to keep Buttons & Bows afloat.

Will seemed to sense the thoughts flitting through my mind. He stretched his arm across the back of the seat and gave my shoulder a gentle squeeze. I smiled at him, relaxing in the comfortable silence between us. Neither one of us needed to fill it with idle chitchat, and once again I had to hand it to Meemaw for her matchmaking skills. What Loretta Mae wanted, Loretta Mae got. She'd wanted Will and me to be a couple, and darned if it hadn't happened. But more than that, it was a good match, and I was grateful to my great-grandmother for knowing what I needed even before I did.

A few minutes later, we'd found the side street Bubba's called home. Bedding flowers lined the walkway to the lobby door, and the parking lot and the repair bays were full of cars. Bubba's Granbury location did a brisker business than its sister site in Bliss. It looked nicer. It was kept up. And I knew better than anyone how important first impressions were. My first impression of a person often sent a vision into my head, and more often than not, the outfit I pictured revealed something about the person, something I might not discover in any other way.

My first impression of Bubba's in Bliss was that it catered to the town's locals and old timers who'd been born and raised in Bliss. On the other hand, my first impression of the Granbury Bubba's was that Suburban-driving moms were just as big a part of the clientele as the good ol' boy network who spent their Saturday afternoons at the barber shop. Flowers told a specific story, and the knock-out roses planted by the door and the beds packed with marigolds said that someone took the time to care for the landscape. Bubba's in Bliss had no such flora love.

A bell dinged as we entered the lobby. Right away we were greeted by a thin man who stood behind the counter. His name patch read MAC. Curly brown hair framed his head and wispy ringlets dusted his sideburns. A gold chain hung at his neck, and I could picture him in a shirt with the collar gaping open. The chin dimple made him look a touch older than he probably was, but he still looked like he was fresh out of high school. He seemed vaguely familiar and I tried to place him, but if I'd met him before, my mind was blank. Aside from Gracie, her friends, and the kids who came into Buttons & Bows, I didn't have much occasion to be around high school kids.

Maybe he just had one of those faces.

"What can I do for you?" Mac asked. His voice was thin and high, and I had an image of him wearing snake-skin boots and a charming grin when he wasn't in his oil-stained coveralls.

Since Bubba from Bliss had already done the annual inspection, I said, "I'm due for an oil change." Buttercup was going to be in tiptop shape by the time this investigation was over.

The young man grabbed a clipboard and pen and ambled out to the parking lot, Will and me on his heels. "No problems with it?" he asked as he wrote down the make and mileage.

"Not a one. Buttercup here is a peach of a truck."

If he thought anything about my name for the old

Ford, he didn't let on. "They made 'em sturdy back then," he said. "We're backed up today. I'll need a good hour."

I saw my opening and jumped. "I bet the loss of Mr. Montgomery has put y'all behind. So tragic."

"Yeah, it has. I'm pretty new here. Never met the guy, but it knocked his partner off the grid. Mr. Blake's taking it real hard."

"Did he get his phone back?"

Mac stared at me, his brows knitting together. "Come again?"

"We were at Chris Montgomery's funeral and his daughter found Mr. Blake's cell phone," Will said.

Mac's lips parted and he dipped his chin. "That explains it. He's missed his shifts and he hasn't been answering our calls. Guess he can't answer if he don't have his phone."

"Do you think he's okay?" I asked. People handled grief in all kinds of ways. Seeing his friend die so tragically could be driving Mr. Blake to face his own mortality.

Mac's eyebrows lifted uncertainly. "Like I said, he's taking his friend's death real hard."

"Will, honey," I said, taking Will's arm. Talking to Chris Montgomery's business partner suddenly seemed vitally important. I assumed that Chris Montgomery's half of the business would probably go to Miss Reba, assuming she'd even want to keep it, but the day-to-day operations would likely fall to Mr. Blake. Maybe that's what he'd wanted. Maybe he wasn't grieving. Maybe guilt had him hiding out or on the lam.

I gave myself a mental head smack for my cynicism. I didn't know the first thing about Eddy Blake, and even

less about how the two Bubba's shops were run and how
Blake might benefit from his friend's death.

"I'm sure you all must be so worried," I said. "We
could go check on him."

Will patted my hand and nodded to Mac. "Absolutely.
Be happy to."

Mac didn't respond, instead turning and ambling back to
the lobby. Will and I followed, an uncertain look passing
between us. "How do we get the address?" I whispered.

Will shrugged. "We can always look in the phone
book, or Google it."

But it turned out we didn't have to do either one. Mac
pulled something up on the computer and a few seconds
later he held out his hand for the truck key. "Be about an
hour," he said as I dropped it in his palm. "5309 Crescent
Street."

I blinked, registering the address.

He turned on his heel, tucking a pen he'd been using
behind his ear and heading toward the door between the
lobby and the garage bays. "Let me know if Mr. Blake's
okay," he said over his shoulder. "We could sure use his
help around here."

"We sure will, Mac," I said. "We sure will."

True to his word, Mac finished up with Buttercup in an
hour, and ten minutes later we stood at the front door of
Mr. Blake's trailer home in the center of a nice mobile
home park on the east side of town. While Christopher
Montgomery lived in a traditional Texas house made of
redbrick, his partner's house was far more modest. It was
a nice mobile home, looking far more permanent than

temporary, with a small patch of grass, a shrub, and a few flowers in front.

"He has a thing for Mustangs," Will commented, pointing to the left of the small house. Five cars were lined up in various states of repair. Clearly, a car to a mechanic was like fabric to a fashion designer.

"Here goes," I said, raising my hand and rapping my knuckles against the door.

In seconds flat, the door yanked open. A woman stood there, her expression shifting from angry to relieved to disappointed, all before I could blink. "Yes?" she asked.

I stepped forward, holding out my hand, hoping I looked more confident than I felt. "Mrs. Blake? I'm Harlow Cassidy. This is Will Flores. I . . . we were just at Bubba's, and Mac said he hadn't seen Mr. Blake lately. We said we'd stop by—" I looked at Will to my left. "To see if he's okay and if y'all need anything."

Her expression changed again, slipping back to a veil of ire. She eyed my hand, but didn't raise hers to shake. "I really can't say if he's okay," she said, anger tingeing her voice. "I haven't seen him in days."

Not what I'd expected to hear. I dropped my arm back to my side and Will took up where I'd left off. "Sounds like he's taking his partner's death pretty hard."

She didn't respond to that, just dropped her gaze, her emotion shifting to a palpable worry. "He is. Harder than I expected."

A red flag went up in my mind from that last sentence. Could Mrs. Blake have had something against Chris Montgomery that led her to kill him, not anticipating the toll the death would take on her own husband? Anything was possible, and I certainly couldn't discount the idea.

"I'm awfully sorry to hear that," I said. "The accident was a shock."

"I heard the car was tampered with and someone forced him off the road." She shook her head as if she still couldn't believe this had all actually happened.

"That's what we heard, too. Something with the steering."

She glanced at the row of cars. "I wouldn't know a steering line from a water line," she said, and I had to wonder if she'd said that to plant a seed about her vehicular ignorance.

"Me neither," I said. "I just need to turn the key so a car will go. Nothing more."

"Me, too. I know my way around a kitchen, and couldn't care less about cars. But they're Eddy's passion."

"As far as it goes," Will said, "cars are a pretty good thing for a man to tinker with."

"I guess," Mrs. Blake said. "He's a good man. He's taking this hard, though. When we lost our daughter, he disappeared on me for a week. Couldn't cope. Drove around looking for her, as if he could bring Sue back to us."

"I'm sorry," I started, but she waved away my sympathy.

"Chris's death, it's a tragedy, but Eddy'll get past it. We'll get through it together, just like we've done with everything. It's what marriage is about, right? For better or worse."

I looked over her shoulder trying to see the pictures framed on a small table to her right. A large photo of a ginger-haired girl sat in the center spot, the rest of the smaller photos grouped around it. There was a family photo, the images too small to make out, and another of the girl in the driver's seat of a gray, dull-looking car. It was Bondoed and primered, but from what I could see, a smile lit up the girl's face.

Instinctively, I moved forward, but Mrs. Blake shifted, blocking my view. "I'm sorry, ma'am," I said, both for the loss of her daughter and her grieving husband.

"Thank you."

We stayed silent. *If you listen, people will talk,* Meemaw used to say. It was true. I'd learned to stand back and let people fill the silence. Mrs. Blake was no different from most other people I'd encountered. She continued. "He'll be back," she said, and I wondered if she was trying to convince herself as much as us. "He stays out a few nights a week, but that's always for work. That business is all-consuming. I sure didn't expect that when he took on a partner and opened another store. But if that makes him happy and it pays the bills, then I'm all for it."

"Sounds like you have a good husband."

She nodded, the anger she'd emanated when we'd first arrived all but gone. "We're a team. We were going to talk about our schedules and simplifying the other night, but then Chris died and now I don't know what'll happen. More late nights than before, I imagine."

"I'm sure you'll work it out once he's back home," I said, trying to sound encouraging.

She gestured to me and Will. "You know how it is. Relationships are about compromise. We've had our share of problems, but he's never done anything like this. Truly, I'm mad as all get-out, but I'm worried sick."

"Could he be at a friend's house? Or a bar? Is he a drinker?"

Her eyes clouded. "He's as sober as the day is long. Oh, don't get me wrong—he has his vices," she said, her gaze straying to the row of cars alongside the house, "but the drink isn't one of them."

"Have you called around to the bars in town, just in case?" Losing someone could play tricks on the mind and send even a sober man to the bottle.

"We've been married twenty years," she said. "I'm under no illusions that my husband is perfect, and if he's turned to whiskey, or whatever, we'll deal with that. But I don't think he's drowned his sorrow in alcohol, I just don't."

She knew her husband better than anyone, so I took her at her word. "I'm sorry about your daughter, Mrs. Blake, and I hope your husband comes home soon. If we can do anything—"

She arched an eyebrow at us. "Who did you say you were again?"

"I'm a friend of Miss Reba's," I said.

She looked blankly at me and once again, I got the feeling that something was off. "Mr. Montgomery's wife," I said.

She shrugged again. "I only met her once or twice, but she's rather . . . I mean we don't have the same . . ." She paused and I got the feeling she didn't want to speak ill of Miss Reba, a new widow. "We don't run in the same circles."

Given the differences in their lifestyles, that was evident. I wondered if this caused friction between Eddy and Chris. Yet another potential motive developed in my mind.

"Again, Mrs. Blake, I'm so sorry about your husband's partner. I hope Eddy'll be home safe and sound real soon," I said, and Will and I took our leave.

Chapter 7

I dropped Will back at his truck. He headed back to work at the town offices, and I drove back to 2112 Mockingbird Lane. Something about the encounter with Mrs. Blake had me on edge, but I couldn't put my finger on it.

I parked under possumwood trees and crossed the driveway, mulling it over, but the answer didn't come to me. Something banged and clacked in the distance. I peered through the trees at Sundance Kids, my grandmother's goat farm directly behind my property. I could make out Nana walking the perimeter of the farm, Thelma Louise, the grand dam of the goatherd, and a few more of Nana's Nubian and La Mancha goats followed her like Nana was the Pied Piper.

I thought about crossing the grass to chat, but my mind was circling around Mr. Montgomery's death, Mr. Blake's absence, Mrs. Blake's distress, and poor Shane. Instead I walked around back, waved at them, and headed up the back porch steps. If only I'd been able to go inside the Blake house. As it was, I knew we'd been lucky Mrs. Blake had talked with us at all, but I felt there was something to be learned there.

Too bad I had no idea what that something was.

A series of bangs stopped me in my tracks. This time they came from inside the house. My stomach coiled. It was an awful lot of noise for Meemaw to be making.

It wasn't Nana, since she was over at Sundance Kids. I stopped just outside the Dutch door, the scent of apples and cinnamon wafting through the open top half of the door. For a split second, I thought it could be my cousin Sandy or her daughter, Libby. While my Cassidy charm centered around the fashion designs I created for people, my cousins' had to do with food. What they cooked softened the edges of the emotions of the people around them, heightening their senses.

But they wouldn't just come into my house and start baking, which brought me back around to Meemaw. Had she learned to bake as a ghost?

I plowed through the Dutch door, noticing three things right away:

1) The kitchen was in disarray. Every bowl had been taken from the cupboards, every mixing spoon used, a light dusting of flour seemed to cover every surface, and what looked like a pile of smashed cornbread muffins sat in a mound about two feet away from the oven;

2) At least thirty-six muffins were cooling on the round pine table, and from what I could tell, there were at least three different flavors;

3) Mama stood bent over the butter yellow replica oven. The oven door was open and another tray of what looked to be streusel-topped blueberry muffins was clutched in her oven-mitted hand.

My breath staggered and a sound must have escaped my lips because Mama's back straightened, she lost her balance, and the tray of muffins tilted right, then left. She managed to keep the tray level, saving the muffins.

"Mama, what in tarnation are you doing?" She had her own kitchen to make a mess in, so why in the world was she in mine?

She whirled around. From the corner of my eye, I caught a glimpse of another figure flickering in and out of visibility like Princess Leia's hologram projected in front of R2-D2 in *Star Wars*.

Meemaw was here, too.

"Mama," I said, looking around the kitchen again. "Why are you making muffins—"

"And cornbread, darlin'."

"And cornbread," I amended, "in my kitchen?"

She set the tray on the counter, turning to face me. Flour was smudged across her cheek and her brown hair was mussed, but she grinned like a Cheshire cat. "My oven's on the fritz, and I had a hankerin' for some muffins."

I stared at her, gauging just how much she wanted muffins versus how much she wanted to know what was going on with Gracie's boyfriend, Shane, and him being a murder suspect. "Is that right?"

"Yup, that's right. Hoss has a hankerin', too, for that matter."

Meemaw's faint form jiggled, and I got the feeling she was laughing. The question was, was she laughing at me, or Mama?

I gestured to the room and muffin debris. "And the mess?"

Mama sighed. "Either I'm losin' my mind, or Meemaw's havin' a little fun at my expense."

"By messing with your muffins?"

"Precisely."

Loretta Mae was full of surprises. I'd seen her use motion to turn the pages of books and magazines. She could move small objects, like a shoe or a spool of thread, from one place to another.

But haunting Mama while she baked in my kitchen was something new. I ignored my great-grandmother's antics and bent to pick up a dropped muffin. "Something's bugging me," I said to Mama.

A damp dishrag sat on the counter. Meemaw. She was a tricky one, bless her heart. I took it and began wiping down the tile.

"What's that, sugar?" Mama asked.

"Will and I went to Granbury—"

"He's a sweet man, Harlow Jane."

I cocked an eyebrow at her, the corner of my mouth raising in a slight grin. We'd been seeing each other for going on a year now. He was everything I wanted in a man . . . and then some. "I know he is, Mama."

"Okay, so, you went to Granbury with him, and . . . ?"

In my peripheral vision, I caught a flicker, like a TV with a bad connection, but when I turned to look, it was gone.

I continued. "I went to Bubba's, and then we went to Granbury to talk to Chris Montgomery's business partner. He wasn't there, so we went to his house."

I paused to shake out the cloth in the sink and rinse it.

Mama wasn't a detective any more than I was, but our curiosity was cut from the same cloth. "And?" she said, her full attention on me.

"He hasn't been home since the funeral. I've been wondering if maybe he has someone on the side, you know?"

An acquiescent moan came from behind me. So Meemaw agreed that my thought wasn't so farfetched. It made sense. Maybe things weren't as great in their marriage as Mrs. Blake thought. If he had another woman, he could very well be seeking solace from her.

Mama stood back and watched as I grabbed the ancient phone from its cradle on the wall—if it ain't broke, don't fix it was one of Loretta Mae's mottos, so I still had the old phone attached to the wall. The long cord stretched as I bent to clean up some more of my great-grandmother's mess. After a few rings, Gavin McClaine picked up with a clipped, "Yup?"

"It's Harlow," I said, cutting to the chase. "Can you find something out for me?"

"Hello to you, too, sis," he said, but his voice was mocking rather than sincere. Siblings we were not.

"Gavin—"

"Deputy," he corrected.

"Eddy Blake hasn't been home since Chris Montgomery was in the car accident. His wife's pretty worried. I was hoping you could trace his credit cards or something to find out where he is."

"Ahead of you there. Not showing at the funeral was a red flag—"

"He was at the reception afterward," I said.

There was a heavy pause, and I could sense his brows furrowing and him tilting back his cowboy hat as he pondered. He was just like his daddy, Hoss, in that way. "You talked to him?"

"No, but Miss Reba said—"

"I can't go by what Miss Reba said. She was distraught. Did anyone talk to him? He might could have dropped a hint at where he was heading."

"Well, I just don't know, Gavin. I didn't talk to everyone. I just know that he left his phone."

"I've been checking on him, Harlow. Wherever he is, he's paying cash or shacking up. His credit cards haven't been used. Now, I know you wanna play at being detective, but if there's nothin' else, I have work to do."

"Sure thing, thanks," I started, making a face at the phone, but Gavin had already hung up. I hung up the receiver, muttering under my breath. Stepbrother or not, he had some nerve hanging up on me. I certainly hoped he was sweeter to Orphie than he was to his newly acquired kin. Namely me.

I needed to go see Miss Reba. Now. A clanking noise sounded from the stove. I whirled around, but all I saw was Mama, a new tray of muffins in her hand ready to place in the oven.

"I'm going to see Miss Reba," I said, knowing exactly what I needed to do. I slung my bag over my shoulder and headed toward the Dutch door, but paused. "I could help you clean up first," I offered, but behind me, as if to say, *not a chance*, an invisible force cradled me, pushing me forward. Meemaw couldn't quite materialize, and she definitely couldn't handle the very physical tasks of cooking, but she could harness the air like nobody's business.

"You just go on," Mama said. "I've got this handled."

"I'll be back," I said, and then I was out the door and heading to find Miss Reba Montgomery.

Chapter 8

Buttercup didn't have the bells and whistles of a new car, and she gave a bumpy ride, but she got me from point A to point B quicker than I could shake a stick, and right now, I wanted to get to Riley's, the furniture store catty-corner to the square. I'd heard through the rumor mill that Miss Reba hadn't wanted to stay at home and wallow in her sorrow so she'd gone back to her job at Riley's.

I rumbled down the street, angling Buttercup into a parking spot in front of the store. Miss Reba saw me through the window and waved me in. She looked this way and that before pulling me to a leather sectional and sitting me down. "Have you found out anything?" she asked.

Cut to the chase. I couldn't mislead her, so I shook my head and waved my hands. "No, no, nothing really. I was in Granbury, though, at Bubba's, and then I saw Mrs. Blake. I just have a question for you."

Her frown deepened, the green of her eyes muting as she waited.

"Mr. Blake is taking Mr. Montgomery's death mighty hard. His wife is really worried."

She stared at me like I'd lost my ever-loving mind. "*He's* taking it hard? I'm his *wife*," she said, pressing an open palm to her chest. "*I'm* taking it hard. Our *kids* are taking it hard. Who the hell is he to take it hard?"

"I know, Miss Reba. It's just, he hasn't been home since the funeral, and I thought if you still have his phone, maybe I could help Mrs. Blake track him down."

Miss Reba was no shrinking wallflower. Her unblinking gaze bore into me. "You said you were going to help clear Shane's name, Harlow. You said you'd help find out what happened to Chris. He did not lose control of his car; someone forced him off the road. Someone did this to him. You're supposed to be helping Shane."

"I'm digging around, Miss Reba. Truly, I am. And that's why I want to find Mr. Blake. They were partners. If someone had a beef against your husband, Eddy Blake might know about it. I think he'll be able to help us."

She threw her hands up in frustration. "I've never even met the man. He and Chris couldn't have been all that close. I don't see how he can possibly help."

"That may be," I said, "but I'd still like to talk to him." Because you never knew. People said things that revealed information they didn't know they had or didn't intend to impart, and people often knew things they didn't realize they knew.

She hemmed and hawed for another minute, but finally waved her hand in front of her as if she were batting at a fly. "It's at the house. Teagen's there. She's refusing to go to school." She shook her head, her aggravation evident. "She won't listen. I know I have to let her grieve, but it's like talking to a brick wall. Go on over and get it, if you want."

"Thank you, ma'am," I said, my good Southern breeding surfacing. But she was in a state and no amount of sweetness was going to help.

"I still don't know what good it'll do, but you're welcome, Harlow. Now, please, find out the truth before that overzealous sheriff's deputy stepbrother of yours puts my Shane behind bars."

Ten minutes later I stood at the Montgomery's front door. I'd rung the bell three times, but Teagen wasn't answering. I dug my cell phone out of my rag quilt bag and dialed Miss Reba at Riley's.

"She's probably in her room with those infernal headphones on and that blasted rap music destroyin' her mind," she said. "Try the front door."

"Are you sure? I don't want to barge in and scare her."

"It's fine. She should be doing her homework, not turnin' her mind off."

My heart went out to Teagen. Her mother had a Southern way about her, but she was as tough as steel. She'd thrown herself back into work, into proving Shane's innocence, and into coping with her loss, but she couldn't assume her daughter was mourning in the same stoic way. She'd lost her father.

It seemed to me that she ought to be allowed to grieve however she needed to. *You can't rush a person's feelings, Harlow,* Meemaw used to tell me when I'd been upset over an argument with Mama or about my unrequited love for some boy I'd crushed on.

I figured Teagen's grief was the same. It had to run its

course, and if a little Rihanna or some Drake helped her cope, then so be it.

"Is it open?"

I blinked at Miss Reba's voice and tried the handle. "It's unlocked," I said.

"Then go on inside. Teagen's room is at the top of the stairs, second door on the right. I think I put the phone in my bedside table." She paused. "Or maybe in the bathroom. I don't know where I put it; just have her find it for you."

For someone who'd seemed so in control, her nonchalance at not remembering where the phone was seemed odd, but I chalked it up to her buried emotions. I'd learned over the years that you could run from what you felt, but you couldn't hide it. Mama's very literal effect on plants was the perfect example. No matter what she felt—or how hard she tried to fight the emotions—the plants responded to her, either withering away from her sadness, growing brittle and thorny from her anger, or blossoming with her joy. That was her Cassidy charm.

I thanked Miss Reba again, then tucked my own phone away before stepping inside. The last time I'd been in the house, the townsfolk had been here mourning Chris Montgomery's death, the buffet table had swayed from the abundance of comfort casseroles, dump cakes, and fried chicken, and I'd agreed to help the Montgomery family—and Gracie—by proving Shane's innocence in his father's death.

The house felt hollow and sad now.

I made my way toward the stairs and started to call for Teagen, but stopped short. If Shane hadn't had anything to do with the car accident, then someone else had.

Someone who knew cars. What if that someone was Miss Reba? Maybe she'd learned from her husband over the years. Maybe *that* was why she was so stoic with her grief. Maybe her own conscience was the thing driving her need to clear her son. And since I was a dressmaker, not a private investigator, she figured the truth was safe with me looking into it. A safe bet to assuage her guilt.

"Oh, Miss Reba," I muttered aloud, "I hope that's not the case."

Miss Reba was a friend and a longtime resident of Bliss. From what she said, she didn't spend any time at Bubba's. Just like Mrs. Blake. Neither one had met the other. As Mrs. Blake said, they didn't run in the same circles. So if she knew anything about cars, it likely wasn't from hanging around her husband's business.

Still, I couldn't let go of the apprehension I felt, a bundle of anxiety settling on my chest like a weight. I debated my options. Could I, in good conscience, poke around the house?

It was my turn to hem and haw. I'd poked around in plenty of places, but it was too big an invasion of privacy to search the Montgomery house. Miss Reba had asked me to clear her son, but she surely hadn't reckoned on me redirecting attention on her in the process.

If anything was amiss, I'd have to find it out more honestly. I mounted the stairs, passing photographs of Shane and Teagen hanging on the wall. Just like at my house, the pictures elbowed their way up the wall, a collection of important moments captured in time. There were few of the kids with Miss Reba, and a handful of the older generation. Everyone smiled.

At the top of the stairs, I called to Teagen. The first

door was wide open. I stopped and peeked inside. Clothes littered the floor, posters of Carrie Underwood, the Eli Young Band, and several classic cars were pinned to the walls. It looked like what I imagined a typical teenage boy's bedroom would look like.

Nothing on the surface that would prove or disprove Shane's innocence.

I hesitated, wanting to sneak in and look around in the closet and his drawers, but I resisted the invisible pull. Butch Cassidy might be my kin, but I was basically a law-abiding citizen. Teagen in the house, possibly happening upon me while snooping, would not be a good scenario.

The second door on the right was closed. I rapped my knuckles against the hollow door. Silence.

I knocked again, louder this time. "Teagen? It's Harlow Cassidy."

Still nothing.

Lifting my hand, I was about to knock again when the door was ripped open by Teagen, with her ginger hair in disarray, one earbud hanging down in front of her body, and a frown that seemed to start at her eyebrows and continue to the corners of her mouth. "Who are you—?" She stopped. "Wait. Ms. Cassidy?"

"I didn't mean to startle you, Teagen." Black eyeliner smudged the area beneath her eyes and dark shadow framed her eyelids. Her fingernails were painted black, a big change from the white and Kelly green they'd been painted just a few days ago. Either Teagen had cleaned up for the funeral, making a big effort to look like the clean-cut good daughter, or that had been the real her and now her grief was sending her hurtling down a black hole. "Your mom asked me to come by—"

She snorted, glaring at me. "Are you kidding me? She sent you to check on me?"

"No, she just said you'd be home—"

She ripped the remaining earbud from her ear and threw the tangled string, along with her iPod, onto the mound of blankets on her bed. Either she hadn't heard, or she wasn't in the mood to listen. "She's completely crazy, you know? Ever since the break-in last month. And now since Daddy died, she's a thousand times worse—and she was pretty bad before."

"Bad how?"

"Way overprotective. She kept me and Shane both on a tight leash, but now? Might as well be in cages."

"But you're here and she's at work and Shane's . . . ?"

"Shane went back to school today, and he's going to Bubba's later. He didn't do what they're saying, you know, but even our mother isn't sure. He just up and left. Said he was going to work on cars just like Dad. She didn't want him to go, but then she went back to work, so she couldn't really argue, could she?"

Guilt gnawed at my gut for even thinking Miss Reba could have had anything to do with her husband's death, but Teagen had presented an opening I couldn't ignore. "I'm sure it's been hard on all of you," I said, not knowing quite how to comfort her. I'd lost my dad long ago, but he hadn't died; he'd walked out on my brother, Red, my Mama, and me once he'd found out about the Cassidy charms. Tristan Walker walked away and never looked back. And that wasn't the same thing at all as having your dad die in a suspicious car accident.

"Yeah, well she's not making it any easier." Her shoulders hunched as she turned and plopped down on an

oversized beanbag chair in the far corner. "She doesn't
get it. I want to go to school. What does it matter, anyway? Everything could end tomorrow. Splat. Done.
Over. So what's the point?"

Aside from the beanbag chair, which Teagen occu-
pied, and the unmade bed, there wasn't a place to sit. I
leaned against the doorframe. "I must have misunderstood your mom. I thought she said you *didn't* want to go
to school."

She huffed, overly dramatic, but effective for convey-
ing her utter frustration with her mom. "*Nooo.* She
doesn't think I can handle people talking about Shane
and our family. She treats me like I'm still eight years
old. Like I can't deal with conflict, you know?"

"Teagen, I'm sure it'll get easier. Just give her some
time."

Her lower lip trembled, making her look more like an
eight-year-old who'd gotten in trouble for using her
mom's makeup than the tortured new teenager she was.
"How much time?"

I crossed the room in five quick strides, crouching
down in front of her. "I'm trying to figure out what happened to your dad. Trying to clear Shane's name. Knowing the truth will help her get through this," I said, hoping
I was right. I could only imagine the dark hole Teagen
would fall into if her mom ended up involved in her
dad's death.

Something she'd said a few minutes ago resurfaced in
my mind. "You said you had a break-in last month? I
don't remember hearing about that."

She ran her fingers under her eyes, whisking away the
tears that had spilled and smudging her eyeliner even

more. "My dad wasn't worried about it. He didn't want to even report it, but it freaked my mom out."

I stood from my crouched position and went to perch on the edge of the bed. "What happened?"

She shrugged. "This is Bliss. No one locks their doors, right?"

"Right." Back in New York, Orphie and I had had three deadbolts and a chain on our loft apartment. Here, people trusted one another, and while it was a bad habit to leave your door unlocked, it was something we were all guilty of.

"Yeah, well, this one night, somebody just walked right in. Guess it wasn't really a break-in since they didn't actually break the lock or anything."

"Did they steal anything?"

She shook her head, but said, "Some of my clothes were missing. A few of Shane's things. His letterman jacket. Some pants. My iPod." She gestured to the one she'd tossed onto the bed, a glaze coating her eyes. She swiped at her nose as she said, "My dad bought me another one the next day."

"Were you here when it happened?"

She spit out a laugh. "Oh yeah. My mom woke up screaming when she saw someone just standing over their bed holding a box, or something. It was all really *Friday the Thirteenth,* minus the blood."

A chill wound through me. I knew what it was like to wake up to weirdness, but my sleep was almost always interrupted by Meemaw, not by a stealthy burglar. "Did the sheriff ever figure out who it was?"

"Nope," she said as she pushed off the beanbag chair and headed for the door. I took one last look around her room before following her.

"I'm going to return Mr. Blake's phone to—" I stopped, not wanting to bring up how distressed he was to Teagen and that I'd be returning it to Mrs. Blake. "Your mom sent me over to collect it."

She paused, one foot in midair on the staircase. "Oh. Well, then . . ." She swung her foot around and headed back into her room, yanking open her top dresser drawer and digging inside. A moment later, she handed over the phone. "Me and Shane were going to take it back to him. We thought maybe he could tell us something more about our dad."

"Like what?"

She shrugged. "Like who'd want to drive him off the road. Maybe Dad was a drug dealer or something and we didn't even really know him."

Oh boy. Teagen had been watching too much TV. I sure didn't see Chris Montgomery as a secret crystal meth cooker, dealer, or anything else remotely similar. Then again, people did have secrets, and he had spent a lot of nights away from home. Anything was possible. . . .

I scrolled through the contacts on the phone looking for Eddy Blake's home number so I could call Mrs. Blake and let her know I'd bring the phone back. When I found it, I pulled my own phone out and dialed, but I looked up as Teagen cleared her throat. The house phone rang, but she didn't make a move to go answer it.

"If you're calling Mr. Blake, it's the wrong number," she said, the phone still ringing somewhere outside her bedroom.

I pressed END. "What?"

She moved back to the door, held it open, and lifted her chin slightly. "It stopped."

"What stopped?"

She turned back to me. "The phone." She flicked her head back, looking at the cell phone in my hand. "It's programmed wrong. Mr. Blake's home phone rings here instead of wherever his house in Granbury is. I bet my dad did it for a joke. He would have thought that was hilarious."

When I'd ended the call, the Montgomery phone had stopped, but to test it again, I dialed HOME from the cell phone. Sure enough, the house phone rang again until I ended the call. "Wonder if he changed anything else," I said, going back to the contact list. Of course there was no way to tell. I ran through the list anyway, looking for anything that might jump out. Reba Montgomery was there under M. Teagen and Shane were both listed, too. Under S was Sue—his missing daughter, I remembered. I could only imagine how awful it had to be to see her name there every day. The only thing more painful would be to actually remove it from the list. Doing so would give her loss a permanence that had to be impossible for a parent to cope with.

"Do you have your dad's phone?" I asked, thinking that if Mr. Blake had Chris's emergency numbers, Mr. Montgomery probably had his partner's numbers, too.

But Teagen shook her head. "He had it with him. The sheriff said it was melted."

The heaviness of the statement hung between us. Neither one of us spoke for about thirty seconds. Finally, I tucked Mr. Blake's phone in my bag and headed down the hallway toward the stairs. "Hang in there, Teagen. I promise, it'll get better. You have to give it some time."

"Ms. Cassidy," she said.

I paused at the door, turning around.

"I heard you're, um, making homecoming mums."

I nodded. "You should see my shop. It's mum city in there."

"You're making one for Shane?"

"And Gracie."

"Is he . . ." Her eyes welled with tears and her lower lip quivered. "Will he be able to go to homecoming? Is he going to be"—her voice hitched as she finished— "arrested?"

Her words felt like a vise around my heart. "I'm making the mums so he and Gracie can wear them. The sheriff is trying to find the truth," I said. "And so am I."

"Do you have time . . . could you . . . I'd really like a . . ."

She stumbled with her words, but I read between the lines. "I would love to make you a mum, Teagen."

Anything to get a little time back at Buttons & Bows, where I could think and weave together the mess of threads of Bliss's latest mystery.

Chapter 9

Quiet time at Buttons & Bows to make a mum for Teagen was not to be. Before I'd even had a chance to start up Buttercup, my cell phone rang.

"We have a problem, Cassidy," Will said when I answered.

I gripped the steering wheel, knowing that Will calling about a problem was no small thing. He wasn't a cry-wolf kind of man, so if he thought something was wrong, something was probably very wrong.

"What is it?" I didn't know which way to drive, so I stayed put in front of the Montgomery house, the truck in idle.

"Gracie called from school. There was an anonymous tip about Shane. Gavin came and searched his locker. They found a flask of vodka, instructions on how to sever the steering linkage in a car, and a shirt they say might be the one he was wearing the day his dad died."

My head spun as he rattled off the evidence piling up against Shane. "How can they be sure it's the shirt he was wearing? And what does that matter, anyway?" I added, trying to gather up the pieces Will had just tossed up into the air.

"The school has surveillance tapes. Apparently the sheriff's office has been going through them all. They saw Shane on Friday's tape. When they found the shirt, they put together that it was the same one."

"But why does that matter?" I asked again.

He hesitated. "There's oil on the sleeve."

I suddenly pictured Otis from Bubba's rubbing his greasy hands on a dirty blue cloth. "Oh no."

I threw the truck into drive and headed toward Bliss High School. The nerves in my gut seized. No matter how I tried to spin it, this didn't look good for Shane.

"Right."

"I'm on my way," I said. Less than eight minutes later, I pulled into the parking lot of the school, tucked the truck into a visitor parking space, and speed walked toward the front office.

I approached the double glass doors and saw that Gavin was there, along with a female deputy named Kate O'Brian. She'd come in to Buttons & Bows several times as a potential customer, but she'd yet to pull the trigger on having me design something for her. Behind the law enforcement officers, Will stood with Gracie, speaking softly and convincing her she needed to go back to class.

My head felt light, as if all the blood was draining from it and pooling in my gut. Between the deputies, hands cuffed behind his back, was Shane. He looked as pale and drawn as I felt, his eyes cast down, his chin slack, a look of disbelief on his face.

"Shane," I said, but my words stopped on my lips. I had a vision of him in a white wide-pin-striped suit, a throwback from the 1920s, looking dapper and irreverent. It wasn't like anything I'd ever made, but that didn't mean it was outside the realm of possibility.

He lifted his gaze to mine, his brown eyes skittish and scared. He was a sixteen-year-old boy, but he looked like a terrified child who was lost in a crowd. "I didn't do it," he said, his voice scarcely above a whisper. "I didn't kill my dad."

Gavin looked at me, his face grim, his lips pressed into a thin line. He shook his head, just barely, and after he'd done it I wasn't entirely sure I'd seen it—or that I'd interpreted it correctly. The message I'd gotten was that he didn't think Shane had done it, either. Maybe I was delusional. Or too close to the situation.

"Let's go," he said to Shane, no bark to his words.

Gavin and I didn't see eye to eye, but like his father, my stepdaddy, Hoss McClaine, he was a fair man and he certainly didn't want to arrest anyone who wasn't actually guilty.

He flattened his palm on the top of Shane's head, guiding him into the back of his cruiser. A minute later, Will and I stood at the curb staring after the disappearing taillights of the car.

Will slipped his arm around me, pulling me close. "I believe him," he said, his gaze still straight ahead on the empty road.

"What did he say about the vodka?" I asked.

"That it's not his."

Of course—what else would he say?

The shirt seemed irrefutable, so I left that one alone,

although there had to be an explanation. The third item found in Shane's locker bothered me the most. "Shane worked at Bubba's. Why would he need instructions on how to cause damage to a car? That doesn't make sense, does it? Wouldn't he know?"

It would be akin to me needing instructions on how to add pleats to a bodice, or how to gather a skirt. It just felt wrong.

"That's just what I was thinking," Will said. "He wouldn't, which means—"

"Someone's trying to frame him," I finished, the words bitter in my mouth. In my mind's eye, I saw the crushed expression on Gracie's face as she stood with her father watching Gavin and Deputy O'Brian lead Shane away. My resolve to help her—to help them both—strengthened. I took out my cell phone and dialed Miss Reba.

"I just heard. I'm on my way to the sheriff's office," she said when she answered.

"He's scared," I said, not wanting to upset her, but not sugarcoating it, either. "The deputy found some things in his locker."

"What's happening, Harlow? Shane didn't do this. He didn't do this!"

"I know, Miss Reba," I said. I just hoped I could figure out why someone was trying to make it look like he had.

Will and I hung around outside the campus until the bell rang and the students were dismissed. A steady stream of kids filed through the front doors. We caught snippets of conversation, some about homecoming, the football game Friday night, and the new restaurant opening in town where half the student population was hoping to get part-time work. The rest centered around the arrest of Shane Montgomery, the discoveries in his locker, and the utter disbelief that he could have killed his father.

"He's, like, the nicest guy," one girl said, wiping a tear from her cheek.

"Doesn't he have an alibi?" the boy with her asked.

"It's not like he was right there when the car crashed. It was tampered with before the accident," another guy said.

"No, but I heard they played chicken . . . and Shane's dad lost."

"Shane. A killer." A group of girls shook their heads in unison as one of them said, "I just can't believe all his bad luck."

They walked off before we could hear any more. "What bad luck?" Will asked.

We moved to the stone half wall and perched while we waited for Gracie. "They had a break-in a few weeks ago," I said, answering his question. "Nothing major was stolen except for Teagen's iPod and Shane's jacket, but some random stuff was taken. Then Miss Reba woke up to the intruder standing over their bed."

"I did hear about that." He went on to say something about there not being any other home invasions or robberies, but my mind slipped back to something Otis had said at Bubba's.

He'd said that Shane and his dad had fought. Maybe he and his dad didn't get along as well as people seemed to think. Otis had thought it was possible Shane had simply snapped. Who was right? Otis, or the kids at school who thought Shane was incapable of hurting anyone, let alone his father?

"Woolgathering?"

"What?"

"You're at it again, Cassidy. Lost in thought, your mind miles and miles away."

I looked up at him sheepishly. "Just trying to make sense of what happened."

We looked up to see Danica and Leslie next to us. Their expressions were somber.

"Girls," I asked them, "did you hear about the burglary at the Montgomery's a few weeks back?"

"Sure," Danica said. "I heard that Mr. Montgomery chased whoever it was down the street, but I don't think they ever found out who broke in."

Leslie shook her head, her brows pulled together. "Pretty scary. Someone just waltzed right in like they owned the place and, from what I heard, scared the bejesus out of Shane's mom."

"Not as scary as murder." Danica looked back at Will and me. "Everyone's saying the sheriff came and arrested Shane. Is he okay?"

Leslie knocked the back of her hand against Danica's arm. "Really? Do you *think* he's okay?"

Danica's eyes flew open wide, the reality of Shane's situation looking like it was hitting her in earnest. She clutched her jacket and fiddled with the strap of her backpack. "No, of course he's not okay. I didn't mean . . . I was just . . ." She gulped, regrouping. "How's Gracie taking it?"

"He's innocent."

This time we all turned, startled by the force of Gracie's voice. She came up on the other side of Will and me, her best friend, Holly Kincaid, by her side.

"Of course he is," Leslie said, while Danica added, "It'll all work out. It has to."

"Shane's mom'll get him a lawyer," Gracie said. Her gaze skittered over each of us and she nodded. "She'll get him the best, and the sheriff'll realize his mistake, and you'll figure out the truth," she said to me, "and it'll all be okay. You'll see."

Will squeezed Gracie's hand. "We'll do what we can to help, sweetheart."

Gracie nodded, but instead of falling apart or looking to her dad for more reassurance, she turned to me, her eyes fiery. "I want to go work on our homecoming mums; is that okay, Harlow? Can I go to Buttons and Bows?"

"Gracie," I said, "are you sure—"

"You don't have to come. I can do it alone," she said quickly. Her eyes glazed over and she dipped her chin, her strength wavering. "Please, Harlow."

"I want to work on mine, too," Leslie said quickly. "And I'd love to see my dress again."

Danica nodded. "Me, too. We can order some pizza and get not *plumb* crazy, but *mum* crazy."

The girls all looked at Danica like she was from Neptune; then they each grinned. It was a silly joke, but it had done the trick of lightening the moment. Even for Gracie.

Holly had her cell phone out, her thumb poised and ready to dial. They all looked at me, their fearless mum leader, to give the okay. At some point, I would trek out to Granbury and return Mr. Blake's phone to his wife, but right now, I wanted to do whatever Gracie needed me to do to help her feel better, and I had to make Teagen her mum. Those two things were more important than anything else.

"Let's go," I said.

An almost enthusiastic cheer went up from the girls, and Holly dialed, stepping aside as she placed a delivery order. The girls split up, each walking to their respective cars. Gracie went with Holly in her Jeep, Danica drove off in her old vintage car, and Leslie walked toward the road. Danica stopped and said something to Leslie through the open passenger window. Leslie nodded and climbed in, the engine revved, and they were off.

A little piece of my heart swelled at the budding of the friendship between the two girls. They'd met because of Zinnia James and her charity, but now they were becoming closer, and that was worth all the dresses in the world.

Will walked me to my truck. "You sure you can handle four teenage girls?"

I laughed. "If I can handle Loretta Mae, I can handle them."

A short while later we were settled around the dining table at Buttons & Bows. I'd already had a base put together, so I spent the first twenty minutes tying on charms, bells, and plastic decorations, including a sparkly pink cell phone.

"For Teagen," I said when the girls asked who it was for.

They nodded in unison, each of them silently acknowledging that, bless her heart, Teagen needed a great mum to help her in her time of need.

It was smaller than the others because she was in middle school, but the way I saw it, she had plenty of time to grow into the enormous creations as she worked through her high school career. Kids had to have something to look forward to, after all.

They kept working on their creations, but I moved on to Danica's dress. There was nothing like working with fabric to help ease my mind and calm my thoughts. But more than anything, what I wanted was inspiration about how to help Shane get out of the shackles he was currently in.

Chapter 10

My dining table had been doubling as a workstation pretty much since I'd moved into the house at 2112 Mockingbird. Thanks to the four teenage girls, now the workspace was spilling into the rest of the kitchen. Half-made mums, strands of ribbon, and small trinkets littered the entire dining area, while lengths of discarded grosgrain coiled like small snakes on the kitchen floor.

As I sewed in my workroom, I listened to the girls' chatter. Holly, Danica, and Leslie worked hard to bolster and distract Gracie. Gracie, for her part, was trying like the dickens to be positive. She was a born and bred Southern girl, which meant, just like the rest of us, she'd been raised to keep a smile on her face, hide whatever might be bothering her, and act like a lady. These tenets were the core beliefs behind the Margaret Moffette Lea Pageant and Ball, an annual event that wasn't quite a debutante ball, but was pretty darn close. Gracie had been part of it recently and had learned the lessons well.

If I looked at her long enough, I could see her lower

lip droop and tremble, but for the most part, she was keeping it together.

The pizza arrived, and I made a pitcher of lemonade and set out a few cans of soda. Holly, Danica, and Gracie each took one piece at a time of the pizza, but Leslie took three, eating quickly, almost as if the food might disappear and she'd be left with nothing. The response of someone who had gone without food, I reckoned.

"He has his mom," Danica was saying. "That's more than you or I have."

She was right about that. Gracie's mom had taken off a long time ago and she'd been raised by her dad. He'd done a great job of rearing a strong, confident young lady, even if she was burying her true feelings at the moment. When we were alone, I hoped I could get her to let down her defenses and fess up to what she was going through.

I still didn't know Danica or Leslie's whole story, but I'd worry about that later. For now, my focus was on Gracie.

"My dad said you went to Bubba's," Gracie said, swallowing a bit of pizza and washing it down with a gulp of lemonade.

"I did. Here and the one in Granbury."

"What did you find out? Do you have a lead?" Her voice rose, her anxiousness to get answers and help Shane lighting all of her nerves. She was like a ball of energy.

I waved my hands so she'd simmer down. "I talked to a guy named Otis. He didn't say much," I said, not mentioning his suggestion that Shane and his dad didn't see eye to eye on things. "He did mention that Mr. Montgomery spent the night at the shop in Granbury sometimes."

The girls all looked to Gracie as if she could corroborate the story. She nodded. "Shane said that, too. His dad would work late and just stay the night instead of driving the narrow country roads in the dark."

"And yet that's how he died," Danica said, shaking her head, her voice sad. "Ironic, isn't it?"

There was no response. The girls just dipped their chins toward their chests, taking a moment of silence.

"My dad wasn't home half the time, either," she continued. She was trying to draw a connection between her and Gracie. Despite the trauma of losing her own parents, she was compassionate and wanting to make her new friend feel better.

"If Shane didn't do it," Leslie said, "then who did? Why would anyone want Mr. Montgomery dead?"

That was a very good question. I listened to them talk, hoping to glean some tidbit of information to help me decide if any of my theories had any merit.

"Maybe Teagen did it," Leslie said. "Maybe she secretly hates her brother and father. She killed her dad and set up Shane—"

"Stop!" Red splotches appeared on Gracie's neck and her temples pulsed. "Teagen didn't kill her father any more than Shane did." She dropped her half-eaten piece of pizza and buried her head in her hands.

Leslie froze, her eyes wide with shame. "Sorry," she said. "I didn't mean anything by it."

"Maybe it was that guy you met, Otis," Danica suggested.

We all looked at her, letting this sink in. "But why would he kill Mr. Montgomery?" I asked.

Her brow furrowed, her jet-black hair falling over her eyes. "He worked for Montgomery, right? Maybe he was stealing from his boss, or maybe Mr. Montgomery was going to fire him?"

Leslie flattened her hands against the tabletop. "Or maybe," she said, "this Otis guy was having an affair with Mrs. Montgomery."

"Shane's mom was *not* having an affair," Gracie said.

"How do you know? If they were, it would be a secret. It's not like people go around talking about their affairs. And if they were, it would be motive, right? Could have been Otis *or* Mrs. Montgomery. Or maybe," Leslie continued, her voice dropping to a conspiratorial tone, "it was both of them together."

I shifted in my seat, trying to figure out how to interject. "Have you met Otis from Bubba's?" I asked Leslie.

"No."

"Have you met Reba Montgomery?"

She shook her head. "No."

I thought about Otis's grease-stained coveralls with the name patch and his slicked-back hair; then an image of Miss Reba came to me with her sweater sets, fashion scarves, and blingy jeans. "I don't really see them together as a couple."

I didn't mention the fact that I couldn't see Miss Reba as an adulterer at all, with Otis or anyone else. The idea of Miss Reba sleeping with another man while her husband spent his nights in Granbury after a long day of work didn't sit well.

Still, I couldn't discount it as a possible motive, and as much as I liked Miss Reba, I knew that how she presented herself to the town of Bliss might not be anywhere close to who she really was. Anyone was capable of anything. Even adultery. And worse, even murder.

The next morning, Buttercup bounced along the bumpy country roads and before long I was back in Granbury and parking in front of Mrs. Blake's mobile home. Things felt different since the last time I'd been here. The Mustangs looked forlorn and unloved. The thatch of grass and flowers had turned scraggly and brown.

I'd come alone this time, hoping Mrs. Blake might be more open to talking without Will looking on. She answered the door after the first knock, as if she were waiting by the door, on edge for some bad news to be delivered. Her skin was sallow, her eye sockets sunken and dark from lack of sleep and worry. "No sign of your husband?" I asked.

She shook her head. "Not a word." Any trace of anger was gone and all that remained was the fear that maybe Eddy Blake wasn't going to be coming home.

"Did you report him missing?"

She slow blinked instead of nodding, but the message was clear. She'd reported it, but there'd been no luck in finding him. Anybody who chose to disappear simply could, and it seemed as if Eddy Blake didn't want to be found.

"I have his phone," I said.

Instead of blocking the entrance to her home as she'd done last time I'd been here, she stepped back and ushered me in. A pall of grief infused in the walls and linoleum of the small house. A lost daughter. A missing husband.

Mrs. Blake had experienced too much sadness. She was living the same experience as Miss Reba, the details of the losses slightly different, but the emotions the same.

My gaze was drawn to the framed photos on the small table just inside the door. It was a shrine to the red-haired girl smiling in the large center frame, the rest of the smaller photos showing the mother and daughter at a park, standing in front of a Christmas tree, and with the girl as a toddler.

Something about the pictures bothered me. I looked at each of them again, studying the smiling faces, and then it hit me. Eddy Blake wasn't in any of them. "Is your husband always the photographer?" I asked.

She looked at the array of photos and nodded. "He doesn't like to be in front of the camera. Doesn't like to have his picture taken at all. Told me he wouldn't be one of those men who have their faces on display on park benches, billboards, or even at his own funeral."

"Maybe that's a male thing," I said, remembering the pictures I'd seen at the Montgomery house. The photos had been of Teagen and Shane, a few with Miss Reba, but I couldn't remember any of them showing Chris Montgomery.

The hairs rose on the back of my neck. Something was off; I just couldn't put my finger on what. I looked around the living room. The place was small, but clean and kempt. Mrs. Blake's distress over her missing husband hadn't stopped her from keeping things picked up. She was like me. Nervous energy always meant I had a clean house.

I plunged my hand into my bag to retrieve Mr. Blake's cell phone. A question crowded into my head. The home number on the phone rang the Montgomery's house. "Did your husband and Chris Montgomery always get along okay?" Teagen had said her dad was a prankster and played jokes on his friend, but the families didn't mingle. The wives didn't know each other. Did Chris Montgomery and Eddy Blake really have an easy, joking friendship, or could that be completely wrong? Maybe Eddy had disappeared because he'd killed his business partner. Maybe they hadn't gotten along at all.

"As far as I know," she said. "They mostly stayed in their own shops, so it's not like I saw them together, or anything. But I'd say that, yes, they get . . . er, got along fine."

"But they each did go to the other's store sometimes, right? I heard Mr. Montgomery came here and spent the night at the shop sometimes. Same for Eddy?"

"Sure, but mostly they handled their own stores. Eddy's place is here in Granbury, and Chris managed Bliss."

Something else I'd been thinking about popped back into my mind. I'd already checked with Gavin and as far as anyone knew, there wasn't a will. Which meant probate, and ultimately a determination of ownership going to Miss Reba and her children as the next of kin.

But what if there *was* a will? And what if that will bequeathed the actual ownership not to Miss Reba, but to Mr. Blake?

I made a mental note to talk to Otis about it. I knew Gavin probably already had, but as Meemaw said, you got more bees with honey, and I was definitely sweeter than the deputy sheriff.

"Do you go to Bubba's very often?" I asked, this time meaning the shop here in Granbury.

She half shook, half nodded her head. "Occasionally. I used to go more often than I do now."

"See, this is why I was wondering if Chris and Eddy got along. Don't you think it's strange that you never met Chris?"

Now she fully shook her head. "No. Eddy doesn't like to mix home and business. When I come, we usually go sit at the picnic table outside. And it's not like I go often. An auto shop isn't where I want to spend my time. I stayed away in the heat of the summer, and in January on through early March. The window of nice weather is pretty small in Texas, I'm sure you know."

"I sure do," I said. Most people thought Texas didn't get all that cold, but they were wrong. The temperature dropped below freezing a good many times during the winter, and we even got snow flurries on occasion. And during the summer, thunder and lightning storms released the humidity that hung heavy in the air, often helping drop the temperature from 100 degrees to a more tolerable 90. But no matter how you sliced the pie, it was hot, and often miserable.

I revisited the thing that had been bothering me since Mr. Montgomery's funeral. "What about company gatherings? Do y'all have those?"

"The holiday parties are usually separate for the two shops. The people here don't know the people in Bliss. Eddy always manages to go down there and make an appearance, but Chris never did come our way, which I didn't like. If Eddy could do it, he ought to have been able to, too, right? One-sided partnership, if you ask me. Eddy deserves the business. I want him to buy out Chris's wife, but of course I haven't had a chance to tell him that."

No, because he hadn't been home. Whenever he finally did show up, I didn't envy him. I got the impression that Mrs. Blake wasn't going to let him off the hook too easily at this point.

Once again, I started to hand over the phone, but for the second time, I stopped. I wished I could put my finger on what was troubling me. Meemaw and I had spent long, lazy summer afternoons creating collages on squares of watercolor paper. Most of the time I found inspiration all around me, particularly with scraps of French fabrics, bits of lace, and figures I'd drawn on text-heavy scrapbook paper. But once in a while, I looked at a page and didn't have a clue what to fill it with. That big question mark I'd felt in those moments was just what I was feeling now. My mind was drawing a big blank.

With my hand curled around Eddy Blake's cell phone, I let my gaze wander the house again. On a back hallway wall, I saw another grouping of photographs. "Mrs. Blake," I said before I could even think, "could I use the restroom?"

"Down the hall to the right," she said. "I'm going to make a cup of coffee. Do you want one?"

"Yes, ma'am," I replied.

"Milk? I only have coconut milk, if that's okay."

"Sure," I said absently, heading off in the direction of the bathroom before she changed her mind and kicked me out. She didn't know me from Sam Houston, after all.

In three steps, she was in the kitchen, removing a sealed carton from the refrigerator, coffee from a can, and pouring water into the receptacle of a Mr. Coffee machine on the counter. I turned and a few seconds later, I was halfway down the hallway. I looked over my shoulder. She had her back to me as she pulled two mugs from the cupboard to the right of the sink. I hurried past the bathroom door, stopping when I got to the pictures on the wall.

The first several weren't all that different from the ones in the nonexistent entry. They were all of mother and daughter, one or two of just daughter, but once again, it appeared that Mr. Blake was the photographer.

A wedding photo caught my attention at the edge of the collection. I checked on Mrs. Blake again, but I needn't have worried. She was sitting at the small, round dining table, her head down and resting on her crossed forearms.

If she minded me looking at the family pictures, she wasn't saying. Not that she would mind. She'd hung them on the wall in the first place, after all. It wasn't as if I was digging around or intruding where I didn't belong.

I raised my gaze back to the wedding picture. Mrs. Blake wore a skirt that fell just above the knees and a tailored white jacket. No froufrou wedding dress for her. I wondered if it had been a shotgun wedding, if they'd been pinching pennies so had opted for something less traditional, or if they just weren't the gregarious types.

I looked at the picture again. Mrs. Blake was fresh-faced and laughing, her new husband nuzzling her neck. Young and in love. It was a natural pose, and I felt a pang of distress at what Mrs. Blake must be going through right now, worrying over where he was and why he'd vanished. Surely the thought that Eddy had had a hand in Chris's death had at least crossed her mind.

I moved on to the rest of the pictures, but nothing jumped out at me that could help me figure out what was going on and where Mr. Blake had gone off to.

After a cup of coffee with Mrs. Blake and no more information to be had, I left, deflated and no closer to any answers.

Chapter 11

It was after noon as I drove away from the Blake home. Something niggled in my thoughts, but I just couldn't put my finger on what it was that was bothering me. I dialed Will, knowing that running the events of the morning and all my thoughts by him would help untangle the threads in my head, but the call went to voice mail. Architecture, I'd realized since meeting him, was a lot like dressmaking. It was controlled creativity, and ultimately, it was about sharing something creative with others.

The function of a space or building didn't define the form, just as the style of a garment didn't define the details. No, we both worked to create balance between form and function, and this very philosophy consumed every one of our projects. Will had recently finished a major renovation of the courthouse on the square, bringing the upper floors, which now housed historic Bliss memorabilia, into focus. He was on to the next pressing town project, a redesign of the building on the east side of the square where Sweet Temptations, a new specialty cupcake bakery, had opened up, and where Riley's Furniture, an orthopedic practice, and a high-end clothing store also had their businesses.

"Trouble with the permits," he'd said the night before. He had to work within the parameters of a blueprint, needed permits to proceed, and, in the case of historic buildings, he had to consider the integrity of the building.

With dressmaking, I had to take into consideration what the client wanted, body shape, and character, but ultimately, it was up to me to decide what would work for a woman's comfort, blending her aesthetic and personality with mine.

I started driving, but pulled over again when I couldn't think straight. Otis kept rising to the top of my thoughts. The girls at the mum party had planted a seed, and it was taking hold. Mr. Blake might be the killer, but what if he wasn't? Otis could be a disgruntled employee. Any motive I could think of for killing his boss was sketchy. Except one.

I dialed Miss Reba on my cell phone, forcing myself to make a little small talk before launching into my question. My mama taught me better than to forgo manners, no matter the situation. She didn't adhere to a lot of Southern rules for ladies like never letting anyone see you cry or always crossing your legs, but compassion, consideration, and chitchat were what she called the three Cs and they were nonnegotiable.

Finally, I was able to ask Miss Reba what I'd called for. "Is Bubba's in good shape financially?"

There was a pause, as if she were trying to figure out just how to answer that. Finally, she said, "It's not a million-dollar business, if that's what you mean, but it does okay. We live pretty well and don't want for anything."

They didn't, but from what I could see, the Blakes didn't live near as well and they might want for quite a bit, comparatively.

"Miss Reba," I asked, broaching the subject I was really interested in, "who inherits your husband's business?"

"His portion, you mean," she said, more as a statement than a question.

"Yes, ma'am."

"I do, of course. A percentage of it is in trust for the kids, and Otis Levon owns ten percent," she added. "I know Chris was thinking about giving him a little more of his ownership, but I honestly don't know if he did."

My thoughts slowed and the threads rearranged themselves in my head. With that one sentence, Otis and Miss Reba were on equal footing as far as motive, as well as Mr. Blake, and possibly even Mrs. Blake. Miss Reba, the Blakes, and Otis all had a stake in the business. So did Shane, for that matter.

I had another thought. "Miss Reba, have there been any withdrawals from your bank account? Could someone have been blackmailing your husband?"

She scoffed. "That's downright absurd, Harlow. Blackmail over what? Chris was an honest man. An upstanding citizen. No one could have *had* anything on him."

"Have you checked?" I pressed.

She heaved a sigh. "Yes. And, no, there's nothing unusual. No withdrawals. Nothing out of the ordinary."

And yet someone had murdered him. Something wasn't adding up.

I drove without thinking, wondering how to get one of the suspects to rise to the top of the list. A short while later I found myself in front of the Granbury location of Bubba's. One word kept circling in my mind. Proof. Maybe I could poke around and find some proof inside that Otis was behind his boss's death. Or maybe I could find something to exonerate him.

Of course I didn't have a deputy's badge or a title, so chances were, no one would let me snoop around in the shop or answer my questions. "I should just go tell Hoss my suspect list," I said under my breath. I started to drive on past Bubba's, but at the last second, I cranked the steering wheel hard to the right and whipped my truck into the parking lot—as much as a vintage Ford can whip. I couldn't simply give Hoss and Gavin a list of people who might have killed Chris Montgomery. Not that they wouldn't have already compiled the same list, anyway, but I didn't want to be responsible for throwing innocent people under the bus.

I channeled Meemaw and her determination, and a moment later I walked up the sidewalk. From the corner of my eye, I spotted the picnic table Mrs. Blake had told me she and her husband sat at when she visited the shop. It was far enough away from the building that no one could hear them talk, yet close enough for Eddy Blake to keep an eye on things.

I drew in a deep breath, grabbed the door handle, and walked into the air-conditioned lobby. A woman about my age sat at the end of one line of chairs, her head bent over her smartphone, her thumbs tapping more quickly than I could spell. A balding man with heavy jowls sat at the opposite end of the chairs, flipping through a car magazine. And at the counter, a young woman, no more than twenty-five, leaned on her elbows, her thumb and her forefinger rubbing her eyelashes.

None of them looked up as I entered.

Maybe the customer service at Bubba's had gone down since one of the owners died.

I cleared my throat as I approached the counter, waiting for the clerk to look up. Finally, she did, peering at me as if I were disturbing her afternoon. "Yeah?" she said. "Help you?"

"I'm looking for Otis," I said, hoping that Otis was in Bliss today and not here at the Granbury store.

She stared blankly at me, as if I'd asked for a ticket to Mars or service for my flying carpet.

"You know, Otis Levon? He works for Bubba's?"

"I know who you mean," she said. "He don't work here. He *owns* here. Or at least part of here."

The hairs on the back of my neck went up, but I smiled and played it off. "Oh?"

"Yep. That's what he says, anyway. Says when everything's settled, he'll collect his part of the business, and it's about time. *It's owed me*," she added in a deep voice, mimicking what Otis must have said over and over.

"I would have thought Mr. Montgomery's wife would have inherited it. . . ."

I trailed off, hoping she'd fill in the blanks. If Miss Reba didn't inherit the majority, it would be big news to her.

"He says he owns it now, but I dunno. Nobody tells me nothin'. And," she continued, "if Mr. Blake don't show up real quick, I heard Otis say he's gonna claim his portion, too." Her gaze skittered to the two people in the aluminum-framed chairs, then back to me. "Can he just do that?" she asked quietly, looking back down at the glass counter.

"I don't think so," I said. "At least not until the police are sure he's not coming back, and not unless it's in the will, but I heard there isn't a will, so . . ."

She shrugged at that and my mind scuttled around the fact that the motive for Otis was growing by the second. *People do what they have to do, when they have to do it.* Those were words Meemaw had lived by, and I believed them. Whatever the reason, people believed they had to murder. It was justified in their minds. A shiver crept up my spine. If Otis had killed Chris Montgomery to claim his portion of the business, he might well have killed Eddy Blake, too.

"He's not here, is he?" I asked again. Bliss was his regular store, but I had to be sure.

She shook her head. "He's in Bliss today," she said.

I caught a glimpse of her name patch: BRANDI, with an I. "When will he be back?" I asked her. I'd be heading back to Bliss, but I hoped I could dig around while he was gone.

She shrugged. "He's managing both stores, now, so I don't know. He hasn't posted his new schedule now that Mr. Montgomery is gone and Mr. Blake is . . . is . . ."

Perfect opening, and I seized it. "Right, I heard he hasn't been around much. That he's worse now than when he lost his daughter." I leaned down, meeting her gaze. "Can I ask you something, Brandi?"

She shrugged again, brushing her auburn hair away from her face.

"I'm a friend of Mrs. Montgomery. She'd love a keepsake of some sort from the business. They started the Bubba's together, didn't they?"

"The Bliss shop. Not here. This one was all Mr. Blake, from what I know. And Otis."

For all I knew, I'd seen Mr. Blake and I didn't even know it. I hadn't wanted to ask his wife to see a photo. Pouring salt on the wound and all that. But maybe Brandi could help. "Is there a picture of them here somewhere?"

Her lips pulled to one side as she thought about it. Finally she gave her head a little shake. "Nope, not that I know of." She waved her arm around. "'Course, it ain't like we got lots of pretty decor here."

I caught a glimpse of a staircase behind her. "Upstairs maybe?" She eyed me suspiciously for the first time. "Who'd you say you are, again? Police?" She gasped. "Are you a detective?"

"No, no, I'm a dressmaker, actually. Buttons and Bows in Bliss?"

She stared at me, a blank expression on her face. Guess word of my business hadn't spread yet to Granbury.

"You probably know that Mr. Montgomery's son is being accused of having something to do with his dad's death?"

This time she nodded.

"I'm a family friend. Just trying to help."

She looked far more alert than she had a few minutes ago. Nothing exciting ever happened in small-town Texas, it seemed, so questions about a suspicious death were of high interest. "I can show you upstairs, if you want," she whispered. "Do you want to see it?"

"Does a seamstress collect fabric?" I said, but from the blank expression on her face, the comparison fell flat. Clearly, she didn't sew. "I'd love to," I amended. "Thank you."

"Your cars'll be ready pretty soon," she called to the two people in the chairs. The woman lifted her head in a slight acknowledgment, and the man wriggled the fingers on one hand, never looking up.

She shrugged—it seemed to be her standard reaction to most everything—crooked her finger at me, and rounded the corner, disappearing from sight. I scurried behind the counter to follow her, mounting the narrow staircase. There was only one room upstairs, and Brandi hadn't waited at the top, so I went in through the open door.

The room was more spacious than I'd anticipated. A navy blue corduroy couch was pushed against the right wall. Opposite that was a short counter, a full-sized refrigerator, and a small, round table with three wood-backed chairs.

"Does that pull out to a bed?" I asked, pointing to the couch.

Brandi plopped down right in the center of it, nodding. "It does, how'd you know?"

"Mrs. Montgomery told me her husband sometimes stayed overnight when he worked late here."

Her right eyebrow arched up. "I never heard that."

"Heard what?"

"About him spending the night."

"Oh. I heard Mr. Blake sometimes spent the night in Bliss, too. Better than driving the dark country roads at night."

"Maybe. I guess. I just never saw Mr. Montgomery here, is all."

I walked around the perimeter of the room, looking through the rack of clothing crammed in the far corner, the pile of magazines on the table, the packets of sugar and sugar-free sweetener scattered on the counter. My attention went back to the rack of clothes, a combination of jeans and button down shirts, a few collared polos, several pairs of navy slacks, and one casual sport coat.

"Mr. Blake keeps clothes here?"

She'd gotten up from the couch and had moved to the doorway, peering out and listening. She might look disengaged from her job, but out of sight didn't mean out of mind. A second later, she came back into the room. "Yeah, weird, right? Any time he goes to Bubba's in Bliss, he changes clothes."

"That's not all that strange," I said. "I design clothes, and if there's one thing I know, it's that people want to look their best when they go into an unfamiliar environment."

"But it's not like it's unfamiliar. He goes there all the time. He does spend the night there, too. I figure that Bliss store has got to be crazy busy all the time since it takes both of them, plus now Otis, to run it. All we have here is Mr. Blake, and once in a while, Otis'll come up. More lately, 'course."

"Of course." I rifled through the clothes, hoping that Otis wouldn't decide to show up now, and doubly hoping that Mr. Blake wouldn't suddenly return from his extended absence to find me poking around the room.

If Otis had killed him, too, that wasn't a possibility, but I had to assume that hadn't happened until I had proof that it had.

Nothing about the clothes was all that interesting, aside from the fact that the jeans were run-of-the-mill over the counter, while the slacks and sport coat were a better-quality brand and were high-quality fabrics. Not unusual, given the different styles, but I might have expected nicer jeans.

"Nobody keeps anything personal here?" I asked, wishing I knew what I was looking for. I had too many suspects and no crystal clear motives, which made my task of helping Miss Reba unfocused. I suddenly understood why Gavin and Hoss narrowed their investigations to the most likely suspect and went from there. If they disproved the suspect, then they could just move on to the next person on the list.

The way I was approaching things was the opposite. I had all the possible suspects in a jumble in my mind, and I felt like a mouse in a maze, following the scent of the cheese, but that cheese kept randomly being moved.

I was confusing myself.

The answer, of course, was that I had to get focused. I had to approach helping Shane the way I liked to approach a new garment project. In a perfect world, I tried to work on that design, and only that design, until I had it nailed down. Sure, other typically mindless tasks from other ongoing projects sometimes interfered, but if I could home in on one thing, my brain was usually happier.

Bringing in other full-fledged designs slowed down my process and sometimes it had the adverse effect of muddying the design concepts of each project until I'd lost my way. Danica and Leslie's dresses were a case in point. Developing Danica's dress concept had been twice as hard and had taken twice as long because I was also thinking about Leslie's. There were times when it couldn't be helped, but ideally, concentrated focus was better.

I needed to apply that rule to what I was doing for Miss Reba and Shane. I'd gotten all I could from Mrs. Blake, and there was nothing relevant here at Bubba's, at least not that I could find. There was no picture of the two owners. I still had no idea where Eddy Blake had disappeared to, or why. Or if he was still alive.

The whole situation didn't set well, but until I could find out more, I would put him on the back burner and move on to another possible suspect, zeroing in my attention.

Otis Levon.

It seemed logical to pay a visit to Mrs. Levon.

Which was exactly what I decided to do next.

Chapter 12

Brandi gave up the Levon address a little too easily, I thought, but I was grateful nonetheless. They lived in the country just outside of Bliss city limits. It took less than twenty-five minutes to find the house after only one near death experience, between me and a motorcycle passing on the shoulder. Minutes later and after a brief introduction, Sally Levon opened her door wide and invited me inside. Southern hospitality at its best.

As I followed her inside, I couldn't help but notice the ill fit of her black pants, the practical, but style-less flats, and the floral blouse topped by a baggy black sweater. This was not a woman filled with confidence, and it was reflected in her clothing.

I'd spent my childhood playing with paper dolls, many old-fashioned ones that Nana color photocopied for me and which I then cut out. Others were perforated, easily punched out from the cardstock, the tabs folded down so I could then hook the clothing onto the paper dolls.

In my mind, I sometimes pictured the people around

me as paper dolls. I would devise a new outfit, fold the mental tabs, and re-dress them with the new outfit I'd devised.

At other times, images simply popped into my head—part of my Cassidy charm—and I knew just what outfit the woman needed in order to reframe the way she thought. In Mrs. Levon's case, I saw her in fitted slacks that accentuated her shape rather than hiding it. A creamy, lightweight blouse and a semifitted jacket, pinched in at the waist with a band at the lower back that was still casual, yet gave her a more pulled-together look. The jacket would have a floral pattern to accent her tawny hair and fair skin.

If only I could make it for her, maybe she and Otis's love would strengthen and he wouldn't sound so surprised when he referred to her as a good woman. Assuming he wasn't a murderer, that is.

She led me into the small kitchen. It was about half the size of Mrs. Blake's, which was half the size of Mrs. Montgomery's, but of the three, the Levon kitchen was the warmest and most welcoming. Red gingham chair cushions sat on top of woven chair seats. A coordinating fabric valance hung from the small window overlooking the postage stamp backyard. Cheery colors and design touches made me want to sit, sip sweet tea, and chew the fat.

Which is just what we did. "I was awful sorry to hear about Mr. Montgomery," she said after she handed me a supersized aqua blue melamine glass filled with sweet tea. I usually preferred unsweetened tea, but Mrs. Levon was weaving a spell, and sipping sweet tea in her kitchen was the most natural thing to do, and it tasted perfect.

"It was definitely a shock," I said. "Miss Reba is just so upset. Rumors are flying about her son, Shane, being involved—"

"Which just can't be true," she said.

"That's why I said I'd help. You see, Shane and a sweet friend of mine—her name's Gracie—are seeing each other. They're going to homecoming," I said. Assuming he was released from police questioning before too long. Surely they couldn't keep him when he hadn't done anything wrong.

She cupped her hands around her glass, listening intently, as if she didn't have a single thing in the world to do other than sit here with me in her kitchen and gossip. "Bless their hearts. We have two kids who just started at Bliss High. They've been fillin' me and Otis in on everything. I can't imagine what those two are goin' through. Poor Shane."

"They're struggling," I said.

"And poor Barbara Ann. She must be worried sick about Eddy. I understand that he's grievin', but he's takin' it too far now."

I'd wanted to get the lowdown on Otis, but I'd file away any information she gave me about Eddy Blake, too. "She's taking it pretty hard. I was over there a little while ago, and she still hasn't heard from him."

"I'm sure they have their problems, but he's always been a spitfire" she said, looking at her hands wrapped around the bright pink plastic glass. "Somehow, I thought they'd make it. Him just goin' off doesn't seem right. I just hope he can get done with his grievin' and move on."

"You've known him for a long time?"

She smiled and small lines formed around her eyes

and curved around the corners of her mouth. "Oh sure, feels like forever. Eddy hired Otis back when he first opened the store in Granbury. Otis helped him open the second store in Bliss. He moved over there to help Mr. Montgomery when he bought into the business."

I absorbed everything she was saying, finally putting a timeline to the two stores and how Chris Montgomery came to be part of it. Chris Montgomery came into Bubba's around the same time he met Miss Reba. "Is that when Otis bought into the stores, too?"

Her grip on her cup tightened. "It took Eddy and Chris Montgomery a good long while to offer Otis ownership. They thought five percent was enough." She scoffed, her cheery disposition fading instantly. "Not nearly enough, not after everythin' Otis did to open that Bliss store. Not after all the back and forth he does workin' both stores. If anyone needs anythin', they call Otis."

"Does he inherit more now that Chris Montgomery is dead? Brandi, in Granbury"—I added, in case she didn't know all the workers—"said he did."

"Him and Eddy both put Otis in their wills. When I first heard that, I thought it was plain stupid. After all, Eddy's young. Same age as me and Otis. I think Mr. Montgomery's around the same. A little older, maybe. I figured Otis wouldn't ever see any of that ownership, but I guess I was wrong."

I guess she was. Maybe I was, too. Instead of gathering evidence against Otis, I was beginning to think I might want to add Sally Levon to the suspect list. She clearly had a thing or two to say about her husband's business partners.

"Were they close, the three of them?" I asked, wanting to keep her talking.

"Eddy and Otis were," she answered.

I waited to see if she'd say more, itching to prompt her with another question. Instead, I stayed quiet. *Just listen.* Meemaw's advice came in handy on a daily basis. *People will talk to fill the silence.*

She was right. It took about thirty seconds before Sally Levon pushed her chair back and stood. "I can show you," she said.

I started to stand, but she stopped me with her hand. "I'll be right back."

I sat back down as she disappeared down the narrow hallway. She was back before I could say Texas Longhorns, a hefty photo album in her arms. She plopped it down on the table in front of me, flipping to the center of the book, going back and forth a few pages. One featured a row of cars that looked as if they had been painstakingly restored. "Those are Eddy's Mustangs," she said.

Finally, she stopped at a section of pictures of people at a picnic. "This is what Bubba's used to be like," she said. "The early days, that's what I call it. This was when it was just Eddy and Otis. When Chris Montgomery came into the business, it all changed."

I looked at the smiling faces in the photos. Otis, looking much younger and thinner, his hair shorter and slightly spiked in the front, was the subject of the first two pages.

The next shot was of a larger group. "That's the whole crew from Bubba's," she said.

"The Bliss store wasn't open yet?" I asked, trying to get the timeframe right.

"No, it opened about a year later."

Otis had his arm around Sally in her jean shorts and

cotton plaid snap-front shirt. It was tied in a knot above her waist. Their heads were thrown back and they were laughing. It was a nice shot.

I studied the rest of the faces, not recognizing any of them. A group in the foreground was in sharp focus. In the background, there were a few people scattered here and there. I glanced at them, returning to the group in front, but a faint feeling of recognition drew me back to the blurred images.

I studied the woman first, and after a few seconds I realized it was Barbara Ann Blake. "Were the Blakes married in this?" I asked, pointing to Mrs. Blake.

"Sure. They were married a good two or three years before then, I'd say. Now there is a couple in love. She's got to be worried sick about Eddy. If she doesn't do it," she said, tapping her fingers against the table, "I'll wring his neck myself whenever he gets himself back here."

"Is one of these men Mr. Blake, then?" I came back to the people in the foreground, looking for the dark hair I'd seen in the wedding picture at the Blake's house. I'd only seen a partial profile, since in the picture he was nuzzling his new wife's neck, so really, there was no way I could tell which one was Chris Montgomery's business partner.

I pushed my glasses more firmly in place as she took a closer look at the photo. "Right there," she pronounced, putting her finger on one of the blurred people in the background.

I pulled the book closer, lifting it to deflect the slight glare from the window. And then I caught my breath.

It couldn't be.

But it was. Oh, it definitely was.

"Oh my gosh," I muttered.

Eddy Blake wasn't out on some bender, drinking away his sorrow at having lost his friend and business partner. And he wasn't dead because Otis—or anybody else— had killed him, too.

No, the man Sally pointed to, the one she identified as Eddy Blake, was the man I'd known as Christopher Montgomery. Eddy hadn't come home to his wife because he was dead, too.

Chapter 13

The ride into town had never felt longer. My head spun with the knowledge that Eddy Blake and Chris Montgomery were the same man. It didn't seem possible, but it had to be.

I headed straight for my mama's house, a large country lot with a log cabin–like house, fauna and flora in abundance everywhere you looked. Just as expected, I found her in her cedar slope-roofed greenhouse out back, her favorite place to be.

She'd added it to her backyard more than ten years ago. I liked to joke and say it was her home away from home since she spent more time in the little outbuilding than she did in the main house. The small structure was tricked out with electricity, water, and rows of benches for her plants, sitting squarely on a cement pad.

Mama's charm worked year-round, and the greenhouse was like her cauldron. I leaned against the doorframe and filled her in on my theory.

She brushed a stray lock of hair away from her eyes, folded her arms, one hand still holding a pair of clippers, and listened. When I was done, she arched one brow and said, "A double life, darlin', are you sure?"

I couldn't blame her for asking. Sure, scenarios like this were in Lifetime movies, but did they honestly happen in real life?

It did sound crazy when I said it out loud, but the bottom line was that I couldn't change the facts. "It was him, Mama, I'm one hundred percent sure of it."

She put down her clippers and peeled off her gardening gloves. Her shiny gold wedding band glistened as it caught the light. I still found myself smiling when I saw the ring and thought about how happy she was. She'd come mighty close to not marrying Hoss McClaine, the cowboy sheriff of her dreams, but my charm had worked its magic, she'd seen the light, and the rest was history.

"So let me just see if I have this straight," she said. Around her, the plants lined up on the shelves of the greenhouse seemed to stand a little perkier, as if they were ready to listen to her recount the story. "You're saying that Eddy Blake, owner of the original Bubba's in Granbury, and Christopher Montgomery, co-owner of both Bubba's shops and husband to Miss Reba, were one and the same?"

"That about sums it up, Mama."

She picked up a galvanized watering can and sprinkled the flowers. "And what's your theory as to why he would do such a low-down dirty thing to both those women, darlin'?"

I ran my finger along a purple petal of a nearby flower. I'd been pondering this very question, and the answer I'd come up with was simple, and it was also the only thing that made sense. "I think he fell in love with Miss Reba, but he still loved Barbara Ann, so instead of forgoing his new love or saying good-bye to his original love, he decided to have his cake and eat it, too."

Mama stared at a lush fern for a good long while. Before my eyes, the tips of the fern's leaves browned and the fronds began to droop. "I found myself a good man, Harlow, but dang it all, some men just can't do right by the women who've stood by them."

I knew she was thinking about my daddy and how he'd turned tail and run when he'd seen the Cassidy magic firsthand. "Mama," I said, breaking her trance.

She blinked, registering the browning fern, and dropped her hands to her sides. Three deep breaths and a good shaking of her arms and hands released the burst of anger she'd been feeling, and the fern started to recover.

I continued with my theory. "From what I've gathered, he was Eddy Blake before he became Chris Montgomery," I said.

"What makes you think so?"

"Otis and Sally. They knew Eddy and have been around since Bubba's in Granbury opened. Chris Montgomery joined the business later, sometime after the Bliss Bubba's opened."

"So it really was because he fell for Miss Reba." Mama snipped away at the newly dead bits of the fern, shaking her head. "If he weren't already passed, he should be strung up by his toes. Those poor women."

"Do you know how Miss Reba met him?" I asked.

Mama stopped clipping and perched her backside on

a stool. She brushed back a lock of hair that had fallen onto her forehead. "You know, I don't rightly remember, Harlow. Reba can tell a good tale, but I don't know that I ever heard that story."

I recounted what Miss Reba had told me at her husband's funeral about meeting him when she went into the Bliss Bubba's for a service, and how he'd swept her off her feet, taking her to Porterhouse on Vine, then to Dairy Queen. "She told me he was a real spitfire. Sally Levon described Eddy the same way. I know I'm right, Mama." I pressed my palm to my chest. "I *know* it."

I took my thinking a little bit further. Living a double life was risky under perfect circumstances, but hiding the truth from everyone in two towns so close together? Would that even be possible? He had to have had help. And there was only one person I could think of who was in a position to help both Eddy and Chris.

Otis Levon.

I'd been pondering a motive for Otis that had to do with ownership shares of Bubba's. If he *did* know the truth, he'd had a lot of leverage and power over his boss.

The more I thought about it, the more convinced I was that Otis had to have been in on the secret. He'd admitted that he'd known both men. He worked at both stores. How could he *not* have known the truth?

The what-ifs started rolling into my brain.

What if Eddy/Chris had offered to buy Otis's silence with part ownership in the business? Of course five percent ownership was hardly enough to keep anyone silent for long.

What if Otis had tried to blackmail Eddy/Chris, something had gone wrong, and Otis had killed his boss?

Or, what if Eddy/Chris had agreed to add Otis to his will, and that had been enough of a motive to kill?

What if I was just whistling Dixie?

"But I'm not," I said under my breath.

"You're not what, Harlow?" Mama said. She'd picked up her gardening shears again and had started trimming back a miniature rose bush.

"Woolgathering?"

My head shot up at the sound of Hoss McClaine's slow Southern voice and the crunch of gravel under his boots.

"More like snake hunting," I answered, glad it was Hoss I would be telling my story to, and not Gavin. They were both stubborn as all get-out, but the elder McClaine, while curmudgeonly, was more levelheaded than his son. Gavin had some big law enforcement shoes to fill, and sometimes he tried just a trifle too hard.

I proceeded to retell my theory about Chris Montgomery and Eddy Blake, their double life, two wives and families, and my suspicion that Otis Levon knew the truth and had helped his friend keep up the ruse.

Hoss was silent for a good long moment, and then simply nodded. "Interesting," he said. After another beat, he added, "Good work, Harlow."

A compliment from Hoss McClaine wasn't given easily, and didn't happen often. I dipped my head and almost felt an *aw shucks* coming. Instead, I smiled and said, "Thanks, Sheriff."

But no matter how proud I felt of what I'd discovered, it didn't change the fact that two women's lives were not what they seemed, that two kids would soon learn that their father had also belonged to another child, and that someone had likely killed him because of the duplicity.

Chapter 14

As I arrived back at Buttons & Bows, my mind was still reeling from my discovery. It was not a normal scenario by any stretch. What I knew for certain was that the suspect pool had now quadrupled. If any of the people in either of the families knew the truth, one of them could have reacted badly and sought their revenge. Suddenly Barbara Ann Blake, Reba Montgomery, and both Shane and Teagen's motives had strengthened.

I'd phoned Will after I left Mama and Hoss and told him I had some news. He said he'd meet me at Buttons & Bows. True to his word, he'd hightailed it over to my house and was there to greet me when I pulled into the long driveway, which ran along the left side of the little yellow farmhouse. I parked under the row of possumwood trees, jumped out of the truck, and practically fell into his arms. "You're never going to believe this," I said to him.

"Try me."

We headed through the gate, walking over the flagstone path. I started at the beginning, telling him about my visit with Mrs. Blake, but as the porch came into view, so did Thelma Louise. The feisty goat stood at the base of the porch steps and raised her nose, her fathomless yellow eyes staring at us nonchalantly. Something hung from her mouth. My heart lurched as I realized what it was.

A mum!

"Oh no!" I took off in a run, clapping and calling her name. "Stop that, Thelma Louise! Shoo! Shoo! *NO!*"

She looked at me like she didn't have a care in the world. Her jaw worked as she continued gnawing at the mum. The nearly completed base with loops of red ribbon to form the flower, and strands of red, black, and white ribbons creating the drape were mashed. I looked more closely, recognizing some of the trinkets: a rhinestone B for Bliss, a miniature vintage car, an enormous cowbell that clinked every time Thelma Louise moved her mouth, a flower clipped onto a wide piece of ribbon, and curly silver trim that added shimmery volume to the strands of the mum. It was Danica's. Another minute or two in the goat's mouth and all her hard work would be ruined. "How did you get that?" I demanded, glaring at Thelma Louise.

She didn't answer, of course, just continued staring at me with her bulbous eyes.

"Don't think you're gonna get out of this," I said, wagging my finger at her. I advanced, holding out my hand to take back the mum.

She backed up, never looking away.

From the corner of my eye, I saw the open window to the dining room. "Ah, so that's how you did it," I said. The mums the girls had been working on had been left on the table. "You stuck your head in there and grabbed one, didn't you?" Under my breath, I said, "Meemaw, why didn't you stop her?"

Of course there was no answer. Loretta Mae, wherever she was, was probably having one good belly laugh right about now. She never had been one for the whole Texas mum tradition, so to see one of Nana's goats chowing down on the ribbon extravaganza probably filled her with all kinds of joy.

But it didn't fill me with any because now I'd have to remake the mum. As it was, half the flower portion was in the goat's mouth. It was a crushed, mushy mess, and I'd never send Danica out with a mum in that state. If I was lucky, I'd be able to salvage the lower half, which was the most unique part. A new base wouldn't take me too long to put together.

But Thelma Louise wasn't going to give up the mum easily. She stared me down, almost taunting me. Behind me, I'd heard Will's truck door slam and the sound of his boots crunching across the path as he came back. "Rope," he said from behind me.

I nodded, keeping my attention squarely on Thelma Louise. If the goat sensed any weakness on my part, she'd take off and I'd never get the mum back. That would never do. At this point, it was personal. *I* was in charge, not the Nubian, and she was not going to abscond with Danica's homecoming mum.

I inched forward, my body cocked forward at the waist. Thelma Louise stood her ground. It felt like it took forever, but we were finally just a foot apart. The trailing ribbons blew in the breeze. I almost grabbed for them, but stopped myself. The staples holding the mum together would give, the ribbons would just yank right off and Thelma Louise would escape with her plunder.

No, I needed to get ahold of the flower base.

Thelma Louise was *not* going to win this battle.

From the corner of my eye, I saw Will skirt around the perimeter of the yard, ready to intercept Thelma Louise if she bolted and leapt down the side steps of the porch. I felt like we were Wyatt Earp and Doc Holliday in a dusty Old West town, arms bent at the ready before a shoot-out. I cocked my arms, slid my feet forward just a tad more, sucked in a deep breath, and . . .

. . . lunged.

My arm shot out and I grabbed hold of the part of the mum base Thelma Louise didn't have in her mouth. I pulled, but she put her weight into it and yanked back, dragging me with her. She shook her head, trying to knock my hand away. She was a wiry thing, and a lot stronger than she looked.

But I was wiry, too, in spirit, if not in physique. I got my other hand around the streaming ribbons, winding the bunch around my hand, gingerly working my way closer, careful not to yank the ribbons right off the base. A minute later, Thelma Louise and I were nose to nose. She flipped her head back, knocking my glasses askew on my face. I couldn't fix them, though. I wouldn't release the mum. No way was the goat winning this battle.

"Darlin'," Will said from behind Thelma Louise. "You can let go. I'm right here."

I peered up at him. Without my glasses on, and being tugged by Thelma Louise's ratcheting head, he was a dark blur more than anything else. "She's not going to win," I said through clenched teeth.

"Neither are you." I couldn't see the smirk, but I could hear it, and it made me dig my heels in and pull harder. "Be careful," he said, and suddenly he was moving toward me. "If Thelma Louise lets go, you're gonna go fl—"

Before he could finish the sentence, the diabolical goat *did* let go. The release of tension was sudden and immediate and I was hurled backward, literally flying through the air just like Will had been in the middle of warning me. But he'd already been on the move, anticipating Thelma Louise's next play. He managed to break my fall before I crashed, back flat, against the porch.

My glasses were knocked clean off my face, I was half sprawled on top of Will, but I clutched the slobbery mum to my chest, clearly the victor in the battle against the grand dam of Nana's herd.

"Take that," I said to her as Will dislodged himself from under me. In seconds flat, he had Thelma Louise contained.

I retrieved my glasses and peered at her, now tethered with the rope Will had brought from his truck. "Do you think she planned all along to let go, or do you think she heard you say it?"

Will arched an eyebrow at me, looking for all the world like he thought I'd gone crazy, but Thelma Louise bared her teeth, either side of her mouth tilting up. That was a guileful goat smile if I'd ever seen one. "Never mind," I said. I had my answer. I V'd my index and middle fingers, directing them at my eyes, then flipped my hand to angle my pointer finger at her. "I'm watching you," I said to her.

"You about done, Mr. Byrnes?" Will said, stifling a laugh at my impersonation of Robert DeNiro in *Meet the Parents*.

"For now." I headed toward the front door, throwing one more warning glance over my shoulder at the goat. Will took her back to my grandmother's property, which butted up against mine. Instead of going inside, I sat in one of the rockers on the front porch. The chair started its back-and-forth rocking motion without the help of my feet pushing off. The other chair rocked, too.

Meemaw.

I bit back the chastisement hovering on the tip of my tongue. *Now* she decided to make an appearance? She couldn't have, say, put a stop to Thelma Louise taking the mum in the first place, or maybe lent a little muscle against the goat when I'd been trying to get it back?

In the distance, I could hear a low chuckle. "Go ahead and have your laugh, Meemaw," I said, the words snatched away by the breeze.

Will got back and sat, not noticing that his chair had been moving. "She behind bars?" I asked, knowing that there were no pens or gates that could contain Thelma Louise.

"She's back at Sundance Kids," he said.

We rocked in silence for a minute. After I let go of my aggravation with Thelma Louise, I went back to the murder and to what I'd been about to tell him before the mum debacle.

I told him about recognizing Eddy Blake as Chris Montgomery in the picture Sally had shown me, and the phone numbers programmed into Eddy Blake's cell phone. "He had two families and they practically lived right under each other's noses," I said, wrapping up my theory. "It's just . . . just . . . worse than . . . than I don't even know what. Worse than a pickled watermelon."

"That's pretty bad," he said, grimacing. He planted his boots on the porch and stopping the rocking motion of his chair. "Maybe they just resemble each other."

"I've tried to convince myself of that, but no. They don't *resemble* each other. They *are* each other," I said. "And there's more. Both wives said their husband stayed overnight at the other shop. Plus neither one liked to be photographed. He was pretty young, right? He told both Reba and Barbara Ann that he didn't want his photo on display at his own funeral. Why would he say that unless he was protecting his secret? So," I finished, "that's why I think Chris Montgomery and Eddy Blake were never in the photos with their families. Bliss and Granbury are both small towns. He couldn't take a chance that someone would recognize him from the wrong photo."

"He was taking a hell of a chance," Will said.

I couldn't agree more. Another thought struck me. I stopped the chair from rocking and my back straightened. "That's why they always sat at the picnic table!"

Will raised a curious eyebrow. "Who're they, and what picnic table?"

"Barbara Ann Blake said that whenever she went to Bubba's, she and Eddy wouldn't ever go inside, they'd go sit at the picnic table. Strange, right?"

"Is it?"

I nodded. "It is." I pointed at him for emphasis. "Unless you don't want the people in the shop to know anything about your personal life."

I shared with him the final bit of discovery. "Otis Levon, aka Bubba, has known Eddy from the beginning. He moved to the Bliss shop to help run things there, so he worked with Chris Montgomery every day. Which means—"

"He knew." Will stared past the front yard at Mockingbird Lane. "So what are you thinking? Otis tampered with Chris's car hoping he'd crash? But why? It's hardly a foolproof murder plan, especially for someone who really knows cars."

That was the one major flaw in the theory. I was sure there were others, I just didn't know what they were yet. "Maybe he got tired of keeping his boss's secret and tried to extort him. Them. *Him*."

"But if he was supporting two families, there wouldn't have been a lot of extra money to go around."

There was another flaw. "Right," I said, feeling my brows pull together.

"I can't think of another reason, though, so let's just go with that theory," he said. "If Otis Levon killed his boss, is he actively trying to frame Shane?"

Good question. Had he planted the flask of vodka, the printout of the steering system, and the shirt in Shane's locker? If he had, there ought to be video of him in the building. I made a mental note to ask Hoss about this, in case he didn't think of it himself.

I needed time to think, which meant I needed to go inside and be surrounded by my sewing and design. Nothing helped me process and untangle my thoughts better than touching fabric, sketching, and simply immersing myself in my work.

"I have some homecoming mums to finish," I said, keeping quiet what we both knew: that there wouldn't be a homecoming for Shane or Gracie if I couldn't prove Shane's innocence.

He caught the door with his hand, squeezed my arm,

and leaned down to give me a kiss. "Be careful," he said, and I knew he wasn't talking about the mum-making.

I didn't know if my charm extended to nonclothing items I created, but it was worth a try. Especially if it would help Gracie, my cousin and the girl I'd come to love as a daughter.

Chapter 15

After Will drove off, I took a deep breath and walked into Buttons & Bows. There was no cinnamon. No scent of apples. No clanking in the kitchen. Meemaw had been outside moving the rocking chairs, but I hadn't sensed hide nor hair of her since Will had come back from returning Thelma Louise to Sundance Kids.

Of course I knew she was around. She couldn't go anywhere. As a ghost, she was trapped, which I knew put a giant hitch in her giddyup.

"Meemaw," I called, heading into the kitchen. No response. I doubled back and peeked my head into the workroom. Leslie's sapphire and confetti-colored dress hung from the dress form. My sketchbook lay open. But, I thought, I hadn't left it open. In fact, I hadn't even left it in my atelier.

There was only one explanation, and her name was Loretta Mae. She wanted to tell me something.

I hurried to the cutting table and grabbed the book.

My sketches were there, from a classic ball gown to a sleek tube dress, and several in between that I'd been toying with.

They'd each been added to. Developed. And colored with watercolor crayons.

Danica's dress had continued to be a mystery to me, but looking at the fleshed out drawings, I was seeing her in a new light. I hadn't been able to get a handle on her and what homecoming design would work, but now one clearly stood out as the right design—mainly because it was circled with a red loop and the name Danica was scrawled in my great-grandmother's shaky cursive.

But even without those clues, it was obvious that the girl would look great in it.

The bubble dress.

Jessica Alba and Kate Beckinsale had both rocked bubble dresses. This modern take on a pouf skirt was more subtle, the tapered hemline billowing gracefully instead of ending in a hard edge. It was perfect. "You're right, Meemaw," I said. "This is it."

I held my breath, waiting and wondering if the sewing machine would start up or if the pipes would moan.

There was nothing but silence. Meemaw, it seemed, had decided to interact with me on a deeper level, first with her more opaque visage, then in the kitchen, and now with offering insight to my designs. I liked this more concrete way of communicating, but I had to admit that I missed the creaks and groans and rustling curtains.

I hurried upstairs to the attic and surveyed the pieces of fabric I had stored there. I zeroed in on the ones with enough yardage and style to make the dress. If I couldn't find what I was looking for, I'd have to take a trip to Fort Worth, something I preferred not to do at this point. I was out of time.

There were several lengths of cotton, one of which was an electric pink and black cheetah print, but after spreading them out and feeling the weight, I discarded them as options. They wouldn't hold the ballooning element, just like silk wouldn't. No, I needed something that could hold its shape.

I scanned the fabrics again, my attention landing on a tangerine microfiber. It had the right weight and wouldn't turn limp at the hemline. And it was wrinkle-free, a bonus. Fashion designer Robert Cavalli said, "Fashion should be fun and put the woman in the spotlight with a little bit of danger." That fit what I was trying to do for Danica—the bold and fun color was perfect for her.

Any dress I made for Danica wasn't going to put the girl in danger, but the tangerine color would certainly draw attention. If it boosted her confidence in the process, it was worth every bit of time, energy, and ounce of creativity I could muster.

"What do you wish for?" I mused aloud, thinking of the possibilities. Danica had no family. She was at the mercy of fairy godmothers like Zinnia James and me to help her get to homecoming. I imagined her greatest desire was to have her family back, and that was one thing my charm couldn't make happen. Her parents couldn't come back from the dead, but if family was her wish, maybe she'd develop one of her choosing. The circle of my family had grown to include Will and Gracie Flores,

Josie Kincaid, Orphie Cates, and Madelyn Brighton. By default, it also included Hoss and Gavin McClaine.

Of course, Danica didn't wallow in sorrow, and she seemed pretty practical from what I'd seen. Maybe finding love or going to college would be her biggest dream. If my design could help her with either of those things, I'd be happy.

As I headed back to the workroom, my thoughts drifted to Leslie. She was much more outwardly confident than Danica, but I got the feeling it was all a show. Deep down, she was injured and being alone got to her. She compensated by trying to woo friends, racing around in a sporty car inherited from her parents' estate while Danica struggled with a fixer-upper that kept breaking down on her.

I couldn't help feeling that Mrs. James's foundation to help girls in need had brought Leslie and Danica together. They were both low mileage, as Meemaw would have said. Young and with a lot of time ahead of them to figure out how things worked and who they were. It was true that they had time, but I couldn't help but hope that maybe Leslie, with her need for friends, and Danica, with her reservations about opening up to anyone, would find a happy balance with each other.

Josie walked in, her baby girl, Molly, in her arms, just as I finished stripping an old design from a dress form in my atelier. The tangerine microfiber lay in a heap on the cutting table, ready to be manipulated into the shape of a homecoming dress.

Right after I'd moved back to Bliss, I'd reconnected with Josie. She'd been Josie Sandoval then, an old friend from elementary school, and had been on the verge of marrying Nate Kincaid. Now she and Nate had a baby girl, a happy marriage, and I had a goddaughter. I took the baby from her and breathed her in. I wouldn't say my maternal clock was ticking, but it wasn't nonexistent in a black hole, either.

Josie dragged a chair from the dining room over to just inside the French doors and collapsed into it. She hadn't quite gotten back to her prepregnancy self, but she was trying, walking every day with the baby in her stroller, putting on a dash of mascara even when she didn't feel like it, catching naps when the baby slept to keep up her energy.

But I knew that she missed working at Seed-n-Bead, the shop she owned on the square. Even with naps, an infant meant short spurts of sleep and a lot of sleepless nights. The dark circles ringing her eyes were proof she wasn't getting enough rest.

Bless her heart, she didn't try to pretend she was. "I'm deprived of sleep and adult conversation," she announced, and for a second I wondered if she'd read my mind.

Molly heard her voice and turned toward her. She fussed, and after a moment, I handed her back to her mama. Josie tugged up her shirt, offering the baby nourishment. Molly settled down, her little legs moving, her hand gripping the collar of Josie's blouse, the soft suckling sound growing rhythmic as her body started to relax. "I need some gossip. I need to hear what's going on in the outside world."

I picked up the first length of microfiber as I launched into all the details about the mystery of Chris Montgomery's death, my theory about who Eddy Blake really was, the homecoming mums, and the dresses I was making for Danica and Leslie.

"So, you're not really up to much of anything," she said, one side of her mouth quirking up in a small grin.

"Nope, nothing exciting," I said with a laugh. I stood in front of a naked dress form, ready to begin the draping process. There were times when I mapped out a pattern, measuring and planning and drawing the pieces of a garment on paper to create a blueprint for a design. But there were also moments, like now, when draping was more appropriate. I could picture the bubble dress I was designing for Danica in my head, a hybrid of what I'd started in my sketchbook and what Meemaw had completed. I had details I still wanted to work out, and right now I needed to see the fabric on a figure to watch it come together.

What I'd learned over the years in my schooling, punctuated by Loretta Mae's lessons, was that simply knowing the principles of patternmaking and design wasn't enough. To really create a design that can be put together in the desired fabric, that is, to translate a garment from conception to execution, took a lot more than patternmaking skill.

"So he's really the same person, Chris and Eddy?" Josie asked.

"I'm ninety-nine percent positive," I said, testing the weight of the fabric in my hands. "Now it makes perfect sense for Eddy Blake's phone to have Teagen and Shane's phone numbers on it. Not to mention that the home number rang the Montgomery house, not the Blake house."

"How did he keep it all straight? Did he ever call his children by the wrong names? Or worse, one of the wives?" She gasped. "Can you imagine!"

I hadn't thought of that, and it wasn't an image I wanted in my mind.

Josie bit her inner cheek, her lips working. It was her thinking expression. A question was coming. "So do you think either of the wives knew?"

I'd been puzzling over that very question and so far, I had no idea. "That's something I plan to find out," I said.

"What if one of them is the killer?" she asked, biting her lower lip. "Harlow, you'll call Hoss or Gavin if you suspect anything, won't you?" We fell silent as I manipulated the fabric, watching it take shape in my hands. As I worked, my decision to use the microfiber was validated. The cotton wouldn't have worked. If I'd doubted it before, I was one hundred percent certain of it now. It would be like a sculptor trying to round the corners of a block of wood instead of using clay, or a painter trying to create a light, ethereal image using heavy oil paint instead of watercolor.

I followed a straightforward process as I draped, beginning with the right length and width of fabric, allowing extra for fullness, flow, and seams. Anchoring the fabric to the core points of the form came next. I pinned the microfiber to the center back, front, waistline, and hips. Then I worked around the dress form, cutting the cloth at the control seams as the elements developed.

"That's for one of Mrs. James's girls?" Josie asked after a few minutes. She held Molly against her, gently patting her back until the baby burped.

"I've been struggling with the design," I said, nodding, "but it's finally coming together."

"Homecoming," she said, the one word sounding a little melancholy.

"What gave it away?" I joked, looking at the mums still hanging from the stair banister.

"I never went to homecoming," she said.

"Me neither." I was more a behind-the-scenes kind of girl. I'd made dresses for my friends, sending them off with their dates and their mums while I moved on to my next design. Nothing had changed as I'd gotten older. I still preferred to be the one making the clothing, not strutting down the catwalk wearing the garments.

As I worked, the design became clearer in my head, the lines flowed, the proportion and balance and detail came together bit by bit. The color and feel of the fabric inspired me. If I closed my eyes, I could see Danica's face, smiling, the dress accentuating her eyes, the curve of her hips, and softness of her form. I let my fingertips manipulate the fabric until I had the look I wanted—the perfect balloon dress for Danica Edwards.

I stood back to survey it once more before I trued up the pattern I'd drawn out as I draped, perfecting the fit based on Danica's proportions and measurements, and duplicating the first side.

"It looks good," Josie said. "Really good."

That melancholy in her voice was still there. Even after nearly fifteen years, she still regretted not attending the dance. The realization reinforced my decision to make the dresses for Danica and Leslie. They wouldn't have Josie's regret.

My thoughts strayed to Gracie. With Shane still under the veil of suspicion, she might be the one with that regret.

Chapter 16

I'd done triage on Danica's mum, the rest were finished, Leslie's dress was complete, and I'd made good progress on Danica's bubble gown. All in all, things were moving along. I checked the wall clock. Four o'clock. Gracie would be here any minute to work on her own homecoming dress. I'd offered to help, but she wanted to do the whole thing herself.

The dress hung from the privacy screen in my workroom, the spaghetti strap bodice complete. She'd used a creamy embossed jacquard and had structured it using darts. The only thing she'd let me help her with was the fitting. She'd had to know it would fit her perfectly before she added the base of the skirt, and it did.

Each day she went home with a bag of materials, and the next day she returned with the same bag full of the flouncy pink, rose, and red rosettes she'd spent hours making the night before. Attaching them to the skirt was slow and painstaking, but she was determined to finish the dress and go to homecoming . . . with Shane.

The mum she'd been working on had miniature rosettes attached to three of the wider ribbons hanging in front, the perfect complement to the skirt of the dress.

I took a closer look at the dress, once again impressed with Gracie's natural talent. As if on cue, the front door of Buttons & Bows opened, the string of bells jingled, and Gracie waltzed in. She smiled at me, released her fingers from the bags she held long enough to give a finger wave, and then zipped past me. She dropped the bags and immediately got to work by moving her dress from the hanger onto the open dress form. She threaded a needle, pulled up a stool, opened the bag, plucked out the first full-sized rosette, and got to work.

I knew Shane was back home. Gavin had questioned and then released him, but he was by no means out of the woods. Still, with the new information I'd given to Hoss, he'd already tracked down Eddy Blake's birth certificate from the Hood County records department. So far, though, he'd found nothing to show Chris Montgomery had ever been born. After he dug a little deeper, maybe Shane could be officially cleared.

I opened my mouth to ask her how Shane was, but closed it again. Something was off. She was too perky, too focused. Gracie normally bounced from room to room, chattered about anything and everything, gave love to Earl Grey, my little teacup pig, and generally brought a lightness to the room.

There was no lightness at the moment, despite the smile that hadn't left her face.

For the second time, I opened my mouth to ask about Shane, but once again, I was tongue-tied.

The third time I tried to broach the subject, I went

forward with a different approach. "Gracie, I discovered something today. I'm not quite sure—"

Her head snapped up. "About Mr. Montgomery?"

I thought about beating around the bush, but decided being direct was better. Hemming and hawing about the truth wouldn't dull the pain once it all came out. "Yes."

She dropped her hands to her lap, yelping when the needle she held pricked her finger. She stuck her finger in her mouth. "What did you find out?" she asked. "Shane's meeting me here. He sounded really upset. What's going on, Harlow?"

I'd told the story to Will and to Josie, but this time there was an emotional element to it. I hesitated, thinking Will should be here, but Shane was coming, *and* he was upset, and I knew that Hoss McClaine had already called the Montgomery family in and broken the news, looking for evidence to support the notion. In a small town, the story of Eddy Blake and Chris Montgomery would be all anyone talked about for days. Weeks. Months. Maybe even longer.

Shane might be Gracie's boyfriend, but *I* wanted to be the one to prepare her for the official announcement the sheriff was sure to make. I knew he'd find hard proof that Eddy and Chris were one and the same. The birth certificate was a start, but it would take a lot of cross-referencing of information to prove it completely. Something I couldn't wait for.

I dragged the second stool next to her and sat. "I believe that Mr. Montgomery had a pretty big secret," I said.

She turned the rosette she was holding over in her hands, stopping and fingering a spot of blood on one of the fabric petals. "Ruined," she muttered, and then heaved the rosette into the trash can.

I cupped my hand over hers. "We'll figure it out," I said.

She bit her lower lip, her chin quivering. Her eyes grew glassy, but she fought against the tears threatening. "What was the secret?"

There was no easy way to say it, so I plunged ahead. "Gracie, I'm pretty sure that he had another family."

She stared. "What do you mean?"

"Another wife. A child."

She stared, slack-jawed. "Like one of those bigamists?"

"Kind of." I took the needle and thread from her, plucked a rosette from the bag, and moved closer to the skirt. I started to sew it on as I told her the full story, hitting the highlights without bogging it down with the extra details of how the Levons and Blakes were friends, how Shane's parents first met, and the phone numbers on the cell phone.

By the time I was done, her mouth gaped open and the tears she'd held back spilled to her cheeks. It might be young love, but her emotions were deep. "Poor Shane," she said softly.

"It's going to be rough for him." Not only dealing with the knowledge that his father had loved another woman and had another family, but also small town gossip. Chris Montgomery would be tried by Bliss's jury of public opinion, and that meant more scrutiny for Shane. People would wonder if he'd known, and then they'd come to the decision that he had to have known, which would lead them to his motive, and voilà! Shane would be guilty in their eyes, whether or not he'd had anything to do with his father's death.

The front door opened again and this time Shane lumbered in, his shoulders slumped. From his body language it was clear he'd heard about his dad's double life, and he wasn't taking it well. He stopped in the doorway, his head hung low.

The instant Gracie saw him, she stood, a trio of rosettes dropping from her lap to the floor. She walked to him without saying a word, and opened her arms wide. He lifted his gaze to her as she reached him, and she curled her arms under his, pulling him close. He lowered his head and they fit together, her head leaning against the hollow of his neck.

My throat tightened and I tried to swallow the lump. If I couldn't prove Shane's innocence, Gracie was going to be devastated.

"I heard," she said after they finally pulled apart. "He really had another family?"

Shane's face was drawn, his eyes hollow and ringed with dark circles. "That's what the sheriff said. I didn't believe it at first, but then . . . I don't know, it started to make sense."

She led him to the little seating area in the front room and sat next to him on the love seat. I sat across from them on the red velvet settee, leaning forward with my elbows on my knees. "How did it start to make sense?" I asked.

He looked up at me, surprised, as if he just realized I was there. "I feel like an idiot. We all believed he was just working so hard, putting in long hours at the Granbury store, but he was with his other family."

His voice dripped with disdain. Any sorrow and love he'd had for his dad had vanished when he'd learned the truth. My heart went out to him, poor thing.

"He loved you, though, Shane," I said. "I know it's not much consolation, but he fell in love with your mother and figured out a way to be with her. In his mind, I think he did what he did so he wouldn't hurt the people he loved."

From the grimace Shane wore, I don't think he believed my more compassionate explanation for his father's betrayal any more than I did.

"How's your mom handling it all?" I asked, knowing it was more of a rhetorical question than anything. She'd just discovered that her whole life with her husband was based on a lie, and that had to be difficult to swallow.

His answer was a halfhearted shrug. "She said she's not up for a visit, but she wanted me to give this to you."

Gracie dropped her arm from around his shoulder as he stood and retrieved something from his back pocket and handed it to me.

It was a square linen paper envelope with *Harlow Cassidy* written in the center in pretty cursive. I peeled open the lightly sealed envelope and slipped out the note-card, an *M* at the top center.

Harlow,

I'm sure by now you've heard the news about Chris and the second life he was leading in Granbury. It has taken me by utter and complete surprise. So far, I have not been able to wrap my head around it. The fact that he could have been lying to me—to the kids—for so long is mind-boggling.

I keep telling myself that maybe there's more to the story. I know the police will look at us with more scrutiny now, wondering if we knew and if that was the reason Chris was killed. Shane . . . I need to protect Shane.

More than anything, I don't want their father's selfish and stupid decisions to define Shane and Teagen's lives. Please, Harlow, keep looking into this horrible situation, and if you find out anything, come straight to me.

Yours,
Reba

"Shane," I said, wanting to ask him one question before I left him and Gracie alone. "Can you think of anything strange your dad did? Anything that didn't strike you as odd then, but now that you know the truth, you see it differently?"

He sat back down and thought for a minute. Gracie rubbed his back with her hand and I could see him sit a bit taller, her compassion infusing him with strength.

"I've been dissecting everything he's done for the past sixteen years," he said, "and I'm seeing *everything* differently. All those nights he said he was staying at Bubba's in Granbury when he was really with his other family. All Teagen's cheerleading competitions he never made because of work, but was he really off watching his other kid play sports? He had two wedding anniversaries. My mom is freaked about that. All these inside jokes and traditions they had, he had with someone else, too. How could he do that to her?"

Despite the horrible circumstances, it was powerful to see Shane so completely concerned with what his father had done to his mother and sister, rather than making it all about him.

He pursed his lips, his nostrils flaring. "I don't know how my mom's going to get over all of that."

"Your mom is strong," I said.

"She is," he said, "but this . . . this is huge. This is monumental. He lied about everything!"

Shane was right—a double life for his entire life was an unfathomable betrayal. There were no ifs, ands, or buts about it. But the Cassidy women adhered to a strict belief that whatever didn't kill us would only make us stronger. It was the truth. We were tested, sometimes mightily, but at the end of the day, you had to recognize all the blessings.

"We might never be able to make sense of it all or understand why your dad made the choices he made, but your mom and your sister are strong, inside and out, and they'll be okay. They will." I looked him squarely in the eyes. "And you will, too."

Barbara Ann Blake was as much a victim as the Montgomery family, I thought, although I didn't say this aloud to Shane. Too much, too soon. She would move on, too. I couldn't help but feel a stronger compassion for Barbara Ann. For whatever it was worth, Miss Reba, Shane, and Teagen had one another. Barbara Ann Blake had no one left, and that was the greatest tragedy of all.

Chapter 17

An hour later, Gracie walked Shane out to his car and I headed to the kitchen to make a late dinner. I perused the refrigerator, then the freezer, waiting for something to entice my appetite. It wasn't quite fall yet, and summers in Texas usually went on and on and on. There were still strawberries in the market, although they were less red and robust than they'd been a few months ago. I'd stocked up on them, and an abundance spilled from a container in the refrigerator. I grabbed the bowl, a red onion, a bunch of cilantro, a package of corn tortillas, and a large piece of mahi mahi from the freezer and set to work.

I soaked the plastic-wrapped fish in cold water to start the defrosting, then cubed it with my sharpest knife, tossing the pieces with cumin, a dash of salt, and garlic powder. Setting aside the fish, I washed and then finely chopped strawberries, half the red onion, the frozen mango and pineapple I'd also grabbed from the freezer, and a large handful of cilantro. Mixing it together released the different aromas, and my stomach growled in response to my creative end-of-summer cooking.

As I sautéed the mahi mahi, I thought about my next steps, both with my sewing projects and with helping Shane. I'd hit a wall with Danica's dress. I had a clearer direction now, but I needed to think on it. Let the design simmer as I worked through the problems I saw with it. She'd be coming by for a fitting before the football game the next day, so my time was limited. At that point, once I knew if any adjustments were needed, I could finish and suggest styling tips to her.

Leslie's dress was all done. The mums were finished, so that was one thing I could check off my list. I wanted to get Gracie to let me finish attaching the rosettes to the skirt of her dress, but so far she'd resisted my help.

But now she was almost out of time.

Tomorrow was Friday, the day of the parade and the homecoming game. The kids would wear their mums all day at school, then take pictures wearing them and their fancy dresses on Saturday night before they headed out in limos or newly washed cars to dinner and then the dance.

I heated up the corn tortillas and warmed up some cilantro-lime rice and black beans I had leftover in the fridge. Just as everything was ready, Gracie came back in the front door and Will's truck pulled up, parking behind mine under the possumwood trees.

Two minutes later, I heard his voice from the back deck. He finished a phone call, gave a quick knock on the Dutch door, which opened from the deck to the kitchen, and walked in. "Ah, just in time for supper, I see," he said with a grin and a kiss on my cheek.

"Yeah, how'd you manage that timing?"

He plucked a cube of sautéed mahi mahi from the pan, and I batted his hand away. We'd grown into a comfortable relationship, and once again I was grateful to Meemaw for having the foresight to know the kind of man who could make me happy, and the kind of woman who could do the same for Will Flores.

He positioned himself behind me at the counter, his head bent, his lips brushing against my neck. I started to sink into him when the pan on the stove literally jumped at the very same time Gracie cleared her throat from the archway between the kitchen and the dining room. "Hello," she said, "teenager present."

And a ghost present, too, I thought, eyeing the frying pan, ready to grab it if it moved again.

Will stepped back, but instead of releasing his hold on me, he pressed his hand on my hip and spun me with him. He'd been grinning, but stopped when he saw Gracie's face. "You heard," he said. Not a question, but a dismayed statement. He couldn't protect his daughter from the real world.

She dipped her head in a slight nod. "I can't even believe it. It's crazy, right? Who does that, has two families?"

She looked at her dad, then at me, as if we had the answers. We didn't yet, but I hoped we soon would.

When we didn't answer, she went on. "Shane left this for you. Told me not to look at it." Gracie handed me a lunch-sized brown paper sack folded down at the top. "It's for my mum."

Once again, I was impressed with the sixteen-year-old. Even in the midst of his world falling apart—the death of his father, the realization of the man's second family, and the accusations hurtling his way—he'd thought about Gracie. I unfolded the bag and peeked inside, half expecting a tiny bear or maybe an eagle, since that was the high school mascot. But I was wrong on both counts. Inside the bag was a miniature antique sewing machine on a sewing table. It had intricate metal details and looked like the perfect accessory for a shadow box or a dollhouse.

I smiled, my admiration for Shane increasing even more. He hadn't just offered up some clichéd mum sentiment, he'd *really* considered her.

The sewing machine would be the perfect centerpiece for the mum.

I folded the bag again and took it to the workroom. It would be a surprise for Gracie.

We ate our dinner of mahi mahi tacos with the strawberry salsa, cleaned up, and a short while later, Will and Gracie got ready to head home. Gracie looked at the homecoming dress she'd abandoned when Shane had arrived, the three rosettes still on the floor. The bag of fabric flowers she'd intended to attach to the skirt to finish the dress right sat where she'd left it.

"Let me work on it, Gracie. I can attach the flowers so you don't have to worry about it."

She hesitated, considering my offer, but after a beat, she shook her head. "No, but thanks. I really want to do this all myself."

She scooped up the wayward rosettes and tossed them in the bag, and then she took the half-flounced dress off the dress form. I helped her put it back on a hanger and zip it up into an inexpensive garment bag so she could get it home safe and sound.

"Let me know if you change your mind," I said as she walked down the porch steps, her arms loaded down. She turned right and followed the flagstone steps through the English flower garden and out the side gate to the driveway.

Will and I watched her. I felt the helplessness emanating from him. There was nothing either of us could do to make her feel better. I took comfort in the fact that she could help herself with her sewing. She was a natural, and the craft that fueled me and had defined my charm was beginning to be what she turned to for comfort, too.

"She's determined," he said.

That she was. She wouldn't let either of us even help her carry her things to the truck. Stubborn might be another word for it, but she was entitled to be dogged if it helped her get through this tough time.

"Don't let her stay up all night," I said.

He gazed after her, watching as she hung the garment bag on the hook in the extended cab portion of the truck. "The distraction is good for her."

"It is, but I'm worried about her," I said. She'd been through a lot for a girl her age.

He sighed, and I knew he was thinking the same thing. Gracie had suffered her share of drama, first when her mother had abandoned her on her unwitting father's doorstep as an infant. Next, when she'd found out her maternal grandparents had been living in the same town with her all these years, unbeknownst to her or them.

The most recent discovery had been that she was a descendant of Butch Cassidy and was charmed.

But now she'd added being the girlfriend of a potential murderer to the list of things she had to recover from. And much as I liked to think fashion was the be-all and end-all that could solve most problems, the reality was that sewing could only do so much.

Chapter 18

I awoke the next morning at the crack of dawn, and dressed quickly in jeans, a peasant blouse I'd recently made, and my go-to red Frye cowboy boots. By seven o'clock, I was on the road, heading for Bliss Park where the mum-exchange photo session was scheduled to take place. Somewhere in Bliss, a mother lay snug in her bed, blissfully unaware of the cameras snapping, the multitude of pictures being taken, and the mums being given and received.

I wasn't a mother, but I was wide awake, what with the excitement of the girls I'd helped with their mums, the mums I'd made myself, and the elation of every teenager in town.

By the time I arrived, it looked like half of Bliss was already there. I searched the crowd looking for Gracie Flores, Holly Kincaid, Danica Edwards, Leslie Downs, or any of the other girls I knew were going to be here. I hadn't been looking for any of the boys, but I saw Shane before I recognized anyone else. He stood away from the group, leaning against a tree with one shoulder, his eyes downcast. It looked like his stint being questioned at the sheriff's station had taken its toll on him.

"Mum delivery," I said, holding out the completed ribbon-flower concoction for him to give to Gracie. I tried to stay positive and grinned. "The sewing machine is perfect. Great thinking!"

He took the mum, mustering a slight smile. "Thanks, Ms. Cassidy—"

"Harlow," I said. At thirty-three I was nineteen years older than the average high school freshman, yet I didn't feel old enough to be a Ms. "Just call me Harlow."

"I tried to talk her out of going to the dance," he said, turning and leaning his whole back against the tree now. He hooked the hanger with the mum over his fingers, gripping the plastic covering the creation in his palm. "I told her everyone's going to be talking about my dad and me and either hanging around us because of it, or avoiding us. Half of them think I did it, and the other half might as well think it, what with all the staring they do."

He was trying to keep his cool and not let his emotions get the better of him, but I could see it was a struggle. His jaw pulsed with the effort and his eyes had a glassy film.

"Shane," I said, looking him in the eyes. I waited until he met my gaze and I was sure he was going to hear and register what I said. "I don't believe you were involved, and I'm going to get to the bottom of it. I promise."

He drew in a deep breath, his jaw relaxing slightly. My heart broke for him and everything he was going through. "You figured it out—about the two families, I mean?" he asked.

"Yes."

He hesitated again, looking around as if he could draw strength from the energy of the homecoming frenzy. "What's she like?"

My gut twisted. This wasn't a conversation I wanted to have, and I didn't think it was one Shane should have, either. Then again, I realized it wasn't my place to make that determination. And he had a right to know, much as I wished I could protect him from the truth.

In the end, I decided to say as little as I could. At least for now.

"Mrs. Blake? She seemed . . . nice," I said. "Nice." It had to be the blandest word in the English language, but honestly, it was true. She'd been irritated at first that her husband was MIA, but after we'd broken the ice, she'd been . . . nice.

I could only imagine the pain she was experiencing now that she knew the truth. Eddy Blake had been her husband first, and now she knew that when he'd met Miss Reba, he'd been willing to risk everything—from his marriage to his business to his freedom—all to be with her.

I was pretty sure those bits of knowledge wouldn't give Miss Reba any solace, but they certainly had to be worse than a prickly thorn in the side of Barbara Ann.

Car doors slammed. Girls and boys, dressed in their everyday jeans and shirts, filed out of the cars carrying mums streaming with ribbons. The quiet morning slowly evaporated, replaced by the excited squeals of the girls as their guys presented them with their mums.

Still, despite the buzz of homecoming, plenty of people shot stray glances at Shane, pointing, leaning close to the person next to them, and whispering something. I'd thought there'd be more compassion toward him from his classmates, but instead they avoided him. They were probably praying for him, but they wouldn't speak to him.

Shane seemed to feel the stares. Sense the whispers. His shoulders curled in and he looked like he wanted to tuck his head in like a turtle and disappear.

I didn't blame him.

Around us, the kids hurled names across the park, the voices rising to be heard above the cacophony. "Susannah!" someone yelled. "Brittany!"

"Heather, is that you? Heather!"

"Carlos!"

"Debbie!"

Slowly but surely, groups found one another and split off. Moms, their back jean pockets sparkling with bling, followed, cameras in hands, to snap a hundred pictures of the homecoming tradition and capture the moment. Through the thinning crowd, Danica, Leslie, Holly, and Gracie appeared like angels materializing through the fog. Gracie was the only one with a date to homecoming, but none of the girls minded. They all grinned, part of a group, which was the only thing that mattered.

Shane pushed off the tree, straightening up. He plastered a smile on his face and leaned down to give Gracie a hug. I looked around for Miss Reba, but she wasn't anywhere I could see.

"My mom's not coming," Shane said, reading my mind. "She couldn't face anyone."

I understood. She had to feel betrayed and humiliated. And if she was guilty, then she had to play her part accurately.

Will had an early meeting, so I told him I'd take pictures of Gracie and Shane with their mums. Holly's mom, Miriam Kincaid, had a bookstore on the square and wasn't able to leave it, and Leslie and Danica were on their own. I was it, the lone parentlike representative.

I clapped my hands and gathered the kids together, unsnapping the cover from my camera. My Canon didn't compare to Madelyn's, but it did what I needed it to do. I could take pictures, like I would that morning at the park, and I could photograph the different stages of my designs, cataloguing them for the Web site I was in the process of creating. Beyond the basics, however, I was lost.

The girls strung their mums around their necks and Shane wore his on his arm, held up by a garter. Ribbons streamed down from each of the girl's concoctions, some nearly dusting the ground. I held the camera up, peering through the eyepiece, snapping away just like the blinged-out moms scattered throughout the park were doing.

Shane pointed out the centerpiece of Gracie's mum—the miniature antique sewing machine—and it was as if the world around them disappeared for a moment. I could see her breathe in, and I watched him watching her, his lips curving up as she gasped, fingering the sloping curves of the gold-flecked machine.

His eyes softened and for a second, it looked like he actually forgot about his troubles. I captured the moment with the digital camera, and then allowed them privacy as I took pictures of Holly, Danica, Leslie, and Carrie.

The girls' voices rose as they chatted about the dance,

their mums, and anything else that came to their minds. Someone in the middle of the group of girls said, "You look so much like this girl I used to go to school with."

I zoomed in, trying to capture candid moments of each girl. Leslie smiled. Danica laughed as she fiddled with one of the charms on her mum, retying a loose knot. Holly ran her fingers under her eyes, cleaning up her eyeliner.

"Well, they do say everybody has a twin," Leslie said.

"True that," Carrie said. She reached her arm out toward Danica. "I *love* your hair."

"Thanks," she said, but she took a step back, just out of Carrie's reach.

"It almost has this blue tint—did you know that? I bet it glows in the dark. Wonder if that would look good on me. Where do you have it done?"

"The Salon on the Square," Danica said, her smile tightening and her barriers going back up. I'd been impressed at how open she was trying to be. She wanted to have fun at homecoming, wanted to be part of the group, but the pressure was taking its toll on her.

From the corner of my eye, I saw Holly plucking at the ribbons and streamers of her mum. I took a few more pictures of Danica, Leslie, and Carrie before I shifted my focus to Holly and started snapping pictures for her mom, Miriam. That line of thought sent another pang of regret through me for Gracie, Leslie, and Danica, none of whom had a mother in their lives.

Meemaw's voice echoed in the back of my mind. *Family is made up of the people you choose.* That was just what Danica had said, and they were both right. I was lucky enough to have both a family through blood that I loved with all my heart, and the family I chose. Danica and Leslie and all the other kids at Helping Hands needed to find people like Orphie, Josie, Madelyn, Will, and Gracie, people who would fill up the space in them reserved for unconditional love and friendship.

I moved the camera back to Danica and Leslie. Carrie was still talking about the friend one of them looked like, and Danica and Leslie both looked like they just wanted to escape. Finally, Leslie pulled out her cell phone and checked the screen. She yelped. "We have to go!"

I looked around and realized that half the kids had already cleared out of the park. School was going to start in fifteen minutes. Cars snaked along the road, heading for Bliss High School.

Gracie gave me a hug, and once again I could see her fighting to restrain the tears glazing her eyes. "Thank you for everything, Harlow," she said. "The mums are perfect."

I had to agree with her. It might be a crazy tradition, but it was a tradition nonetheless, and the kids loved every second of it.

Danica, Leslie, and Holly gave me quick hugs, too, before heading to their cars. Shane stopped short of a hug, instead inclining his head. "I know you're trying to help," he said, the sadness and anxiety back in his eyes.

"I am," I said, "and I won't give up."

My phone rang as they headed off. Miss Reba. "Shane and Gracie looked beautiful," I said when I answered, but she didn't seem to hear me.

"Harlow, I found something," she said, her voice muffled as if she'd been crying. She blew her nose and I knew I was right.

"What's that, Miss Reba?" I didn't offer reassurances or sympathies. I'd already done that and it only went so far. No, what I needed to offer her now were answers.

"Letters," she said. "Chris kept a box filled with letters *she'd* written to him. I don't want them in my house. I *can't* have them in my house. Harlow," she said, "please come get them."

Chapter 19

I made it to Miss Reba's house in record time, my curiosity spurring me on. "You need to call the sheriff," I told her.

"I don't want all our dirty laundry out there for people to chew on," she said, sniffling, although I sensed the strength back in her voice.

"But it could be evidence. The sheriff needs to see it."

"I want to show you first," she said. "If you think we should turn them over after you see them, we will. But not before."

I let out a heavy sigh. "I'm just a dressmaker, Miss Reba. I'm not—"

"You're the only one I trust, Harlow. You're not judging my family, and I know you can sort out the truth. Hell, you already did. Thanks to you, we know about Chris's double life. The sheriff didn't do that. *You* did that."

She made me sound like some superdetective, and I was afraid that in her mind, that's what I was becoming.

She believed that I could somehow find all the answers she sought and make everything okay for her and her kids in the end.

It was a tall order for a small-town fashion designer.

"Will you look at them?" she asked, pressing the nondescript shoebox at me.

I hemmed and hawed for another minute, but finally took the box and followed her into the living room. Plush brown couches were arranged around a square high-gloss coffee table. A stack of oversized books sat at an artistic angle on one side; a basket with a shallow vase of flowers inside was on the other side. Our styles were different, but I could recognize her eye for decorating and balance.

Even more apparent was the difference in decor between the Montgomery house and the Blake house. It was as if when Chris had been here, he'd lived the high life, and when he'd been Eddy Blake, he was blue collar and survived on less.

I couldn't help but wonder if he'd preferred one lifestyle to the other, and if so, which one? Knowing that could help explain his thinking and why he'd chosen to live the two lives he did, but it was something none of us would ever really understand or know the answer to.

Miss Reba and I sat next to each other, her body turned toward me. I set the box between us. She'd given it to me, but I wanted her to take the lead.

She didn't miss a beat, quickly flipping the lid back to reveal the stack of letters stored inside.

She'd regained her composure, the only sign she'd been crying her red-rimmed eyes. "Go on," she said, nudging the box closer to me.

"Are you sure?" I asked one more time. One thing I didn't want was to be given the green light to read Chris Montgomery's private letters, then discover something else sordid, only to have Miss Reba change her mind and end up upset that she'd ever shared something so personal.

"Harlow Cassidy, for heaven's sake. I want you to read them. I just can't do it. Not yet, anyway. And I wouldn't ever subject Teagen or Shane to their father's other life. But if there's something there that can help you, well then, you need to read them."

I didn't bother trying to convince her to share them with the sheriff instead. She'd already declined and I didn't see her changing her mind.

My glasses slipped. I pushed them back up and tucked my hair behind my ears. "You want me to read them all right now?"

"Pshaw," she said, fluttering her hand. "I'm not going to torture myself by watching Chris's other life unfold before your eyes."

Instantly, I felt as if a huge weight had been lifted. Another issue still remained—after all, I had agreed to read the letters—but at least I could do it privately and without Miss Reba watching my every reaction. I closed the lid and stood, tucking the box under my arm. "I'll start tonight," I said.

She followed me to the door, and from her expression, I thought for a second that she might change her mind. But she didn't. As I drove off, I saw her in my rear-view mirror still standing on her stone porch. One car crash had changed her entire life. The box on the seat next to me might give her solace. Or it could do the opposite, digging the knife in deeper and then twisting it. I didn't blame her for not wanting to read them herself.

But I wondered how I'd become Bliss's de facto sleuth, and if I'd help her, or if I'd end up letting her down.

The day loomed before me. I made a mental list of everything I needed to do, and the order in which I needed to do it. I headed back to Buttons & Bows, set the box of letters on my own coffee table, plugged the SD card from my camera into my computer to let the homecoming photos upload, and then headed to my workroom.

I'd meant to ask Gracie if she'd finished attaching her rosettes, but the kids had all run off so quickly that I'd forgotten. If she needed help, I'd stay up all night with her, but for now I had to concentrate on finishing Danica's dress. Homecoming was tomorrow.

The bells on the front door jingled as the door opened. Madelyn Brighton breezed in, her camera bag slung over her shoulder. For someone with short hair, she had a hundred and one hairstyles. Today it was gelled and artfully spiked. She wore a pair of jeans, a wide fold at the ankle, jeweled sandals, a flowing white T-shirt, and a hot pink tailored jacket. Against her mocha-colored skin, the white top was fresh and crisp and the jacket popped.

"You look ready for the boardwalk on the beach," I said when she came into the workroom.

"If I project, do you think a beach will appear?" she said in her lovely British accent.

It was still hot enough that Madelyn and I both longed for surf and sand, but Bliss was nestled on the southern end of North Texas, so the nearest beach was down far away at the Gulf.

She glanced around, stepping back to peek through the French doors toward the dining room. "No more mums?"

I grinned. "No more mums." I'd cleaned up the supplies, organizing the ribbons, backings, and charms in plastic bins, storing them in the attic. Thankfully, mums were just a once-a-year project. "The kids all met at the park this morning and, you'll be very proud of me . . . I took pictures."

Her pink-tinged lips curved into a happy smile. Pictures were her life, and there were never enough subjects for her taste. With an absence of portrait work, she'd recently taken an interest in macrophotography, stalking flower gardens in search of spiderwebs—"They are incredibly perfect," she'd explained—and unmarred flower petals—"Each one is a work of art."

"Let me see," she said, looking around for the camera.

I pointed toward the dining room and the little computer table in the corner. "They're uploading."

She scooted off, and I went back to Danica's dress. It hung on the dress form, still not quite right. I walked around it, my hand cupped at my chin, thinking. Something wasn't working with the tangerine microfiber. It was too . . . orange. With nothing to break up the color, I was worried it would overpower Danica's subdued personality. The right design could help bring out the subtle elements of someone's personality, but if it was too much, it could backfire. This, I was afraid, was going to backfire big-time.

It was holding the bubble flounce at the hem, but it needed something to diffuse the overwhelming tangerine color. An idea hit me suddenly. "It could work," I muttered. I snatched up my phone and dialed Josie. I explained my dilemma to her, my plan, then what I needed.

"Black beads?" she asked, mulling over my solution to all the orange.

"No. Black and orange is too much like Halloween. The fabric's pretty vibrant, so I think a blue glass would look great. I'll attach them to the straps, and make an accessory for the waist. If you can make a necklace, that'll complete the outfit."

The other end of the phone was silent.

"Hello? Josie? You still there?"

"Oh! Sorry. I was thinking. I just sketched out a rough design. I think it'll be perfect!"

"It should come to a point, maybe with a larger bead hanging from the center?"

"Exactly what I was thinking. I'll work on it right now," she said, an excitement in her voice that I hadn't heard for a while. She loved motherhood and adored her baby girl and her husband, but having someone else need you for something was a good feeling. The task of making a necklace for Danica was small, but it was something she did brilliantly, and I needed her. I could sense her spirit bolstered because of it.

I hung up with Josie just as Madelyn came back into the workroom. "Remind me to show you how to frame a person in photograph," she said.

I feigned shock and hurt, pressing my flattened palm to my chest. "Are my subjects poorly framed?"

"Funny girl. Quite poorly framed, if I must be honest. You have some far too close up, and others are so far away you see no details. I can tell you tried to create groups. Grouping friends, siblings, boyfriend/girlfriend together is a brilliant idea, but not if you can't draw connections from the subjects or if the shots themselves aren't that interesting."

"Thanks for the pep talk, Mads," I said. "You could be a football coach with that skill."

She smiled, throwing her shoulders back a little, completely missing my sarcasm. Then she saw the mock hurt expression on my face and rushed forward. "I'm sorry, love. You're a brilliant dress designer. All I'm saying is don't give that up for photography."

"I hadn't planned on it, but now I know for sure." I smiled, showing her no harm, no foul. I got what she was saying. I didn't have the eye to capture reflections or to frame a photograph interestingly, but then again, it wasn't my passion. Give me a garbage bag, some trim, and some time, and I could create a killer dress.

I couldn't do much more on Danica's dress until Josie came by with the beads. Leslie's was done. I didn't know the status of Gracie's. And I didn't have to help with the Helping Hands brunch until morning. My gaze trailed to the coffee table and, just like that, Miss Reba's shoe box full of letters rose to the top of my To Do list.

My coffee table had once been an old door. Now it sat squarely between the love seat, sofa, and settee, and squarely on *it* was the box. I sat down on the settee, pulled the box to the edge of the table, and flipped the lid back.

Madelyn moved to the corner of the sofa nearest the settee. "What do you have there?"

I filled her in, taking my sweet time telling the story. It was a good stall tactic, but it didn't last for long. It wasn't a long story, but by the time I was done, she had scooted to the edge of her seat. "Let's have a look-see then."

I couldn't think of a single reason not to at this point. I took the first envelope out of the box. The name "Eddy" was written in neat cursive across the front with a curvy line scrawled underneath it. The paper inside was a single trifolded page. I opened it up and started to read. There was no date on the page.

Dear Eddy~

Happy Anniversary! Twenty years. Are you tired of my letters yet?

I hope not because I will never stop writing them, even though my words don't always flow from my heart through my fingertips the way I wish they would. I love you more today than I did in the first years of our life together. I feel blessed because not everyone can say that. Sometimes I think that my life began the day that we met. You are the love of my life. We may no longer have the thrill of a first kiss, and this letter may lack the excitement of new love, but what we do have is the trust and the years together and the knowledge that we will never break each other's hearts.

Long days at work and time apart strained our foundation. We both know that. We've experienced the joys and trials of every family. Sue leaving us brought untold challenges that I sometimes thought I'd never overcome. It's only because of you that I survived losing my only child. But you

were there, and we did survive. We still have each
other. You know what commitment really means,
and through you I know that men can be kind and
compassionate and truly loving.

Eddy, I love you.

Forever and always,
Barbara Ann

The hairs on the back of my neck stood up. Reading
Barbara Ann's private letter to her husband was bad
enough. But I knew the truth about Eddy, and by now
she had to know it, too. My stomach twisted as two
thoughts raced into my head. On the one hand, Barbara
Ann's heart could be breaking right this second as she
tried to process what had happened to the man she
thought she could trust.

On the other hand, her heart might have broken
months ago, or years ago, when she first found out. She
might have already processed her pain and progressed to
revenge.

Barbara Ann really *could* be the killer. It made sense.

"What's it say?" Madelyn asked, her gaze wary.

How could I summarize all the love Barbara Ann
Blake had poured into the letter to her husband, and all
the betrayal she must now feel? "She loved her husband.
She trusted him." My eyes glazed as I tried to find the
right words. "And I bet she feels like she's been run over
by a Mac truck."

"So it's a love letter, then?"

I trusted Madelyn, and I needed someone else's perspective, so I handed it to her. As she read it, her brow

furrowed and her lips parted. When she finished, she folded it neatly and replaced it in the envelope. "You think maybe she found out and killed him."

I stared at her. "How did you know that?"

She tapped her right temple with the pad of her index finger, and then pointed at me. "You forget. I know you."

She did. We hadn't been friends for very long, but sometimes you just clicked with a person. Madelyn was one of those people for me. She knew the Cassidy secrets, and she hadn't run away screaming about witches and magic. She was funny and smart, and she'd become one of my best friends.

"I guess you do," I said. "And, yes, that's exactly what I was thinking." I leaned forward, anxious to talk through the possibility. I nodded toward the letter we'd both read. "If this is how she felt about Eddy, she really, really loved him. We think she just found out the truth, but what if she somehow found out a month ago, or a week ago? She might have snapped. I mean, her whole world fell apart before her eyes."

I held the shoebox on either end. "Everything she wrote to him would have been based on lies because he wasn't truthful and he wasn't faithful."

There was only one way to know if Barbara Ann's sentiments in the letter we'd read were consistent throughout her letter writing. Read another one.

I didn't know if they were in any kind of order, and I wanted a random selection, thinking that would somehow give me a truer view of Barbara Ann and her feelings. The next envelope had Eddy's name across it, a curved line scrolled underneath the name, just like the previous one. I dove right in.

*Eddy, how can she be gone? If I close my eyes, I
can still see her dimpled face, her huge grin, the
braids in her hair. Did I do something wrong? Fail
as a mother? I can't see through my tears, and
they're blurring the ink. I want to curl up and disappear. No more dreams of your race-car-driving
daughter. No more Sue. No more McQueen. What
are we going to do without her?*

It was as if the letters to Eddy were Barbara Ann's
personal journal. She wrote what she felt at that moment, examining the things going on in her life.

I handed the brief letter to Madelyn. It took her all of
ten seconds to read. "Who's Sue? Who's McQueen?"

"Sue was their daughter. McQueen must be a nickname. I can't even imagine . . ."

"Poor thing."

"Yeah."

I reached for another letter, wondering if I'd find a
sad Barbara Ann, a loving Barbara Ann, or someone in
between. This one was in a gray envelope and instead of
Eddy's name on the front, Chris's name was.

"He kept his life separate, but mixed his letters," I said
as I opened the envelope. A single notecard slipped out,
and this one also took less than ten seconds to read.

I know who you really are and what you're doing.

"Oh my God!" I dropped the card and recoiled. Madelyn arched an eyebrow as she reached for it, but my
hand shot out, grabbing her wrist. "Don't touch it."

"What?"

"We have to call the sheriff."

"Your stepfather? Why? What in the world—?" But she broke off when she craned her head around and read the one, brief sentence.

She drew in a sharp breath and looked at me.

I looked at her.

And together we said, "The killer."

Chapter 20

I waffled back and forth between suspects as I waited for the sheriff to come and take the box of letters. I'd immediately assumed that Barbara Ann Blake could have found out the truth about Eddy and snapped, messing with his car and killing him.

But the letters had been in the Montgomery house, so it just as easily could have been Miss Reba who'd discovered the truth and had done in her husband.

"Or maybe," I told Madelyn, "it's like that Carrie Underwood song 'Two Black Cadillacs.' Maybe they both learned the truth and conspired together to kill him."

"That's a good song," she said.

I nodded my agreement. Carrie could sing, and maybe she was onto something with the two women in the black veils. They hadn't bothered to cry because they were guilty of murder. Had I seen Miss Reba or Barbara Ann cry?

I couldn't say that I had, but I couldn't draw a straight

line between that little fact and the car accident. Otis Levon and his wife, Sally, lingered in the back of my mind as possible suspects. Blackmail was a dangerous game, and either one of them could have orchestrated that with Eddy/Chris.

Each of the four of them had motive. There was no way to pinpoint when the car had been tampered with, so any one of them might have had the opportunity.

And then there was the means. Otis knew cars inside and out, so messing with the steering would have been a no-brainer for him.

But what did Miss Reba, Barbara Ann, or Sally Levon know about cars? That was a big fat question mark.

A short while later, Hoss McClaine sauntered through the front door of Buttons & Bows, pulling off his cowboy hat as he entered. His curmudgeonly tendencies couldn't hide his Southern gentleman upbringing. He dipped his chin in greeting and in one fell swoop, he seemed to take in the room, his eyes landing on the box still sitting on the coffee table.

"Ladies," he said. He ambled toward us, and though one corner of his mouth lifted, it wasn't really a smile and it definitely didn't reach his eyes.

"Sheriff," we said in unison. Hoss McClaine was newly married to my mama, but when he was on duty, he was sheriff. Come to think of it, whenever he wasn't on duty, he was still the sheriff, too.

"That it?" he asked, nodding toward the box, his drawl as thick as molasses.

I nodded. "Miss Reba gave it to me this morning. I read a few of the letters from Barbara Ann Blake to her husband, but then I saw that one." I pointed to the gray card with the single sentence. The writing was nondescript, as if whoever wrote it had tried to disguise it.

"You didn't look at the rest of them?"

"No," I said.

Madelyn and I sat back down and the sheriff took a seat in the center of the love seat. "So you touched the box, and those three letters."

He'd said it as a statement, but it was really a question. "Right. I took one from the center of the pile, so I may have touched a few more."

If he was disappointed, he didn't say. Instead, he pulled a wad of something lavender from his pocket. He unwound the mass, peeling off what I realized were gloves. Purple latex gloves. He tossed a set to me, one to Madelyn, and kept a set for himself. "First rule of investigation is not to contaminate the evidence."

"I didn't know it was evidence," I said. That was a little bit of a fib. I'd thought about calling the sheriff the moment Miss Reba had told me about the letters, but I'd let her talk me out of it. Now my fingerprints were all over the note to Chris Montgomery, a note that might have come from his killer.

"Put the gloves on," Hoss told us. "We need to do two things. One: Read each and every one of these letters. And two: Sort by date."

"The ones we read weren't dated," I said, "but we could try to organize them based on things happening in their lives."

"You want me to help, Sheriff?" Madelyn reminded me of Tigger, nearly bouncing off her seat. She was the sheriff's staff photographer, taking pictures of crime scenes, but she also worked for the city of Bliss, capturing moments in time, doing macrophotography along the walking trails, and any other job that involved photography.

His response was a raised bushy gray eyebrow.

It was all Madelyn needed to pull on the gloves, snap them at the wrist, stretch her fingers wide, and charge ahead. She took a letter from the pile inside the box and started reading.

I did the same, though I didn't muster quite as much gusto as Madelyn had.

One by one, we read the letters written by Barbara Ann Blake to her husband, Eddy. The tone of each letter was similar . . . Eddy was her true love, and while they'd suffered trials and tribulations, together they'd survived. There were plenty of letters where she was angry at him for staying out at the Bliss store overnight, more than a few about the challenges they had with their daughter, whom she always referred to as McQueen. It seemed Eddy really had thought she'd be a successful race-car driver. They'd nicknamed her McQueen when she'd been a little girl, after Lightning McQueen, from the Disney movie she'd been obsessed with. The name stuck and she'd gone on to compete at the track as a seventeen-year-old . . . just before they'd lost her.

Madelyn gasped, waving the letter she'd been reading over the center of the table. "Listen to this." She cleared her throat and read.

> *Eddy, after twenty years I can tell when something's wrong. If you can't talk to me, then what do we have together?*

She looked at me, and then the sheriff. "This one has a date. The week before the accident, exactly."

"Keep reading," Hoss said.

I saw Reba Montgomery in Granbury today. She'd come by Bubba's to pick something up for Chris, she said. She went to the fabric shop on the square. That's where I ran into her. I was picking up some new fabric for an apron. I never pictured her as a woman who sews, but maybe I was wrong about her. She bought some yardage of three different prints, not at all what I would have imagined her choosing.

I can't say as I like the woman . . . too uppity for my taste, but she was pleasant enough and we chatted for a few minutes. For some reason, she confided in me. She said Chris had been acting strange. Distant. And she seemed really worried.

It got me thinking about you and me and how we've been distant, too. It got me wondering if I should be worried. I know you love me, but sometimes I wonder if love is enough.

"She was beginning to realize something was wrong," Madelyn said.

"Maybe they both were. From that letter, Miss Reba sensed it with Chris, too." I suddenly remembered something Miss Reba had said after her husband's funeral. She'd told me and Will that Chris had called her from the car and asked her to wait up for him, that he had something he wanted to talk about. Had the guilt of his dou-

ble life gotten to him? Or had he fallen out of love with
one of his wives?

Had he made it home to the Blake house in Granbury, talked to Barbara Ann, and crashed on the way
back to Bliss? Or had he never made it to Granbury in
the first place?

There were too many unanswered questions, and the
only person who could answer them was dead.

We kept on with the letters. There were no references
to Barbara Ann discovering that Eddy had created a new
identity as Chris Montgomery, no other mention of Miss
Reba, only the occasional lamentation about Eddy's late
nights at the Bliss store. There was nothing else to shed
any light on whether Barbara Ann had discovered the
truth.

At the very bottom of the box lay one last envelope.
My heart skipped a beat when I realized it was gray, just
like the other one that seemed like it might be from the
killer. I picked it up, looking at Hoss and Madelyn.
Slowly, I opened it and pulled out the single notecard.

I read it silently before handing it to the sheriff.

*Dear Chris . . . or should I say Eddy? Tony
Stewart—you know who he is, right? Won the All-
state 400 in 2005. He said, and I quote, "If I died
right now, my life would be complete." If you died
tomorrow, would your life be complete? I think
you should answer that question. Say good-bye to
your wives. Your kids. Your cars.*

    Say good-bye.

                                See you tomorrow.

As he read it aloud in his slow Southern drawl, a chill worked its way up my spine. It was a death threat. There was no other way to look at it. Someone knew the truth, and Eddy Blake, aka Chris Montgomery, knew he was going to die.

Chapter 21

An hour later, Hoss and Madelyn had gone and I had moved back to my workroom. Hoss had taken the letters with him. The way the last letter was phrased made us all think it hadn't been written by either Barbara Ann Blake or Reba Montgomery—why would either one of them refer to herself in the third person? Then again, it could have been intentional.

Hoss didn't share his investigative plan, but I had a feeling he'd be paying a visit to Barbara Ann Blake, Reba Montgomery, and to Otis and Sally Levon. If it was up to me, that's what I would do, anyway. They all had motive. Was one of them guilty?

I moved the garment bag with Leslie's dress to the front room. She'd be here anytime to pick it up. Next, I moved the dress form with Danica's dress next to the cutting table. Josie was on her way with the beads to complete the garment.

Until one of them arrived, I had time to think. I flipped open my newest sketchbook, turning to the last page so I could jot down my notes. I reached for a pencil, stopping when I saw that it wasn't blank. Lines of familiar writing filled the page. Loretta Mae's shaky script.

"Meemaw," I said to the empty room, "you're messing with my sketchbook again."

The latch on the window lifted and the window slid up. I watched, riveted, as the air rippled. Her form started to take shape, but before it really looked like her, it shimmied and scattered into a million sparkles. "Someday, Meemaw," I said. I knew she'd keep trying to find a way to be more present, but today wasn't that day.

I talked to her when I was alone, filling her in on my life, the things happening around Bliss, and lately, the murder of Eddy Blake, aka Chris Montgomery. The simple one-sided conversations helped me gain some semblance of order with my thoughts, and she knew me better than anyone.

And right now she was trying to help me. I pulled the sketchbook toward me and turned to a blank page.

The sparkles that had been her rippling form a minute ago now circled around me, finally funneling like a tornado over the open sketchbook. She wanted me to write, as I'd done in the past, to help me make sense of all the information.

"Good thinking, Meemaw." I picked up the pencil that suddenly appeared next to the sketchbook and started writing.

Eddy Blake marries Barbara Ann.
Eddy opens Bubba's in Granbury.
Otis joins Bubba's and becomes Eddy's right-hand
man.

*Otis is given ownership in Bubba's when the Bliss
    store opens.*
Eddy and Barbara have a daughter, Sue.
At the Bliss store, Eddy meets Reba.
*Enter Chris Montgomery. Eddy creates the new
    identity to pursue a relationship with Reba.*
After a whirlwind courtship, they marry.
Shane is born.
Teagen is born.
Sue dies.
Otis Levon must know the truth.
Otis must know.
Does Sally?

I reread the last few lines I'd scribbled almost without
thinking. With Miss Reba's discovery of her husband's letters, and the question of whether or not she or Barbara
Ann could have known the truth, I'd almost forgotten
about the fact that Otis Levon had to have known and
been an accomplice in Eddy's double life. Someone had
to have been there to cover for him, to raise the alarm
when one of the wives called—or worse—showed up, and
to help him keep up the ruse with the other employees.

That could only have been Otis. I'd thought, briefly, that
Otis could have told his wife, Sally, the truth, and that
maybe Sally could have been blackmailing Eddy. But so far,
I'd found nothing to indicate blackmail. Miss Reba had said
she hadn't noticed money missing from their account, but
Eddy/Chris would have had at least two accounts.

I looked up Barbara Ann Blake's number and dialed.
"Mrs. Blake," I said when she answered, "I'm so sorry
about everything that's happened."

"I have nothing to say."

"I'm trying to help, ma'am," I said, hoping she wouldn't remember that when I first met her, I'd told her that I was friends with Miss Reba.

"What? What do you want? Reporters have been calling. The police have been here. I just want to be left alone. I'm just alone."

"One question, Mrs. Blake." I forged ahead before she could say no, or worse, hang up. "Do you think someone might have known about . . . about your husband's . . . activities and was blackmailing him? Was any money missing from your account?"

There was no response, but I could hear her ragged breath. Finally, she answered. "When the Bliss Bubba's opened, we were supposed to see an increase in our income, but that never happened. We're in worse shape now than ever before. And do you know why?"

Everyone knew why. Mrs. Blake had no more secrets, and couldn't escape the lies and betrayal of her husband. But it was a rhetorical question because she went on, not waiting for me to answer.

"Because," she said, "he married someone else, had a whole 'nother family. What kind of house do *they* live in?" she asked.

"Mrs. Blake, don't—"

"Don't what? He broke my heart! He stole everything from me. Every memory I have of him is tainted. It's all lies.

"Let me tell you where they live. It's not a trailer park. There aren't stupid Mustangs parked everywhere. They have a pool and a gardener and God knows what else. That other family got everything that should have been ours. Those kids have iPods and cars and all the name-brand clothes they could ever want."

She was ranting, but she was one hundred percent right. Because Eddy had become Chris Montgomery, he siphoned off half, or maybe more, of his income to support Reba and the Montgomery kids. No matter how anyone tried to spin that, Mrs. Blake was the most injured party. A cold feeling rushed through me knowing that she'd driven to Bliss and had seen the Montgomery house. I didn't blame her, but on the other hand, the knowledge scared me. I hadn't pictured Barbara Ann Blake as a take-action kind of person, but she had sought out her husband's other family.

Had Miss Reba done the same? And if she did, what did she think of the Blake household?

The blackmail angle had been a bust, but—my thoughts halted. She'd mentioned the Montgomery kids' iPods. Was that coincidence, or did she know that they'd had them because *she'd* broken into their house? Could she have been the one standing over Miss Reba in her bed?

Oh boy. Maybe Barbara Ann Blake really had killed her husband.

Chapter 22

Josie, Leslie, and Danica converged on Buttons & Bows at the same time. The girls had taken off their mums for the time being. Leslie held the door and Molly's car seat, while Danica, who cradled baby Molly, and Josie, who was loaded down with her sturdy plastic tackle box filled with beads and a canvas tote emblazoned with her Seed-n-Bead logo, filed in.

"We were like a race-car convoy, only I'm in a mini-van instead of a cool ride," Josie said as they came in.

"Minivans come with being a mommy," I said, wondering how I'd feel about trading in Buttercup for one. I hadn't ever given much thought to being a mother. Work had always come first. The life of a fashion designer in New York wasn't conducive to relationships, let alone motherhood.

But now I was settled in Bliss, and Will and I had a good thing going. I looked at Josie's baby. Maybe someday . . .

Molly cooed and Danica fluttered her index finger under the baby's chin. "She's so precious."

She was. Tiny and delicate and vulnerable. I couldn't quite imagine what it would be like to bring a life into the world, to be responsible for it, the worry and the joy. Eddy and Barbara Ann Blake had suffered, losing their daughter. Was it better to have had and loved her, only to have lost her, or not to have had her at all and never known that kind of pain?

I tucked my wayward thoughts into the back of my mind. I couldn't answer that question, but from the adoration on Josie's face when she looked at her baby girl, and the awe on Danica's as she cuddled her, I thought I knew what their answers would be.

"The mums were a hit?" I asked.

Both the girls nodded, grinning. "Gracie's was the best with that sewing machine in the center," Danica said, "but ours were awesome. I've never had a mum like that. I'm going to hang it on my bedroom wall after the game tonight."

The pregame homecoming activities would start in a few hours, so we had no time to waste. I ushered them all into the workroom, handing Leslie her dress. "It's all done," I said.

She took the garment bag and hugged it close, smiling. "Thank you, Harlow. I love it so much!"

A rush of pride filled me. There was no better feeling than giving someone so deserving what she wanted. "I'm so glad."

She unzipped the garment bag, staring in awe at the dress. Her fingers dusted the sapphire blue semisheer fabric. Seeing the happy look on her face, I knew that whatever her dreams were, they'd come true. She would be the belle of the ball.

"It's beautiful," Danica said. She'd shifted Molly's position, holding her against her chest, gently rubbing her back.

Leslie pointed to the tangerine dress on the dress form. "Danica, look. Yours is gorgeous," she said, and once again, I was grateful that these two girls had found each other.

"We need to do the final fitting," I said, "and we have some beadwork to finish up."

Danica's eyes widened. "Beads?"

Josie had placed her tackle box on the cutting board and removed a gray beading board, small cutters, needle-nose pliers, and round-nose pliers. She took out a second plush-lined tray and carefully laid down an intricately beaded belt made with deep blue glass beads.

"What's that for?" Danica asked.

"It'll complete the dress," I said. I wrapped my hands around Molly's torso and gently took her from Danica, cradling her in my arms. She was in a twilight sleep, her eyes fluttering open, her mouth forming a small O at the movement. I rocked her back and forth and she settled back to sleep. "Go try on the dress," I told Danica.

She got it off the dress form easily. Almost too easily, and I wondered if Meemaw was around, helping. She loved to be in the thick of the action, but she was usually not so subtle. I looked around for a ripple in the air, a flutter of the curtains, or any other of Loretta Mae's tell-tale signs.

My gaze hitched on the window. Thelma Louise had her nose pressed against the glass. I opened my mouth to shoo her away, but Molly stirred in my arms so I stopped, waving instead as if the Nubian goat would respond, nar-

.rowing my eyes to tell her that I still had my eye on her after her mum thievery.

She didn't budge, defiant thing. She did what she wanted, and I didn't reckon that was going to change now just because I wanted it to.

Josie was showing Leslie the beading for Danica's dress. I started to turn toward them, but stopped when I caught a reflection in the window. It was faint, almost hidden by Thelma Louise, but the more I concentrated on the image, the more it came into focus and the goat faded. Loretta Mae was here, and while I couldn't see her figure in the room, her faint reflection was there in the window. I couldn't make out details, but my mind filled in the blanks. The snaps on her plaid cowgirl shirt, her curly ginger hair with the blond streak sprouting from her temple, and her mischievous grin made me shake my head and smile. God love her.

I snuck a look around the room to see if any of my guests had noticed the ghost in the window. They hadn't. Josie and Leslie were enthralled in their beading discussion. "You might could apply for a part-time job at Seed-n-Bead," Josie was saying. "I've cut back my hours, what with the baby and all. And you seem to be a natural."

Leslie looked like she'd just won a five-million-dollar lottery. She nodded, an excited smile gracing her lips. Pink splotches colored her cheeks, giving her mocha skin a lovely glow. "Really? A natural?"

Josie ran her fingers along the beads Leslie had just strung. "Oh yeah, I'd say so."

Maybe this was what Leslie wanted—to fit in and be part of the community. If it was, the dress I'd made her was already working its charm. And if she wanted something else, then she was getting a bonus with Josie.

Danica was behind the privacy screen trying on her dress. I hoped there was no way she'd seen my great-grandmother's ghost. If any one of my visitors had, Buttons & Bows would get a reputation for being haunted—not something that would be good for business.

I winked at the reflection, grateful to see Loretta Mae, and equally thankful that she'd figured out how to be present without being obvious.

Leslie had set Molly's car seat just inside the door. I gently laid her in it, carrying it to just outside the work-room where we could see her, but where she'd be away from the hustle and bustle of the final fitting and the final beading.

Danica emerged from behind the fitting screen, a vision in tangerine. The V-neck, one inch strap, and the fit of the bodice accentuated her waistline and the curves of her breasts, while the bottom of the dress hung perfectly, hitting her just above the knees and falling in soft, lush billows. The subtle structure of the microfiber combined with the softness of the bubble hem made it seem as if the dress floated around her legs.

We all stared. Leslie's jaw dropped. Josie shot a quick glance at Molly. Looking back at Danica, she drew in a deep breath, and I got the sense she was imagining her daughter in sixteen years getting ready for homecoming, the belle of the ball.

Carefully, I picked up the completed beaded belt. Danica stepped onto the fitting platform. "I can't breathe," she whispered.

I lost my own breath at that. The seams lay flat and

nothing looked amiss. I knew my measurements were correct. "It's too tight?"

She laughed. "No! It's perfect. I just mean, oh my God, I can't breathe, you know? I've never had anything like this. I feel like a princess."

I released the air I'd been holding, relieved. "You *look* like a princess."

Ten minutes later, I'd marked a few small adjustments to make to the bodice and I'd figured out how to attach the beads to accent the dress and add just the right amount of interest without overwhelming the design.

Josie and Leslie had almost completed the necklace Danica would wear, and by the time she went back behind the privacy screen to change into her regular clothes, we all felt like her fairy godmothers.

"I'll bring it to the brunch in the morning," I told her when she emerged again. I took the dress and put it back on the dress form. I couldn't see Meemaw next to me, but I caught the reflection of her backside in the window. The dress slid onto the dress form like butter.

"Is Gracie's done?" Leslie asked.

I wish I knew. I'd tried to call her earlier, but she hadn't answered. "I hope so."

"Bless her heart," Josie said. "How's she holding up?"

"As best she can. It's been tough on both her and Shane."

"Are they any closer to finding out who did it?"

I didn't think Hoss McClaine would want me talking about the letters Miss Reba had discovered, so I just said, "I can't say for sure. I don't want to believe it, but it seems to me like Mrs. Blake has the strongest motive."

"They say it's usually the wife or the husband, don't they?" Leslie asked.

"Or someone the victim knows." I sighed. "I think I have it figured out; then something else pops into my head that opens up a new possibility."

"Like who?" Danica sat on a stool at the cutting table, fingering the beads on the beading tray. "If it wasn't Mrs. Blake, then who was it?"

I couldn't throw out the names of all the suspects for them to chew on, so I dodged the question. "The sheriff'll figure it out. He's got some other leads."

Danica fiddled with the beads, sucking her lips in over her teeth. She lifted her gaze to me. "Like what? Other suspects?"

Once again, the letters popped into my mind, but I just shrugged. I didn't want to give out confidential information. That's just how rumors started, and suddenly different stories got melded together until not a single one of them was right.

"I read the paper," Leslie said, a hint of pride in her voice. "And I saw that Otis Levon is a partner in the business, and he's going to inherit a big part of it. Mrs. Blake and Miss Reba split the rest equally, with portions going into a trust for their kids. So Shane'll get something, I guess."

"I still can't believe the guy had two families," Josie said. "As if one isn't hard enough."

"With Sue Blake dead," I said, "I imagine her trust will revert back to Mrs. Blake."

"Is that their daughter?"

I nodded. "Their only child."

Leslie's voice grew soft and distant. "Oh my God, I hadn't heard that."

"How . . . horrible," Danica said, the words catching in her throat. She sounded even sadder than Leslie had.

I could see the talk about loss of family was seeping into her, bringing back whatever she felt about losing her own family. These poor girls were too young to have to deal with the pain they had.

"What a tragedy," Josie said. Her cheeks were hollow and her skin had grown pale. I knew she was blindsided by the very idea of losing her precious daughter. It was unfathomable, and my heart ached for Barbara Ann Blake all over again.

A heavy damper lay over us. We worked in silence for a while longer, wrapping up the beading. The home phone rang while we cleaned up. "Ms. Cassidy?" a young woman's voice said when I answered. "This is Brandi. From—"

"Yes, from Bubba's," I said. "I remember." She could only be calling me for two reasons. One, she had some dressmaking need, which seemed highly unlikely since she'd indicated she hadn't heard of my shop, or two, she had some information about Chris Montgomery's death.

I'd lay down money it was number two.

"Right. I hope it's okay I'm calling. You mentioned your shop. I looked it up to get your number."

"It's fine. Call anytime." Once again I employed Meemaw's be quiet and listen tactic, hoping she'd cut to the chase.

"You said to let you know if I thought of anything."

The excitement I'd tried to contain spilled over. "I did. I do. I'm so glad you called. Did you remember something? Otis . . . ?"

She paused and I heard her draw in a bolstering breath.

"No. Well, yes, he . . . but that's not why I'm calling. You said something when you were here and it's been bugging me."

"I did? What did I say?"

Josie, Danica, and Leslie had all stopped what they were doing and stared at me, not even pretending not to listen.

There was silence on the other end of the line. "Brandi? Are you there?"

"I shouldn't even get involved. It's not my business and it doesn't mean anything anyway."

"Do you know something that could help?" I asked.

"I think Otis does. It's about the burglary at the Montgomery's." She paused again and I could almost hear the wheels of her mind turning as she thought. "You know what? Never mind. He'll have my hide if he finds out I called. Forget it," she said, and then the line went dead.

"Hello?" I jiggled the hook on the phone, trying to get the connection back. Nothing. She was gone.

"What was that about?" Josie asked after I hung the phone back on the wall.

"She started to say something, but then she changed her mind," I said. I wanted to find out what she'd intended to say, but I also didn't want to spook her by charging over to Granbury to confront her and demand to know why she'd called. By the time I got there, the store would be closed anyway.

No, I needed to think about what to do and how to approach it. Maybe I needed to go straight to Otis.

"What'd she say?" Josie asked.

Danica and Leslie both waited, Leslie finally adding, "Yeah, why'd she call?"

"I don't know. It was nothing, I guess," I said, although I sure didn't believe that. I ushered the girls toward the door. "Come on. Let's get y'all on your way to the game."

Their faces fell, their disappointment at not hearing more about the conversation evident, but they let it drop. Leslie carried her garment bag over her arm, Danica held Josie's tote bag, Josie had the car seat with Molly strapped in, and I brought up the rear with the tackle box. We headed out the front door, down the porch steps, and to the row of cars in front of the house.

Josie was still a new mom, so it took her a few minutes to get Molly's seat properly buckled in. Danica and I set the tote bag and box in the deep trunk of the minivan. After a quick hug, Josie pulled out, her taillights disappearing down Mockingbird Lane.

"Thank you again." Leslie said it first, then Danica, the same melancholy, yet grateful look on both their faces. Part of friendship was empathy, and they were both experiencing that in spades. It was hard to feel happy when friends were suffering.

"Have fun at the game," I said as they each got into their cars.

"I will," Leslie called through her open window.

"Me, too. Thank you, Harlow." Danica put her hand out and waved. They sped off in different directions, and I sent a silent wish after them that they'd both have a great time at the Bliss homecoming game.

Then I went inside to call Will and pitch my plan to go pay another visit to Otis Levon.

Chapter 23

"You have no idea what she was going to tell you?" Will asked me from the driver's side of his truck. A car zoomed past us in the opposite direction, its brights momentarily blinding us.

"None," I said after the car had passed and the stars I had been seeing dissipated. After the others had left, I'd tried to call Brandi back at the Granbury store, but it had gone straight to voice mail. "She said something I'd said was bothering her, and then she said Otis knew something that could help. She said it had to do with the burglary at the Montgomerys'."

"And he told this girl Brandi?"

"Or she figured it out? I have no idea." I threw my hands in the air, frustrated that I couldn't seem to get anything concrete to help Shane. "She just changed her mind and hung up."

"Simmer down, darlin'," he said, giving my leg a reassuring squeeze. "We'll just go talk to him and see what we can find out."

I ran my fingers through my hair. "But we're out of time. The dance is tomorrow—"

"Cassidy, you've given Hoss plenty to think on. He's not going to arrest Shane anytime soon. There are too many other possibilities. This is no slam dunk."

"I was just hoping to figure this all out before the dance so none of it would hang over him and Gracie."

"You're being too hard on yourself. There's only so much you can do."

I tried to take that to heart as we entered Bubba's. The place was deserted. Homecoming in a small town was a huge event—the parade, the presentation of the court, the crowning of the king and queen, and the big game. The entire town would turn out for the event . . . which meant no one was at Bubba's getting their car worked on.

The door had dinged when we entered. We waited for a few minutes, but the place was graveyard silent. No one came to help us. "Is anyone here?" I whispered.

Will looked around, puzzled. "Doesn't seem like it."

"Hello?" I called.

Nothing.

An eerie feeling came over me. Something wasn't right. It was still business hours, but the doors to the garage bay were closed. I peeked through the window to the garage, but it was dark. The lobby door was unlocked, yet no one was here.

There was no upstairs in this shop, but behind the counter there was a small room. I headed right to it, turned on the light, and looked around. It was a smaller version of the Granbury location. A rack of clothes was pushed against the wall in the corner, just like in the

Granbury shop, and a sleeper sofa was up against the opposite wall. A small refrigerator stood next to the sofa. A microwave was on a portable stand.

Will had come up behind me, but now I scooted around him and backtracked to the lobby. I opened the door to the garage bay and stepped inside. The light sensor activated and the space was illuminated.

I walked deeper in, moving past some of the equipment and tools. A car was parked in the center bay. I skirted around it . . . and stopped dead in my tracks.

A man was sprawled awkwardly on the ground, legs spread, one of them cocked at an unnatural angle. If I drew a line of chalk around him, he'd look just like the stereotypical dead body drawing on TV.

Otis? I slapped my hand over my mouth. "No," I whispered. He couldn't be dead.

Behind me, Will was already calling nine-one-one.

We tiptoed closer to get a better look. I hoped against hope that I was wrong and that it wasn't Otis. And that he wasn't as dead as he looked.

Will and I leaned down. I used the flashlight app on my smartphone to illuminate his face. I didn't know if he was dead, but it was definitely Otis Levon.

Chapter 24

The sheriff's station wasn't where I wanted to be, yet here I was. Will had called Hoss after he'd phoned emergency, and it had taken less than ten minutes for the EMTs, Hoss, Gavin, Madelyn, and a whole slew of other people to arrive. Will and I were taken outside while the sheriff's team processed the garage bay.

"Take 'em to the Church," Hoss told Gavin, pointing to Will and me. The Church was Hoss's nickname for the sheriff's station. The current department had once been owned by the old Methodist church. When the church moved to their new building, the town bought the old place and moved the city offices.

Gavin started to protest, but Hoss was already sauntering back to the garage bay, lost in his thoughts. Gavin ripped his cowboy hat off his head, slapping it against his thigh, muttering under his breath. "Dammit . . . babysitter . . . stepdaddy . . ."

"We know where the Church is," I said. "We can get there ourselves and you can stay here." The last thing I wanted was to be babysat . . . or questioned . . . by Gavin McClaine.

"Nice try, Harlow, but, uh, no." He held his arm out, his hat still clutched in his hand, and ushered us toward Will's truck. At least he was going to let us drive ourselves, which meant neither Hoss nor Gavin thought we were actual suspects.

Small consolation.

Now we sat at a table in a nondescript room. The gray walls made it feel smaller than it was, but natural light streamed in through the square window. Gavin sat across from us.

"Okay, Harlow, let's hear it."

"Where do you want me to start?"

He heaved a frustrated sigh. "The beginning."

If I'd had a cowboy hat of my own, I'd have snatched it from my head and whacked it against my thigh. I wanted to know what had happened to Otis, too, but berating me wasn't going to get Gavin any closer to any answers.

"Any day now, Harlow. I have a crime I'm investigatin'."

I simmered down and told him about the call from Brandi in Granbury and how that had led me to Bubba's to talk to Otis Levon. Before I finished my last sentence, he interrupted me with a curt, "And you met her how?"

I swallowed. Gavin wouldn't take kindly to me poking my nose in where it didn't belong, but there was nothing I could do about it. My nose was in one hundred and ten percent. "I happened to be in Granbury the other day and stopped in for an oil change."

"Uh-huh. And why did you happen to be in the area? Just a coincidence, I'm sure, right?"

Will and Gavin both watched me. I felt my face go slack as I tried to come up with a lie. But I couldn't do it. Meemaw had adhered to the rule that given a sticky situation over something you'd done, one should ask for forgiveness, not permission.

Currently, I felt like a fly stuck to a very tacky spiderweb, and forgiveness was my only way out.

"I went to see Barbara Ann Blake, Gavin." I hurried on before he could get the words out that I could see were on the tip of his tongue. "I know I shouldn't have, and before you say anything, I know I'm butting in where I shouldn't have been, but Miss Reba asked me for help. She's worried about Shane. And, well, I just couldn't say no, Gavin, now could I? So I'm sorry, but I'd do it again. I had to do whatever I could to help prove Shane is innocent."

"And did you?"

I stared. "Did I what?"

"Did you prove Shane is innocent?"

"Well, not exactly, but I've got reasonable doubt. And," I added, "maybe he has an alibi for whenever Otis was assaulted."

Gavin steepled his fingers together in front of his chin. "He does, as it turns out. Have an alibi, I mean."

Will leaned forward, hands folded on the table in front of him. "What is it?"

"He was workin' on the float for the homecoming parade. He's been there since school ended at three thirty."

The parade! I'd forgotten about the Bliss High School homecoming parade. It would start on Magnolia Street, winding through the neighborhood behind the school, finally ending at the football field. The marching band would lead the way, followed by floats made by the different clubs on campus, the sports teams, the scouts, and even the peewee football league. The streets would be lined with families, candy would be tossed to them from the people on the floats, and at the end of it all, after the football game, there'd be a big bonfire at the high school to celebrate.

Homecoming was a big deal in Texas.

"So Shane's in the clear?"

"For Otis, yes, but so far we don't have evidence that whoever attempted to kill Otis also killed Chris Montgomery . . . or Eddy Blake." With his steepled his fingers, he looked just like his daddy, Hoss. Like father, like son. "Back to this girl, Brandi," he said.

I sat back in my chair, crossing my legs. I couldn't contain my nervous energy and my red Frye-booted foot moved back and forth double time. "She said she had something to tell me. She told me that Otis knew something about the burglary at the Montgomery's, but then she changed her mind and hung up."

"And that's when you decided, instead of callin' the authorities, to take matters into your own hands."

"That's when I . . ." I glanced at Will. "When *we* decided we might could use an oil change."

Gavin smirked. "Gimme a break, Harlow. You went to—what did you say a minute ago?—to poke your nose in where it didn't belong."

I folded my arms over my chest and met his chastising gaze. "Maybe so, Gavin, but because we did, Otis might have a chance to survive, and you also know that there's a crazy person running around Bliss right this very minute."

His upper lip curled up, but he swallowed whatever

he was about to say, blew out a breath, and said, "I'll give you that."

"Thank you."

"And you have no idea what this Brandi was talkin' about?"

"None. We could call her—"

"Uh-uh," Gavin said, wagging his finger at me. "*I* can call her . . . and I did."

I leaned forward. "You did? And?"

"And nothin'. Ain't reached her yet. And until I do, you stay away from her. Stay away from Granbury. In fact," he said, "why don't you stay right here in Bliss, Harlow, and keep yourself out of trouble?"

"I'll see to that, Gavin," Will said. A look passed between them that spoke to some understanding they had. I smarted, but after a second of thought, I just smiled and said, "Yes, sir, Deputy, sir."

I didn't need to be watched by anyone, but if anyone was going to watch me, I'd definitely choose Will Flores.

Chapter 25

Despite Will's promise to Gavin, he was slipping at the job of watching me. We sat on one of the top rows of the Bliss High School bleachers cheering on the Bliss Eagles. The majority of his attention was firmly on the football game, the halftime show with the marching band, and the presentation of the homecoming court. Carrie, the girl I'd first seen with Leslie in my shop, then again at the park, had been named the sophomore class homecoming princess. Her jaw dropped when her name was announced, tears flooding her eyes as she was crowned and accepted the sash and a bouquet of flowers.

She wasn't the cheerleader type, or even an athlete, so hadn't been a shoo-in for the honor. I might have been off base, but to see her chosen by the student body as their homecoming princess felt like encouragement for the underdog.

Everyone around us wore red and black and white, the school colors, including Will and me. My shirt was missing the Eagle emblem and was custom made, but it *was* red and was as close as I had to school spirit wear. Will, on the other hand, had a collared black shirt with the red school logo on the left chest. He had a collection of men's Eagles shirts, just like every other father in Bliss. He was nothing if not a Texas dad. And I loved him more for that.

The people around us waved pompoms attached to foot-long sticks. From our position high in the bleachers, we had a good view of all the activity. Gracie sat with Holly and Libby, all three of them sporting their mums. They laughed and cheered, and for the first time in days, Gracie looked happy.

I scanned the crowd looking for people I knew or recognized. The school administration, school board, and a few teachers sat in the center section of the bleachers just under the press box. It was prime real estate for the football games.

Leslie, Carrie, and Danica walked toward the concession stand. The three of them wore their mums, just as proud as every other girl here. The ribbons streamed down their legs, whipping around as they walked. They stopped to talk to their friends, and once again I was grateful I'd been able to be part of making their night special by helping them fit in with their mums.

Kids of all ages milled around. Cheerleaders, elementary school football players already dreaming of having their chance on the field, and every other town member seemed to be here. If someone wanted to burglarize a house in Bliss, doing it on a Friday night during the homecoming game was a sure bet.

The burglary at the Montgomery house came back to me. That had happened in the middle of the night, and whoever had done it hadn't chosen a time when the house would be empty. Had they *wanted* someone to be home?

Whoever had broken in had stood over Miss Reba in her bed. That was personal. Barbara Ann Blake. Once again, my finger pointed at her. If she'd discovered the truth about her husband, would she want to exact revenge against the woman who'd stolen the rest of her married life?

I wouldn't be surprised if she had.

A roar went up in the stadium. A wave started at one end of the stadium, traveling through the crowd. People lifted their arms, stood, and then sat back down as the next section repeated the action. I acted without thinking, standing and cheering when our turn came, my mind coming back to the game. I knocked Will on the shoulder with the back of my hand and pointed to number thirty-two on the field. "Is that Shane?"

"Yeah. He looks good tonight."

"Must be directing all his anger and frustration to the game," I said, half to myself.

But Will agreed with me. "I think you're right."

The next play started. Will talked through what the team was doing, and why. The quarterback held the ball, falling back and searching for a receiver. "Shane's wide open," Will said, pointing.

"Throw it!" someone nearby hollered.

The quarterback made a decision in the nick of time, hurling the ball through the air like a missile. It headed straight for Shane. Shane ran, jetting left to adjust for the trajectory of the ball. He lifted his arms, never taking his eyes off the ball, and then he caught it and darted into the end zone.

"Touchdown!" Will whirled around and grabbed me in his arms, lifting me clear off my feet.

We were at eye level, but he let me go and I slid down until my toes touched the plastic-coated bleacher floor. I stayed on tiptoes, lifting my lips to his. We kissed, and for just a minute, the entire stadium disappeared.

Will and I waited by his truck for Gracie. She split off from Holly and Libby when she saw us, waving to them as they headed to Holly's car. I looked for Leslie and Danica, but they'd been enveloped by the crowd. I'd see them at the brunch in the morning, and I'd already decided I'd help them, as well as Gracie, Holly, and Libby, get ready for the dance. It felt almost as if *I* were going to homecoming, making up for choosing dressmaking over a social life in high school.

But truthfully, I preferred being a spectator and was happy to cheer on Gracie and her friends.

"It was a good game, wasn't it?" she asked as she came up to us. She mindlessly twirled the ribbons of her mum, her smile fading now that she was with us instead of her friends.

"It was a great game," Will said. "Shane made that touchdown look like he was taking candy from a baby."

She smiled, but it didn't reach her eyes. "Yeah."

"Let's get out of here." Will opened the passenger door for us before circling around to the driver's side of the truck.

I stopped Gracie before she got in and climbed to the back. "Are you okay?"

Her chin quivered, but she met my gaze and nodded. "I'm fine."

She was not fine. Anyone with eyes could see that, and I had the added benefit of knowing her . . . and knowing her well. "Gracie?"

"He's acting like a different person. I don't know if he suddenly doesn't like me anymore, or what's going on. It's like he won't even hardly talk to me."

I wanted to fold my arms around her and draw her into a comforting hug, but the high schoolers milling around stopped me. Embarrassing her wouldn't help. "Darlin', he's going through a rough time, that's all. Boys handle stress differently than girls."

She looked at me expectantly, waiting for me to go on. "We want to talk about things, to hash it all out, sometimes over and over and over again."

She nodded, her eyes clearing and showing she completely agreed with me.

"Boys, on the other hand," I continued, "can often tuck something away in the back of their minds and not think about it, but from my experience, that means they also withdraw a little bit. Shane can't deal with everything that's going on right now, so he's just not, but you're part of that."

A tear slipped down her cheek and she bit her lower lip. "I just want him to talk to me," she said, her voice quavering.

"Baby, he will. Give him time."

"How much time? The dance is tomorrow. I don't know if—"

She broke off, leaning against the truck. Will waited in the cab. I caught his eye and held up one finger, telling him it would be another minute. He nodded, that look of fatherly concern I'd come to know so well slipping onto his face.

"Did he say he doesn't want to go to the dance?" I asked.

She shook her head. "Not lately, but he hasn't said he still wants to go. And now with Mr. Levon . . ."

I leaned one shoulder against the truck next to her. "Gracie, darlin', you can't do that. He didn't have anything to do with Otis Levon, so put that out of your head. He already asked you to the dance. You're boyfriend and girlfriend. He's struggling right now, but if he hasn't said he's changed his mind, don't put words in his mouth. Nothing's changed with the dance. You two will go and, yes, it may be tough for him, and for you, but you'll get through it and you'll have a good time."

She wiped away the tears staining her cheeks and nodded. "We will. You're right, Harlow."

This time I did hug her, teenagers be damned. She didn't seem to mind and, in fact, she wrapped her arms around me and hugged me back. "Thank you," she said.

"You're welcome." I held the truck's door open for her and ushered her into the backseat of the extended cab. "Now," I said, "what's the status of your homecoming dress?"

She grinned sheepishly. "I tried, Harlow, I really did, but can you . . . would you mind . . . I could use some help," she finally said. "I'd like the company."

A zing went through me, and for a moment I felt as if Meemaw had invaded my body, filling me up and making me stand taller. Gracie needed me, and I knew it wasn't just for the sewing help. She'd confided in me about Shane and what she'd been feeling, and she wanted to spend the evening with me. This was what it felt like to have the love of a child, and to be needed and wanted. It was a feeling so completely different from being loved by your family, or the love of a man.

Gracie's love filled my heart so completely that it spilled over. My eyes pricked with tears and for a second, I lost my breath. The love of a child. It was new to me, and I was grateful for it.

She took off her mum to climb into the extended cab of the truck. As I slid into the passenger seat, Will shot me a look, raising one eyebrow in a silent question. Was his daughter okay?

I nodded, smiling, and took his hand. We were all okay.

Chapter 26

Helping Hands was the organization Mrs. James had founded to help kids in Bliss. It was a low-mileage foundation. It might be young, but Mrs. James never did anything halfway, and Helping Hands was no exception. She aimed to create friendships among the girls who might be struggling because of their family circumstances. Girls who'd been Margarets or were in the high school honor society could participate as part of their community service, and Mrs. James's hope was that strong bonds would form between the girls.

From what I'd seen with Leslie, Danica, Gracie, and Holly, Mrs. James was right. Spending time together making their mums had created a bond between them, one I hoped would be long-lasting.

Mrs. James had solicited donations to fund the charity from her husband's political circles and from her group of wealthy and connected friends. It was growing more slowly than she liked, but it was helping kids, and that was her mission.

I'd brought the materials for the centerpieces of the tables and had arrived a few minutes early to help Mama unload the vases once she arrived. I didn't have to wait long. Her truck pulled up in the roundabout driveway. She stopped and hopped out, crooking her finger and beckoning to me.

"What in the devil is going on with you?" she asked.

"That's a nice way to greet your daughter." I gave her a peck on the cheek anyway.

"All I'm sayin' is you look like you didn't get a wink of sleep last night." She leaned closer, as if proximity could give her some answer to my ragtag appearance. "I called you at home, you know. No answer."

She looked me up and down. "You're looking a little worn."

"Thanks, Mama," I said with a grimace. But I caught a glimpse of myself in the glass of the front door of the Grange. Truth be told, I *was* looking a little worse for wear. As I'd helped Gracie with her dress the night before, I'd mulled over the letters Miss Reba had given me. There seemed to me to be no question that the final note we'd found in the box was from the killer, and that it was a blatant warning that Eddy, aka Chris, was going to die. I really hadn't slept after that.

My glasses hid the dark circles framing my eyes, but my cheeks looked gaunt and my hair seemed dull. Even the Cassidy streak of blond seemed darker and less magical.

"Where were you?" Mama asked.

She was no babe in the woods, and she knew that the sun rose in the east and set in the west, so why she was asking a question she most likely felt she knew the answer to was beyond me. "I was at the Flores home, Mama, and before you go countin' your unborn grandbabies, I was helping Gracie with her homecoming dress. All night."

She cocked a brow. "*All* night?"

"Yes, Mama, *all night*." Which was why my eyelids were drooping and I felt like the walking dead instead of a spritely thirty-three-year-old dressmaker volunteering to do a good deed for some disadvantaged kids.

"Well, damn, girl, you're not gettin' any younger."

I stared at my mother. "Who *are* you?"

She ignored me. "All I'm sayin' is that that man has it bad for you, and you have it just as bad for him. I don't know what y'all are waitin' for."

Will and I weren't waiting on anything in particular, except time. We were still pretty new in the scheme of relationships.

"Not so long ago, you were practically running from the altar," I said. "Pot calling the kettle black, and all that."

"Pshaw." She waved away my argument. She'd married Hoss, so in her mind, whatever hesitation she'd had was old news. "Help me with the vases, darlin'."

I grabbed a box from the back of her truck and carried it into the Grange, setting it on a portable rectangular table Mrs. James had had set up. Mama put the second box next to it, and one by one, we took out the wide-bottomed glass vases and set them in the center of each plain table.

She'd filled each one with white jointweed and pink starfruit flowers. With their white tablecloths, the mounds of delicate pastel tulle I added, the metallic pink plastic chargers at each place setting, and the sparkle of the confetti, the tables suddenly looked happy and festive.

"Lovely," Mrs. James said. She came to stand next to Mama, gazing at the transformation of the room. We talked about the brunch and the food Sandra had made for the event. I imagined the girls at the brunch today would have a heightened sense of romance and anticipation about the dance tonight after eating the finger sandwiches, quiche, fruit, and salad made by my cousin.

Mama gave me a hug, pinching my cheek. "Get some rest," she said.

"I will." But I knew I couldn't really rest until Chris Montgomery's murder and the attack on Otis Levon were solved. Even if Gavin wasn't convinced the two were related, I was.

Mama left us to the brunch. Just as she pulled out, her truck rumbling away, my cell phone pinged as a text came in. I pulled it out from my bag, read it, and grinned. *Remember the Hill Country*, it said. Will.

The trip to the Hill Country bed-and-breakfast had been pushed to the back of my mind, but now it was front and center again. I texted back. *Counting the days*. I just didn't know how many days there were left to count before I got to the truth and was able to forget everything and have a weekend getaway with the man I loved.

I tucked my phone away, holding on to Mama's words. *That man has it bad for you*. Had Eddy had it bad for Barbara Ann at one point? After he met Miss Reba, did his feelings for his first wife change, or did he simply have it bad for two women? At what point did a man decide to cheat—or create a separate identity, as the case may be—versus being true to his vows and the woman he'd committed to?

Mrs. James interrupted my thoughts. She was in a suit, this one pink with black trim, truthfully more reminiscent of Jackie Kennedy than Nancy Reagan, whom she normally channeled. Her short silver hair was neatly coiffed, and her lipstick muted. She Botoxed and used fillers and looked damn good for her age. Only the papery quality of her skin gave her away, but no matter. She was aging gracefully, if with assistance.

But at the moment, tiny lines ran up and down above her upper lip, a telltale sign of her stress. "One of the servers called in sick," she said to me.

I hesitated only for a second. The truth was, I'd hoped to sneak in a quick nap before helping the girls get ready for the dance, but instead I smiled and said, "I'll fill in, Mrs. James."

She swiveled her gaze back to me, zeroing in on the dark spots I knew were under my eyes. "Darlin', you're a peach, but no. You're working too hard as it is."

"Mrs. James, I want to help." And I did. Either I was a glutton for punishment, or I thought I might learn something useful.

She squeezed my arm. "Zinnia. How many times must I tell you?"

"Till the cows come home," I said with a laugh. "I just can't do it."

She pursed her lips, but there was a smile behind them. "I'll keep trying," she said.

"You do that."

"Are you certain about helping?"

I'd done a few stints of waitressing during college. I

could spend two hours schlepping quiche to teenagers and maybe still have time to sneak in a nap afterward. "Yes, ma'am. One hundred percent."

"You may be crazier than a hornet, Harlow, but you're a lifesaver." She handed me two stacks of cards and a few strips of paper. "Libby was supposed to come help with this, but she's running late and I want her to have a good time today, not be racing around working."

Libby was my cousin Sandra's daughter, and Mrs. James's granddaughter. Bliss was a small town with an intertwined family tree. "Sure thing," I said, taking the cards.

"These," she said, tapping the smaller, creased stack, "are the place cards. Put one at each place. Then refer back to the bigger ones and see if there are any special dietary requests."

"Got it. And these?" I asked, holding up the strips.

"If there's a dietary request, put the strip at the place. Vegetarian. Gluten-free. Dairy-free. God love 'em, but these girls are persnickety."

I wouldn't have thought there were many vegetarians in Texas, the land of cattle and beef, but from the number of strips, it looked like the lifestyle was booming in Bliss, at least amidst the younger crowd. "Any particular arrangement?"

"Not as far as I'm concerned. You decide. Ta-ta!" she said with a wave, and she wandered off to check on the ETA of Sandra and the food.

I didn't know most of the girls, so I went with random placement. I supposed they could switch them around if they really wanted to sit with someone in particular.

I read each card, placing the corresponding strip, if

there was one, on the center of the charger. One out of three had a request. Poor Sandra. No wonder she was behind.

There were a total of thirty girls. Five tables of six. I had to squint to read some of the writing on the cards. Penmanship wasn't a class at the school. After some shuffling around, I managed to put Leslie, Danica, Holly, Gracie, and Libby together at one table. I added Carrie as the sixth person.

I only glanced at the cards briefly as I worked, scanning the requests. Danica was dairy-free, and Carrie was vegetarian, but the normal brunch worked for the rest of the girls.

The next hour was spent helping Sandra in the kitchen. She had her red hair pulled back with bobby pins, her lips shimmered with gloss, and she wore a clean white apron. I'd never seen her in a dirty apron, and I wondered if she simply didn't make a mess when she cooked. Her aprons were like Nana's pristine white socks, and both were a mystery to me.

Sandra had prepared delicate green salads topped with strawberries and almonds. "This is the first course," she said as she added a lavender pansy to the top of each mound. "The flower's edible."

Sandra couldn't make plants grow like my mother could, but she knew the meaning behind flowers and somehow her charm was related to those meanings.

"Don't pansies have to do with people from your past?" I asked.

She nodded. "Remembrance. But they also mean togetherness. As in friendship."

Ah, that made perfect sense. So when the girls ate the

petals from the pansies, the friendships they were developing would grow stronger. The charm was so similar to mine, yet far more focused. I didn't know what I was sewing into the seams of the clothing I made, only that deep desires would be realized. If Sandra wanted someone to feel something specific, she could use a food's properties to tailor responses and enhance emotions.

It was a nifty component of her charm that I sometimes wished I had. Then again, there was something exhilarating about the unknown, and wondering how my magic had impacted someone's life. If it had a negative effect, I think I preferred not knowing.

The girls started arriving a short time later. They milled around, gossiping, describing their homecoming dresses, and talking about the parade, the game, and the homecoming court from the night before. Girl after girl after girl congratulated Carrie as the homecoming princess, giving her hugs and supportive pats on the back, but something was wrong. I'd only seen her a handful of times, but Carrie normally had an easy air about her. Right now, though, her dimpled smile and the glow in her cheeks were gone. The dark circles under her red-rimmed eyes looked worse than mine, and her skin was pasty. I circulated in the room, carrying a tray of iced tea and water glasses, passing them out to the different groups of people, glancing back at Carrie.

I walked the perimeter of the room, listening to snippets of conversations. Leslie was describing her confetti-colored dress to Carrie, and then Danica gave a rundown of her tangerine bubble dress with the custom beads.

"It sounds beautiful," Carrie said, but her voice cracked. It was a reminder that what Shane and Gracie were going through, what the Montgomery, Levon, and Blake families were experiencing, affected others in the community, too. There was a murderer in Bliss, and that had to scare everyone.

"I've been to two proms and three homecomings," Carrie continued. "Granbury, well, they just don't have a custom dressmaker in town." She laughed, her dimple materializing, but the sound was hollow. Forced. She was trying hard to control whatever emotions she was experiencing. Poor thing.

The other girls laughed, but Carrie had stopped, her smile drooping.

"Ladies." Mrs. James's voice interrupted the girls' conversations. The girls in the room seemed to swivel in unison to face their benefactor. Someone started to clap, and before long, the entire room of thirty girls was clapping, honoring her.

Mrs. James was usually cool as a cucumber. She was a politician's wife and had been around the block enough times to know how to school her emotions. But this group of girls had gotten to her. Her cheeks turned as pink as her suit and splotches of red marked her neck just under her collar.

After a minute, the applause died down and she cleared her throat. "I appreciate that," she said to the girls. "As many of you know, I'm married to Jeb James, state senator."

A few of the girls nodded, and she continued. "But as a girl, I wasn't always able to do the things I wanted, and believe me when I say that I had plenty of help along the way. I grew up here in Bliss, on the other side of the tracks, you might say. Do y'all know what that means?"

She paused. Some of the girls dipped their heads. Leslie and Danica, as well as a few others, nodded.

Mrs. James explained to the rest of them. "It means not having the things you need, let alone the extras in life. I mean the things you *want*.

"Helping Hands is meant to be just what the name says—hands that can help. A group that supports you, without judgment. It's about you, for you, for your here and now and for your future. It's thanks to the wonderful women of Bliss—"

Mrs. Abernathy, my grandmother, Mama, Mrs. Mcafferty, and several other women seemed to appear out of nowhere. They stepped out of the shadows and formed a wide circle around the girls. Mrs. Abernathy held a mound of something in her arms. She began to unfold it, holding one end while passing the mound to Nana. Nana unwound more of it, and I realized it was netting. Mrs. Mcafferty took the ball of netting, unwinding it and handing it off. On and on it went. Clear across the room, Sally Levon appeared at the circle. She was pale, and I could see her red nose and glassy eyes from across the room. Her husband had been gravely injured, but she was here supporting her daughter and the girls of Helping Hands.

Her daughter. Oh my God. I suddenly realized who her daughter was. The familiarity I felt when I saw her was from the photo Otis Levon had shown me. And the hugs she was getting? Oh Lord, it all made sense now.

I searched the group of girls in the center of the circle, my focus landing on Carrie. She had her gaze locked on her mother, Sally; they were lifelines for one another. Carrie Levon—she was Otis's daughter. No wonder she had dark circles and pale skin and was barely holding her emotions in check. She didn't know if her father was going to live or die.

I wanted to charge across the room and wrap her and her mother up in a hug.

After the circle, I'd do just that.

Sandra came out of the kitchen and joined the circle. Finally, it came to Mrs. James. She took what was left of the netting and looked around the room until she spotted me. Crooking her finger, she beckoned me toward her, handing me the last section of the netting. Mrs. Abernathy reached out, offering the tail end of what she had. I took it, completing the circle.

The thirty teenagers were in the center, surrounded by the netting.

"We are your support," Mrs. James said. "We'll catch you when you fall. We'll hold you up and help you soar. We'll be there for you, from today forward."

Tears pricked my eyes. I wasn't a girl in need. I never had been. I'd had my brother, Red, Mama, Nana and Granddaddy, and Meemaw. They'd always been, and continued to be, my net, and I theirs. Some of these girls—the Danicas and the Leslies—didn't have the good fortune of a family that was still with them, but now they had Helping Hands. They had other girls and women who would be there for them.

Mrs. James had done an amazing thing by creating this group, and from the tears of the girls in the inner circle, they felt the power of what was happening, too.

We were part of something bigger than any one of us. I looked for Gracie in the circle, catching her eye and giving her a wink. Her eyes glistened from tears, but she smiled and winked back. My net had grown to include her and Will. I'd be there for them, no matter what, and I knew they felt the same.

They were the family I'd chosen.

Chapter 27

Sally and Carrie Levon were gone before I had a chance to talk to either of them. My sympathies would have to wait. Tonight was already committed to the homecoming dance.

By the time the brunch was over, the afternoon was half gone. The kids planned to gather at Gracie's house to take pictures before the dance at five o'clock. From there, they'd go to dinner, ending the evening at the dance. Will had agreed to host the after-party. "We'll just play spoons and watch movies," Gracie had said.

"I'd rather have her home where I can keep an eye on what's happening," he'd told me later.

"You're not being overprotective?" I asked him when he stopped by Buttons & Bows.

"Maybe, but I'm allowed. I'm her dad." He paused before flashing that wicked smile of his, the one that reminded me of Rhett Butler—one quarter sincere and three quarters sly charm. His eyes sparkled and that goatee gave him enough edge to make him dangerous—in the most enticing way imaginable.

"You know I need you, right?"

A zing went through my body. "Mmm, you do?"

"Of course. All those girls in one place? I can handle the boys, and Gracie, but the rest of them? Not so much."

I knew how he felt, so I tried not to let disappointment seep into my voice. "Ah, you need me at the after-party."

Instead of answering, he slipped his arms around my waist and pulled me close. "No, I need you always, Cassidy. Life before you was dull. No Thelma Louise. No Meemaw. No charms." He paused, smirking. "No murder."

"Yeah, because murder's so appealing."

"No, but your cleverness is."

"Except that this time, I'm really stymied. I can't figure it out. Sometimes I think it's Barbara Ann Blake. Other times I think it's Miss Reba. I thought for a while it might be Otis."

"Guess he's out."

"Yeah. If I discount Shane and Teagen, that still leaves Sally Levon, Otis's wife."

"So all three main suspects are wives. Kind of a scary statement about marriage, don't you think?"

It was. But try as I might, I couldn't think of any other suspects. No one else benefitted from the deaths. No one else had a motive. And each of the three wives had pretty good motives.

"I'm missing something," I said, "but I have no idea what."

All the ruminating I'd been doing hadn't brought me any closer to answers, so I pushed it all aside, grabbed Will's hand, and dragged him to the computer. "The pictures from the park," I explained. I hadn't viewed them yet, and he hadn't seen the sweet shots of Gracie and Shane.

He crouched beside me as I pulled the collection up and scrolled through them. "There were so many kids there," I said just as a panoramic shot showing just how many had been there popped up, "and Madelyn says I can't frame a shot, but I think they're pretty good."

Other than a single "Whoa" at the first shot of the group with the rest of the groups in the background, he was rendered speechless for a few seconds. "Will there be that many tonight?" he asked after he recovered.

I laughed. "No. This was the hot spot for photos. Lots of different groups were there. Tonight it'll just be Gracie's core friends. Holly. Libby. She invited Danica and Leslie. Carrie," I said, pointing to the girl who'd suddenly become part of the group. "And the boys, of course."

"Of course."

The next picture was one of the six girls, each with their mums. It was a candid shot and most of the girls were looking at something other than the camera. Carrie looked at Danica. Danica looked off to the left. Leslie looked to the other side. Libby and Holly looked at each other, ginning.

Only Gracie looked at the camera, but her face was haunted rather than joyful. No smile. No glee. Her eyes looked hollow and my heart just ached for her.

Will stared at the picture, a similar sadness washing across his face. He couldn't stand to see his daughter hurting, but looking at her in the picture, there was no doubt that's what was happening.

I didn't know what to say to help him see that she'd be all right after a while. A knock at the door stopped me from trying and jolted us both out of our thoughts.

I'd recently realized something about Buttons & Bows. Half the time, people just walked in, thinking the house was an ordinary shop and not realizing it was also where I lived. The other half waited patiently at the door, thinking it was by appointment only.

Right now, with a murderer on the loose, I was glad people weren't just barging in, and I was also glad Will stood up to go answer the door. I stayed put, mesmerized by Gracie's face.

"Oh. Hello. I . . . I'm looking for Harlow Cassidy," a hesitant voice said. "Is this her . . . er . . . is she here?"

Will moved aside, and a moment later Barbara Ann Blake stepped in. She was dressed in black from head to toe. In my experience, people no longer adhered to the strict rules of wearing mourning clothes, but it looked as if Barbara Ann had a different idea. I imagined her selecting her long black maxi skirt and the black blouse she had belted around her waist to represent her grief. The one thing I couldn't say was whether she was mourning the loss of Eddy or the fact that the life she knew had been a complete sham.

I closed my eyes for a split second, summoning up a vision of her in something else. I still had no idea if she was innocent or guilty, but I wanted to assume she was innocent, and I wanted to see the potential peace of her future after she began to heal from all her loss.

She moved next to the dress form I'd recently positioned in front of the large front window behind the settee. You could see it from the sidewalk, and while it wasn't quite the same as dressing a storefront window, it gave a hint about the dressmaking that went on inside Buttons & Bows.

"Mrs. Blake," I said, standing. I started to move away from the computer to come greet her, but she stopped me with her hand, palm facing me. Okay. So she wanted to operate at her own pace. Fair enough. She was here for a reason, and I had to assume that she'd fill me in on that reason before too long. I stayed put, waiting, my heart pounding because if she was the killer, she wouldn't hesitate to do it again.

Of course she had no reason to want to kill me. I didn't know anything. Or at least nothing concrete.

Still, anxiety twisted my insides.

I wondered if Will had the same thought, because he hadn't moved from the door and was keeping his eyes trained on her. But Barbara Ann was either clueless, a diabolically clever actress, or innocent. She didn't seem to notice the pall of tension in the air. She was enraptured by the whispery sage blue fabric of the dress she was looking at. I'd made it as a sample so people passing by might put together that I made custom frocks of all kinds, including party and dance dresses.

She reached out to touch the fabric, closing her eyes for a moment as if she were picturing herself in the dress, twirling across a ballroom floor. A faint smile graced her lips, but then her nostrils flared and her breath grew ragged. It was a comfortable temperature in the shop, but a visible shiver passed through her. Her smile faded and a pained look came over her. She wasn't picturing herself, I realized. She was picturing her daughter, Sue.

From the corner of my eye, I saw the air ripple. Will started, peering at the space as he leaned forward slightly. He saw it, too. Seeing evidence of Meemaw always sent a physical zing through my body. I could only imagine what Will felt seeing evidence of a ghost in the house.

The rippling air took shape, and before long, it looked like a figure. Barbara Ann's back was to Meemaw. Good thing, because Meemaw made a beeline for her, passing right through the dress form. She stopped just behind Barbara Ann. In the blink of an eye, Meemaw's form split into a million specks, like slivers of glass exploding through the air. The shimmers enveloped Barbara Ann, circling around her, passing through her, and after another few seconds, Barbara Ann's shivering stopped and a calmness seemed to settle over her.

I had a sudden intuition that nobody could see Meemaw except people who knew about her. Barbara Ann certainly seemed to have no clue, so maybe I was right.

Barbara Ann snapped out of the trance she'd been in. She turned away from the window, coming up the steps to the dining room where I sat with the computer. "I'm sorry to barge in—"

I waved the apology away. "Don't be sorry. I did it to you . . . twice."

"Yes, you did," she said with a smile. She took the bag off her shoulder and for a second, I tensed, wondering if she was pulling out a gun or some other weapon. Will was right behind her. We locked eyes for a second and I knew he was ready to grab her in a chokehold, if necessary.

But it wasn't a gun she pulled out of the bag. It was a Bliss High School letterman jacket. "I was going through Eddy's closet," she began, pausing long enough to swallow and keep her voice steady. "I found this. I assume it must belong to one of his . . . his . . . other kids. I didn't know who else to bring it to, so I came here. I . . . I hope that's okay."

She handed over the jacket, and then pulled a plaid button-down shirt, a pair of sunglasses, and a ball cap from the bag, setting them all on the table. Finally, she withdrew a framed picture of Miss Reba, Shane, and Teagen, and a metallic pink iPod.

All things taken from the Montgomery household the night of the burglary. Why in the world would Eddy have broken into his own house and stolen things that belonged to his own family?

The other possibility was that Barbara Ann had been the one to break into the Montgomery house, and now she was playing a twisted game by pretending she'd discovered the things amongst her husband's effects.

Her gaze strayed to the computer screen and the picture of Gracie I still had pulled up. She was riveted by it.

"That's Will's daughter," I said.

"She's . . . lovely," Mrs. Blake said. She blinked, moving closer. "It looks just like—"

She broke off, tears swimming in her eyes. "My daughter."

I kicked myself for thinking this woman could be a cold-blooded killer. Her pain was palpable. I couldn't imagine what she had to be feeling, seeing a group of girls dressed for homecoming, something she'd never experience with her own daughter. I quickly put the computer to sleep and steered her away from it.

She snapped out of her reverie, snatched up the letter jacket again, and handed it to me. It took only about five seconds to know for certain that it was Shane's. Which seemed to confirm that I'd been looking at the burglary at the Montgomery house all wrong. It had to have been Eddy, aka Chris, pretending to break in and take his children's things, standing over Miss Reba in bed.

But why? Why would he break into his own house and steal his children's things?

I couldn't answer that, and all I knew was that it didn't make a lick of sense.

Chapter 28

Will and I managed to get Barbara Ann Blake on her way before the teenage girls converged on Buttons & Bows to get ready for the dance. I didn't want to put her through more unnecessary grief by having to see the girls, memories of her own daughter and lost opportunities flooding her. How did a mother get past that grief?

She'd glanced at the computer one last time, then at the pile of things she'd left on the table. "I'll take care of them," I told her.

A million expressions crossed over her face, ranging from utter despair to understanding and acceptance. Finally, her face took on a determined edge. Had she made the decision right then and there to accept her losses and move on? Or maybe she had determined to remember her daughter in her own way.

Either way, she stood a little straighter, throwing back her shoulders, and with a quick thank-you to me, she scooted out the door.

Not five minutes later, Gracie, Danica, and Leslie arrived. Libby, Carrie, and Holly were getting ready at their own houses, and the girls would all meet up at Gracie's house, ready for more pictures.

"I feel for her," Will was saying as the girls plowed through the door, giggling. "What she's going through isn't easy."

The girls stopped, looking from Will to me. "Who?" Gracie asked.

"Mrs. Blake," Will said.

The color drained from Gracie's face. "The other wife?"

Her dad nodded. "She was here. Left a few minutes ago."

Gracie looked around as if she feared Shane were here and would see his father's other wife. She walked up the steps to the dining room. We were almost the same height, standing eye to eye. "Why? Why was she here?" she asked, her voice sounding small and fearful.

I hated what this situation with Shane was doing to her. Fear and unease had become an everyday experience for her. If only I could erase those feelings and bring her back to being the happy girl she'd been before all of this had happened.

But I couldn't. All I could do was try to help Shane, like she and Miss Reba had asked me to. I pulled out a chair for her. She sank into it, and I sat next to her. Will, Leslie, and Danica all came and stood next to us, each of them looking at me with different expressions on their faces. Leslie looked curious. Nothing seemed to faze her, and she always wanted all the gossip. Danica, on the other hand, looked spooked. More than anyone, she empathized with Gracie, knowing fear and uncertainty firsthand. Will's expression held a slight warning. He didn't want Gracie hurting any more than she already was. If he could have, I knew he'd have asked me to be careful with my words.

He didn't need to ask.

I stuck to the facts. "Her husband had some of Shane's things," I said, putting my hand on the pile of clothes. "She brought them here so I could get them back to him."

All eyes turned to the pile on the table. Gracie reached out and put her hand on top of the letterman jacket. "It's his."

The other two girls leaned closer, peering at the pile of clothes and the picture in the frame as if it were a snake that might strike at any second. "I don't think so. How'd she get it?" Danica asked.

Leslie gasped. "The burglary! Maybe she was the one who broke into Shane's house—"

"*Pft.* Why would she do that?" Danica asked.

"If she found out about the other family," Leslie said, "maybe she wanted to see it for herself. See what the competition was."

"Competition?" Danica stood back up, folding her arms over her chest. "I don't think it was a competition."

"It may have been to her." Leslie glanced at Will, and then turned to me. "If you two were married and you suddenly discovered that he had another family, wouldn't you see the other wife as your enemy? Wouldn't you want to find out what you could and, I don't know"—she glared at Will, her hands clenched as if she were choking him—"get back at him?"

"Hey," Will said, holding up his hands in innocence. "I'm a good guy."

I took his hand. The girls were processing what had happened the best way they knew how. "You're the best guy," I said.

"But seriously." Leslie looked at each of us. "Wouldn't you want revenge?"

Slowly, Danica nodded her head. "I would. But I don't see how breaking in and stealing Shane and Teagen's stuff is getting revenge."

Gracie piped up before Leslie could come up with a reason. "Because she wanted to show her husband that she knew."

Leslie snapped her fingers, pointing her index finger at Gracie. "Right! She must have found out, but she couldn't just ask him, so she went to see the other family. Makes total sense."

Gracie looked stricken. "So you think she did it? She killed her husband and rammed Carrie's dad with her car?"

Leslie nodded, but Will put his hand on her shoulder. "We don't know who did it, sweetheart. It's anybody's guess at this point."

Danica didn't look like she was buying the story. "She's the victim, though. *She* was married to the guy first, and then *he* met someone else. I mean, who does that? She didn't do anything wrong. You can't just turn her into the villain here."

"Right," I said. "You can't just turn anyone into the villain. Miss Reba's a victim, too."

Danica shook her head again. "Are you sure Miss Reba didn't know, though?"

"I don't think so." I'd spoken with her shortly after she found out. She could have been faking her shock and grief, but if she had been, she was just as good an actress as Barbara Ann Blake was if she was the guilty one.

Someone deserved an Academy Award for Best Actress. I just didn't know who.

"Maybe it was Mr. Levon's wife," Danica said. "She's the only one left."

I'd seen Sally's grief at the brunch that morning, and I'd heard Otis say what a good woman she was, despite the shotgun wedding and unexpected family. They'd grown into, rather than away from, each other. "But what would the motive be?"

They fell silent, thinking about my question.

"Money," Danica said. "She must have wanted her husband's share of the business, or something, right?"

She'd come to the only possible conclusion. "He didn't own that much, though."

"Not enough to murder him over?" Danica asked.

"Is there ever something that's good enough to warrant murder?" It was a question I'd had to ask myself several times, and I never got a different answer. There was never a good enough reason.

The girls didn't know how to respond. They'd grown up watching too much TV showing cavalier murder and mayhem. It had to affect their perspective.

"Hey, y'all," I said, leaving Shane's things on the table and heading to the front room. "Time to get ready. Who needs makeup and hair?"

All three girls raised their hands. Will gave a sheepish grin and raised his, too.

Gracie swatted at him. "Dad, you do not," she said,

but she smiled for the first time since she'd heard Mrs. Blake had been here.

"I'm gonna go tackle that gate while all y'all get beautified," he said. He headed out the front door, leaving us to blush, mascara, curling wands, and homecoming dresses.

An hour later, they were ready. Gracie's chestnut hair was a mass of ringlets, she had a single rosette secured with a bobby pin behind her ear, and with her cream-colored dress of handmade rosettes, she looked like a princess straight out of a fairy tale. The only thing missing was the tiara.

Mrs. James had taken Danica to buy blue wedge heels to complement the blue beaded accents of her dress. A light glitter dusted her cheeks and with the bright tangerine bubble dress, she looked like a fairy.

Leslie's dark hair was pulled back and secured with a sapphire blue headband I'd made from a scrap of her dress fabric. I'd lined her eyes in sapphire, which made them look cornflower blue against her chocolate skin. She'd found strappy metallic sandals at a secondhand store off the square, and with the tiered hem of her dress, she was a vision of iridescent color.

I ushered them out to the porch for a few prepicture pictures, positioning them in front of the red door, a red slatted bench Will had made for me off to their left, Meemaw's old white rocking chairs to their right. I hurried down the steps, adjusted the focus and aperture on my camera, framed them as best I could, and snapped away.

Before I could check to see if any of them had turned

out, the girls were piling into their cars to follow Will to his ranch. It was a caravan of old cars following Will's pickup truck. "I'll be along in a minute!" I called. Will stuck his arm out the driver's window and waved.

Back inside, I cleaned up, changed into a fresh blouse, and quickly uploaded the pictures I'd just taken. Out of the shots, only three looked halfway decent. If this was how it went for three girls, imagine how hard it would be with a much larger group. Thank goodness Madelyn had agreed to go to Will's and take the photos of the homecoming couples.

I went through them again, deleting the shots that had Leslie blinking, Danica looking off into the distance, all three of the girls frowning, Gracie brushing a wayward strand of hair away from her face. On and on they went, bad shot after bad shot.

I felt a swirl of warm air behind me and spun around. The pile of things Barbara Ann Blake had brought still sat on the table, but they'd been relocated to the opposite side.

"Right, Meemaw, and I'm not giving dressmaking up any time soon for photography," I said. "I couldn't even get them to focus on me. Too much distraction with all the passing cars."

I poised my finger over the delete key, ready to depress it. I stopped. Something was bothering me about the pictures, but I couldn't pinpoint what it was. The composition? The dresses? I peered more closely, but the girls all looked gorgeous, and I couldn't find anything amiss with the garments, the shoes, the hair, or the accessories.

An invisible force pressed on my shoulder. "Jussst thinnnnk," Meemaw said.

Good advice. I'd hoped the murderer would be identified before the dance, but it didn't look like that was going to happen. I needed time to ponder all the things that were bothering me—and that list was growing long.

I took my camera and ran out the door.

Chapter 29

I passed Clevis Johnson's ranch, a memory of me wreaking havoc with his weather vane crashing into my head. Some things were better left forgotten. As cars passed by going the opposite direction, I recognized a few of the parents of Gracie's friends. Then I thought I saw Sally Levon zoom past.

Part of me wanted to turn around and chase her down so she wouldn't be alone right now. Her heart had been broken, just like Barbara Ann Blake's and Reba Montgomery's. But after I passed the car, I wasn't even positive it had actually been her. Common sense prevailed. After all, she might be guilty as sin. She was definitely a suspect in the murder of Chris Montgomery.

I pulled up to the Flores house. The kids weren't in the front yard, although there were about eight cars parked along the grassy shoulder. The driveway was long, and there was plenty of room to park there, so I opted for that, pulling up as far as I could.

Cattle fencing blocked off the backyard and acreage.

Instead of hiking around until I found a gate or a way to pass through, I headed up the asphalt driveway, along the cement sidewalk leading to the front porch of the ranch house. I let myself in when no one answered in response to my knocking.

Inside, the entry opened up into a big family room. An enormous table sat on the right side of the room. I knew that Will used this for architectural projects. Once he'd built a miniature version of Bliss's town square, including a few of the peripheral streets like Mockingbird Lane. That model was now housed in the museum at the courthouse on the square.

Right now, the table was piled high with materials for whatever his next project would be. He and I were the same, both passionate and creative. Only our outlets were different. I used garment design and fabric to evoke emotions and to convey ideas, to give people comfort and style, and help them define themselves. He used shape and structure and building elements to do the same things.

The rest of the house was an ode to design. It was comfortable, but minimalistic, with clean lines and simple shapes. Our styles weren't the same, but they complemented each other. I had a preference for anything old, the history that seeped into objects giving them character and meaning. Will liked to create things that would eventually have history. It was a different perspective and approach, but the end goal was the same.

Large windows lined the back of the room, bringing the outdoors in, the green of the grass reflected in the pale green interior walls. I headed out the back door and to the photo session. The kids were in all their finery.

Madelyn was directing the girls, grouping them together first. I saw Shane leaning against the back fence, off to himself. Miss Reba was here, camera in hand, but just like her son, she had isolated herself. Life . . . and death . . . was taking its toll on both of them.

The other moms and a few dads, including Will, also snapped pictures, but Madelyn was clearly in charge. "Time to add in the boys," she announced, ushering them over and waiting while they positioned themselves next to their dates. Everyone was paired up. "We're just going as friends," Danica had said about her date with Tony Franco. "Us, too," Leslie said about Jim McDaniels, but the glimmer in her eyes told me she was hoping they'd be more than friends by the time the dance was over.

Shane ambled toward the group, sliding into place behind Gracie. "Look happy!" Madelyn said. I scanned the group. They all tried, bless 'em, but the pall of death and fear hung over each one of them, especially Gracie and Shane. Their smiles were halfhearted, at best. I snuck a glance at Miss Reba. She was on her cell phone, her back turned to Shane and his friends.

I went into stealth mode, edging toward her, getting as close as I dared. It didn't matter. She was doing more listening than talking and I couldn't hear a thing. Then my cell phone rang, and that was that. My spying was over.

I glanced at the screen, hesitating when I saw Gavin McClaine's name pop up. Did I really want to talk to my stepbrother right now?

The answer was no, but the smart thing to do was answer in case he had some information to impart. "Hey,

Deputy," I said, trying to sound more upbeat than I felt. Miss Reba, Gracie, and Shane's dejected attitude was spilling over to me. I'd vowed to myself to get Shane off the hook by tonight so he and Gracie could enjoy the dance. I'd failed.

"Sis." Gavin's heavy Southern drawl came through on even the smallest word, stretching the three letters out until the word sounded like two syllables.

"What's up, Gavin?"

He didn't beat around the bush. "We have some news. Looks like your boy is in the clear."

"What?" I said, barely holding back a shriek. Behind me, Miss Reba started sobbing. If Gavin was on the phone with me, I reckoned Hoss must be on the phone with her. "Who?" I asked, but even as the question came out, I knew the answer. "Oh my gosh, it's Barbara Ann Blake, isn't it?"

"How'd you know?"

Good question. "A hunch." She'd been front and center in my mind since her surprise visit to Buttons & Bows.

I lowered my voice, talking loud enough for Gavin to hear, but making sure no one around me could. "She stopped by the shop today. Brought some of the things that had been taken from the Montgomery house during the burglary last month, and it got me thinking. She said she'd found them with her husband's things, but that made no sense."

"Not a lick."

"Right. Because why would he break into his own house, steal things from his own kids, and then hide it at his other house? Unless," I said, "she was trying to throw us off her trail."

But then why would she confess? I was stunned.

I looked up as Miss Reba walked past me, making a beeline for Shane. "Thanks for the update, Gavin," I said. I hung up and tucked the phone back in my bag, following Miss Reba. I wanted to see Shane's reaction, hopeful that the worry and despondency that he'd worn like a veil since hearing of his dad's death would lift and float away.

She drew close. As if Shane sensed her, he turned his head toward her, his lips parting. "It's over," she said.

He stared, lifting his eyebrows. Gracie had turned, too. "What?" she asked.

"The other wife . . . Barbara Ann Blake," Miss Reba said, shaking her head as if she still couldn't believe it. "She just confessed to everything."

A collective gasp went up from the kids, and the tight group separated, then drew back together in a new configuration, closing in protectively around Shane. One of the guys whooped and hollered. The stunned expression on Gracie's face slowly melted away, replaced by disbelief and then relief.

"She killed her husband?" Leslie asked.

Danica looked between Miss Reba and me, her hand on her chest. "And Mr. Levon?"

"I just spoke to the sheriff, and he said she confessed to all of it, including the attack on Mr. Levon."

"So Shane is . . . They know he's . . . It's all okay now?" Gracie asked, finally finding the right words.

Miss Reba swiped away the tears that fell, her smile shaky, but in no danger of fading. "He is . . . and it is," she said. "As okay as it can be."

This time, there was a tinge of regret in her voice. Her

children were still without their father, her husband had still led a second, secret life, and it would take a long time to pick up the pieces, but the hope was there that they'd get through it. A mother's love for her child was different from her love for her husband, and while I knew the betrayal still cut deep, all that was pushed aside to rejoice in her son being freed from suspicion. She'd hoped beyond hope that her son was innocent, and now she knew that to be true.

Madelyn circled behind me, her camera to her face. She turned the lens, focusing, capturing every moment with the pictures she took.

"I can't believe she just up and confessed like that," I said to her a short while later. As many times as I'd considered Mrs. Blake as a suspect, it didn't sit well that she'd actually done it.

"She messed with her husband's car?" Madelyn asked.

"They were married for a long time. She must have picked up some of his automotive skills over the years . . ."

"And she clobbered that other man?"

"More like ran him over. Pinned him to the wall in Bubba's garage," I said. I was seeing Barbara Ann in a whole new light, and the fact that I'd been alone with her several time sent a shiver down my spine. "Did you see how relieved Miss Reba was?"

Madelyn's carefully shorn hair, artfully messy, didn't move one bit when she nodded. The woman had some powerful hairspray. "Like the weight of the world had just fallen off her," she said.

Exactly what I'd been thinking. Gracie had the same

relieved look. Her entire body had relaxed, her shoulders, which had been tense, were now dropped, her jaw was loose, and her hands were no longer fisted. She hugged Shane, burying her face in his shoulder as he lowered his chin to the top of her head.

Madelyn quickly lifted her camera and snapped the picture. It was a moment in time that showed the past falling away and the future spread out before them.

After another few minutes, the kids piled into the limo they'd all chipped in to rent and left for their dinner at Giselle's off the Square, one of Bliss's finer restaurants.

"Let's go sort through this mess," Madelyn said, holding up her camera.

"Perfect."

Will came up to us, grinning. I slipped my arm around him, the sides of our bodies pressed together. Just as Miss Reba had wanted Shane free, he wanted Gracie to be happy—no matter what it took. "I never thought I'd be so happy to have a murder solved," he said.

It was true there was still a lot of sadness, grief, and healing to get through, but for just a moment, we reveled in the fact that Gracie and Shane had a wonderful, stress-free night ahead of them.

"Dinner?" I asked Will and Madelyn.

Will looked toward the back pasture. "You two go ahead. I have to repair the fence while there's still light," he said. "I'll see you later?"

The after-party. I wouldn't miss it for the world. "I'll be back here at eleven," I said, and Madelyn and I headed off to her house to sort the homecoming pictures.

*　　　*　　　*

Madelyn lived in a section of Bliss called Idiot's Hill. Back when the town was a fraction of its current population, all the homes were situated around the courthouse square. Until, that is, a builder decided to develop an area north of the town's center. "Only an idiot would buy way out there," he was told, but he went ahead anyway, sure that his vision was sound. Meemaw had told him it would be a success, after all, and everyone knew Meemaw was never wrong.

Just like in *Field of Dreams,* he built it and they came, but the area was forever burdened with the name Idiot's Hill. The people who lived there didn't mind. They had greenbelts, a pond, and a tight-knit neighborhood with people who watched out for one another.

Madelyn and Billy's house was a plain brick single-story rancher. They weren't much for gardening, so the front lawn was more weeds than grass, and the abundance of flowers visible in my yard was absent here.

But Madelyn didn't mind. "I have enough hobbies and interests," she told me once. "No time to take up gardening. I just need your mum to come and visit," she added.

Her home office was a photographer's dream. It was small, but she had everything she could want or need for her vocation. She had a high-end photo-quality printer on a small table, stacks of paper and replacement ink on the shelves below the printer itself. Four corkboards hung on one wall, prints of some of her recent spiderweb shots, a hummingbird in flight, and a reflection in a bird bath, among others, pinned to them. On the large worn oak desk was a computer with an enormous screen, stackable trays for her paperwork, and a digital frame scrolling through her most recent uploads.

She sat at the desk and went to work, removing the SD card from the camera and plugging it into a gadget attached to the computer via a USB port in the back. I dragged a chair over to sit next to her. I looked around in awe. I was always amazed coming in here. Everywhere I looked I saw evidence of her passion.

"Ready?" she asked.

I scooted the chair forward and pushed my glasses back into place. "Ready."

She scrolled through the photos, just as I had with the ones I'd taken on my front porch, deleting the ones that were clearly no good, glancing at me for confirmation on the ones she didn't care for, and pausing on ones we weren't sure about. Once the collection had been whittled down, she cycled through them again.

My stomach felt tight looking at the pictures. Before the confession, and after the confession. Miss Reba stepping into the mix was a defining moment, and it had changed everything for the group.

"I can crop them," she said, demonstrating how she could eliminate the blurred background elements. She chose a picture that focused on Carrie and her date, selecting the section of the photo she wanted to keep. She pressed a button and, voilà, the background disappeared and all that was left was the smiling couple.

Carrie had on a striking green organza dress with long ruffles, spaghetti straps, and rhinestone crystals along the bodice. Netting underneath gave the skirt volume.

"Not sure about that one," I said. The photo would have been perfect had Carrie been looking at the camera, but her eyes were angled to the side, her expression . . . I couldn't say exactly *what* her expression was.

The best word was wary, but I had no idea what she'd be wary about.

Madelyn pressed the arrow key and moved to the next picture. This one was of Holly and Libby, each stunning in their homecoming dresses, arms looped around each other like sisters.

"Keeper," I said, knowing their mothers, Miriam and Sandra, would want copies.

The next several were good as is. She adjusted the exposure on a few, cropped the background out of another several of the couple shots, and then we were on to the group pictures. "Getting a shot where everyone is smiling and looks good is the most challenging aspect," Madelyn said. She pointed to one of the boys on the screen. "Everyone looks great here, except for this young man. I'll keep it, though, until we know if we have a better one."

One by one, we went through them. In each photo, someone blinked or made a strange face or looked away. In most of the early group shots, Shane and Gracie looked tortured. Madelyn kept cycling through the shots. After another few, something changed. The group started to split apart. Bodies turned toward Shane. Madelyn moved through the frames quickly, as if she was operating the camera in sport mode.

She moved backward through the frames. The kids lurched awkwardly. I couldn't help but laugh. It made the moment when Miss Reba stepped into the frame to announce her news about Mrs. Blake's confession all the sweeter.

Madelyn went backward and forward a few more times before stopping on one of the earlier group photos.

"Look at each person's face. That's the only way to start eliminating."

I did, moving my attention from face to face to face. Everyone except Gracie and Shane looked perfect, if slightly sad. In this early picture, they each still carried the weight of their burden. "Not that one," I said.

She didn't delete it, but moved it to a maybe file. The next one popped up on the screen. It was the same setup. Leslie's expression was off, and Gracie and Shane were still doused with sadness. "Nope," she said, before I had the chance.

The next several were crossed off for the same reason. The next one showed Miss Reba's shoulder, Shane's jaw dropped open, and Gracie turned toward her. The rest of the group was unaware, still smiling away.

"Delete," Madelyn said, but I stopped her.

"Wait. Go to the next one."

This time, Miss Reba was completely in the frame, her back to the camera. Shane was smiling, and Gracie's mouth was drawn into a circle. I scanned the rest of the group. They all looked stunned, and I imagined them hearing the news. *The other wife confessed! Shane, everything's going to be okay!*

Okay, she hadn't said it with quite so much enthusiasm, but the sentiment was there. The murderer was behind bars.

"Here's the next one," Madelyn said. She had shifted the angle of her camera so it captured only half the group. Gracie and Shane were in focus, their embrace captured by Madelyn. The rest of the visible kids were blurred in the background.

I scanned them, expecting to see relief and true smiles

lighting up their faces. On most of the kids, that's exactly what I saw. Except . . .

I stared at the photo. Looked at the expression and tried to make sense of it. A hundred tidbits of information careened around in my head suddenly, pieces that hadn't stood out as significant before now. My heart dropped.

I looked at the photo again, hating the direction of my thoughts, but I couldn't stop them. Couldn't prevent the truth from barreling into my mind and taking hold with clamps that wouldn't let go.

I suddenly knew that Barbara Ann Blake hadn't killed her husband, Eddy, or tried to kill Otis Levon.

And I suddenly knew who the real culprit might be.

Chapter 30

"Are you sure?" Madelyn asked from her shotgun seat in Buttercup.

"Not one hundred percent," I said, "which is why we need to talk to her."

"And you're just as sure that this Barbara Ann Blake woman didn't do it, then?"

I'd been going over it all in my head, and the more ways I twisted and turned it, the more certain I was that Barbara Ann was as innocent of killing Eddy Blake and hurting Otis Levon as I was. "Yes."

"And you brought me along as, what, your bodyguard?" There was a lilt in her voice, so I knew she wasn't serious. In conjunction with her photography, she wanted to be an investigative journalist and had even written an article on women in business, which had included me. She was also writing a book on the historic homes in Bliss, which also included my little yellow and redbrick farmhouse.

"I brought you along because you wouldn't have

stayed away for anything," I said, chiding her. "In fact, didn't you practically hurl yourself into the truck because you thought I was leaving without you?"

"You are prone to exaggeration, Harlow," she said, the indignation as manufactured as the boots on her feet.

"Maybe, yet here you are."

I parked in the driveway and ten seconds later, Sally Levon was letting us into her house. From the look of things, plenty of people had been around in the last few hours. A few bouquets of flowers sat in green glass vases amongst the casserole dishes lined up on the kitchen counter. Her fingers dusted the flower petals. If it had been Mama touching them after the ordeal she'd just gone through, the flowers would have withered and died on the spot. But for Sally, they bounced back from her touch, as colorful and uplifting as ever.

"This is the first time I've gotten flowers," she said with a sad smile. "I don't think it ever crossed Otis's mind to get them for me. Not even on Valentine's Day. But you know what he *would* do?"

Madelyn and I both shook our heads. She needed to talk. To share. And we'd let her do just that.

"When I worked late at the dry cleaner's, he'd keep my dinner warmed up on a plate in the oven. Sure, it dried out the chicken, or whatever we were havin', but he thought about me. Thought about the fact that I'd be hungry when I got home."

"Very sweet of him," I said, trying to merge the rough and rugged Otis Levon I'd met with the thoughtful husband he tried to be.

She offered us a seat at the kitchen table, pouring us each a cup of coffee and offering cream and sugar. "Help yourself," she said, taking a seat and wrapping her hands around her mug. She shivered, the warmth of the ceramic not doing much to warm her.

"We're so sorry about Otis," I began.

She nodded, biting back tears. "The doctors think he'll make a full recovery. I'm praying."

I couldn't help but heave a relieved sigh. "Sally, that's great news."

She clamped her lower lip to stop it from quivering and nodded. "It's a miracle. You're the one who found him?"

I spread my fingers on the table, then intertwined them. Being the bearer of bad news wasn't something I liked. "Yes."

"Was he . . . was it horrible?" Her voice cracked with emotion, but she swallowed and kept herself together. "Did he suffer?"

I was certain he had. He'd been rammed with a car, pinned to the back wall before crumbling to the ground, and left for dead. I couldn't tell her that, though. Instead, I reached my hand across the table and laid it on top of hers. "Try not to think about it, Sally. Hold on to the fact that he'll be back here with you before too long."

She pulled her hands away, burying her face in them. "We made it through," she said through her sobs. "The kids . . . they're devastated. I made Carrie go to the dance tonight. Forced her. She put up a fight, but finally she went." She looked at us, her face streaked with her tears. "Was that wrong? Maybe I should have kept her home."

I could imagine the range of emotions Carrie was experiencing. Someone had tried to kill her father, she was homecoming princess, and she was barely keeping it together.

Sally's sobs started again, her body racked with her grief.

"He's going to make it," Madelyn said, her British accent strong and authoritative. She stood, coming to stand beside Sally. "You're the rock in this family. You'll help them all get through."

Sally wiped her eyes and looked up at Madelyn, nodding. "I will." She trained her eyes on me. "He's a good man."

Tears pricked my eyes, and Madelyn's glassed over. This poor family. I couldn't begin to imagine their pain. "Yes, he is. And he told me, that first day I met him, what a good woman you are and how lucky he and the kids were to have you. You need to hold on to that, Sally."

She sucked in a deep breath. "What did you need to talk about?" she asked, getting to the point of our late-night visit.

"Your husband showed me a picture of your children. Carrie looks so different now."

"When we moved from Granbury to Bliss, she wanted a new look to go with the new town. She cut her hair, bleached it, and it was like she was a different person. She's still shy, but she's made friends. Gracie, Libby, Holly, Danica, and Leslie. I've never seen her so happy. She was voted homecoming princess for the sophomore class, for heaven's sake. That never would have happened in Granbury. It's like she's discovered something strong and solid inside herself."

She'd undergone a major transformation. The realization of this when I'd put together who she was, opened up another thought process in my mind, which led to a question I hadn't specifically asked.

I took the pictures Madelyn had printed and slid them to Sally. "Madelyn took these before the dance at Gracie's."

She nodded. "I dropped her off, but I just couldn't stay."

So it *had* been her I'd passed on the way to Will's house.

"I'll get you copies of everything," Madelyn said. "You just give me your e-mail, and I'll send them. I have some wonderful shots of Carrie."

But Sally shook her head. "I don't know if we want to remember today. Looking at the pictures of homecoming'll always be a reminder to her of what was done to her dad, won't it?"

"It might," I said, "but a reminder isn't always a bad thing." I said it, but I wasn't sure I believed it. I had the luxury of remembering Meemaw on a daily basis. If someone I'd loved had been horribly hurt, wouldn't I want to forget that day?

My mind circled back to my question. "Do you recognize any of these kids?" I asked Sally.

She stood up and got a pair of reading glasses from a drawer, giving a sheepish, halfhearted smile. "Need these now."

I automatically pushed my own glasses into place. "Me, too."

She picked up the picture and studied each face. "I haven't met all of these kids. Carrie's really blossomed this year, but she doesn't bring a lot of kids home."

Her lips quivered as if she were fast-forwarding to see her daughter in a backward slide, closing in upon herself after the blow of what had happened to her father. "Sally," I said, "you heard that Mrs. Blake confessed to killing Eddy and hurting your husband?"

She nodded, tears pooling in her eyes, hovering there but not spilling over.

"I don't think she did it. I think she's protecting someone."

She drew back. "Protecting who?"

I finally asked the question I'd been mulling over for the last several hours. Since I'd first met Barbara Ann, and then when I'd read the letters she'd written to her husband, I'd assumed that her daughter was dead, but what if she'd simply left. Run away and, like Carrie, transformed herself? "Did Mrs. Blake's daughter—"

"Sue?"

"Yes, Sue. Did she die?"

She sputtered. "Did she die? Good grief, I don't think so."

And there it was. A shift in everything I'd thought so far. Sue Blake wasn't dead. She was very much alive, and I was one hundred percent sure she was living in Bliss. And I was pretty sure I knew who she was.

"Carrie wasn't friends with her," Sally continued, "but I do remember that something happened. Rumors were that there was trouble at home, but no one ever really knew. She just vanished one day. Left some sort of a note and ran away."

A note that said, *I know the truth,* I thought, remembering the card in the box of letters from Mrs. Montgomery. A thought crashed into my head. The handwriting. I could picture it—how distinct it was and how I'd seen it somewhere else.

The next second, it came to me. I'd seen the same handwriting on one of the cards from the Helping Hands luncheon. I racked my brain to remember the details. All I could think of was the no-dairy designation and then coconut milk came to my mind.

Barbara Ann Blake had had coconut milk at her house. Because her daughter didn't eat dairy, and old habits died hard. Another series of thoughts careened into my head and a chill wound through me. Oh my God, could it really be her?

My skin went cold. I touched the edge of the photograph. "Are any of these girls Sue Blake?"

Sally dropped her gaze again. She puckered her lips, but after a long minute, she shook her head. "I don't know. I don't think so. She has long red hair. She was on the chunky side, if I'm remembering right."

I came around next to her and pointed to the girl I suddenly suspected was Sue Blake. "Imagine her with longer hair and in jeans. Maybe a little heavier."

Sally's face tightened as she thought. "Maybe," she finally said.

She stood suddenly, walked briskly from the kitchen, and returned a minute later carrying a thin hardcover book. "Carrie's yearbook from Granbury," she said, flipping it open and turning the pages. She stood up straighter, confidence pouring into her. When she found what she was looking for, she turned the book and pointed. "That's Sue Blake. You think it's the same girl?"

I studied the faces, first of the yearbook picture, then one of the shots from Madelyn's prints. "No, I don't think so," I said. Upsetting Sally further was the last thing I wanted to do, but in my mind, I was sure the girl in the pictures was Sue Blake, the person who'd driven her car into Bubba's and rammed Otis until he nearly died. The girl whose mother had confessed to protect her. The person who was most likely guilty of killing Chris Montgomery.

Would I have done the same thing? Would I have lied to protect my child if my child was a killer? I closed my eyes for a beat, but I couldn't answer that question. All I knew was that people went to great lengths to protect their children. I felt protective of my nephews, and Gracie. In his own twisted way, Eddy Blake had tried to protect his children by keeping their worlds separate. But it had backfired when his daughter Sue had somehow discovered the truth.

My concern at the moment, however, was figuring out how to intercept the kids. I hadn't been able to define the look I'd seen on Carrie's face in the picture after Miss Reba announced Barbara Ann's confession. But now I understood it. She knew the truth. She knew who'd hurt her father, which meant Sue Blake's secrets were in the hands of someone else.

Sally's house phone rang. She picked up and barely said hello before whoever was on the other end interrupted her. Her eyes grew wide and turned to stare at me as she continued to listen.

"Okay, baby, calm down," she said after another few seconds. "Tell me what happened."

She fell silent again, but mouthed to me, *Carrie*.

Carrie was upset and calling her from the homecoming dance. Sue Blake had already killed. And now, every fiber of my being told me that Carrie Levon was in horrible danger of becoming another victim.

Chapter 31

I texted Gracie right away to tell her my suspicions and warn her to keep her eyes open and stay safe. And then I drove, pedal to the metal, while Madelyn made phone calls, first to the sheriff's office, then to Will, and finally to her husband, Billy. She filled each one in on different information.

"We're worried about Carrie Levon," she told Gavin, filling him in on what we'd discovered. "We're on our way to the high school. Her mom, too. Carrie's supposed to meet her at the door, but you may need to be there."

"The school won't release her until the dance is over," I said. Gracie had told me how strict the rules were. Once you were at the dance, you were there until it was over. These were extenuating circumstances, but I still felt sure we'd need the sheriff to do the heavy lifting with the school's admin team to allow Carrie to leave.

"On my way," Gavin said. No ifs, ands, or buts from

him, which was unusual. Instead of being a comfort, it filled me with more unease. What if we were too late?

She called Will next, putting him on speaker. Once again, we told the story of what we'd discovered. "So Sue Blake isn't dead? You think she killed her father, attacked Otis, and now she may target Carrie?"

I took the next right, following the farm-to-market road to the high school. While prom was usually held at a hotel ballroom in a nearby city, homecoming was all about celebrating hometown. "I think Carrie recognized Sue Blake," I said. "They both went to Granbury High School." I didn't say what we both knew . . . that Sue Blake *knew* Carrie recognized her, which meant Carrie was probably scared out of her mind and worried for her own safety.

"I'll meet you at the school," he said, and then he was gone.

Somewhere between Sally's house and the farm-to-market road, Sally's taillights had disappeared into the darkness. She didn't care about speeding, or driving the dark country roads in the dark, or about anything but getting to Carrie.

I gave the old truck more gas. Two knights in shining armor were on their way to the school, that was good, but there was no time to waste. Madelyn and I would be at Bliss High before either Will or Gavin made it—and we couldn't be too late. Madelyn left a message for her husband. "Off on a case with Harlow, love. Catching another murderer. When you moved me from London to a small Texas town, you undersold it."

She hung up and put her phone into her camera bag,

something she never left home without. She hung on to the door handle as I took a sharp turn. "He's teaching tonight," she said. "He hates the night classes at the university, but it does leave me time to sleuth with you."

I didn't know how to answer that. Sleuthing took time away from sewing, and right now, I longed for a drawn-out boring day in my workroom.

It felt like an eternity, but we actually made it to the school in record time. The roundabout was filled with limos rented for the night, so I hightailed it to the football parking lot, found a spot, and Madelyn and I piled out, running across the asphalt to the front entrance.

"Oh. My. God." Madelyn doubled over, panting, at the front door. I had to work to catch my breath, but was in better shape than she was. All my years of walking in Manhattan hadn't worn off yet, and living off the square meant that I walked everywhere I could in Bliss, too.

I grabbed the door handle and pulled, but the thing didn't budge. "Buttoned up tight."

"Odd," Madelyn said.

"Odder that two childless women want in, I reckon." Still, I cupped my hands and peered through the glass, hoping to see a teacher or parent chaperone.

A face suddenly appeared on the other side of the glass, startling me. I jumped back, clutching my chest, a distinct feeling that we were in the midst of a horror movie coming over me.

"Doors are locked until the dance is over," the woman said through the glass.

"They lock the kids in?" Madelyn stared at her as if it

were the woman's personal decision to have such tight security.

"Standard practice. Helps us keep the kids safe from leaving without permission, and keeps people who don't belong here"—she looked Madelyn and me up and down, the implication heavy in her eyes—"from coming inside."

And then, before we could cajole her to make an exception, she was gone.

"Great. The homecoming dance lock-in."

I turned around. Where was Sally? Had she managed to get around the security system? Had Carrie been snuck out, and were they already gone, Carrie safe and sound?

I peered at the high school's driveway. One way in and one way out. We'd have passed each other on the farm-to-market road if she'd already collected her daughter. So Sally and Carrie had to be here somewhere.

"Come on." I headed across the lawn toward the indoor gym where I knew there was a second entrance.

"Maybe I should wait here," Madelyn said, still panting. "In case someone comes by, you know."

"No, you're not staying here!" I went back, grabbed her by the wrist, and yanked her forward. "We are sticking together. Murderer, remember?"

"She's a girl—"

"Who's killed one man and injured another."

She looked over her shoulder as if she were longing to stay put, but she trudged along with me instead. Madelyn was no fool. If Sue Blake got to her car, she could ram either of us down. Whether it was true or not, I felt stronger as a pair, and I suspected that Madelyn did, too.

"Aren't the doors all going to be locked?" she asked.

"They didn't use to be, but I guess things have changed, haven't they?"

"It's a scary world out there."

We made it to the gym door and tried the handle. Locked. I peered through the glass. "Look, someone's there," I said. I waved, but whoever was there didn't see us.

I pushed my glasses to the top of my head and rubbed my eyes. "Think," I muttered. "How are we going to get in?" How could we get into the building? If it was secure against teenagers, it was certainly secure against two thirtysomething women.

We traipsed along the perimeter of the school, heading toward the one possible flaw in the security system I remembered from high school. The band director's window. Mr. Campbell was an institution at Bliss High. He'd been a smoker back when I'd been in school, and I was willing to bet he hadn't kicked the habit. The school had been, and still was, a nonsmoking campus, so Mr. Campbell had cracked open the window in his office, lit up, and blown the smoke out. All the kids knew, but Mr. Campbell was like everyone's favorite uncle, so no one ratted him out.

My brother, Red, and I had snuck onto campus once or twice using this very path. Not our finest moments, but memorable. I could have found the window with my eyes closed, and in minutes, we were standing in front of it. "Our way in," I said, gesturing toward the small opening. "Mr. Campbell never remembers to close the window after his smoke break."

"Top-notch security," Madelyn whispered to me.

"Thank heavens for bad habits."

I pushed the window up and scurried up and over the windowsill with all the aplomb of an over-the-hill gymnast. Madelyn's entry was less graceful—and that was saying a lot. I pulled her arms as she flung one leg over the sill, then the other, finally tumbling to the floor inside the office.

"Remind me next time that the dangerous part of tracking down a killer is the breaking and entering . . . minus the breaking."

Of course, there wouldn't be a next time—how many murders could one small town have, and how many could I help solve?—but I didn't mention that now.

We followed the *thrump thrump thrump* of the music's baseline echoing in the building, but I couldn't pinpoint the direction. Madelyn tiptoed ahead, peering down the different hallways. She looked at me over her shoulder. "So, Detective Cassidy, where to?"

"They've remodeled since I went here," I said, not knowing how to follow the yellow brick road. "The dances used to be in the cafeteria." I pointed down the center hallway. "Down there, I think."

We walked, our feet sounding hollow against the floor. The music grew louder and louder. At the end of the corridor, we made a right turn and there it was: the homecoming dance. The entrance to the cafeteria was decorated with scalloped crepe paper and streamers in black, red, and white. Enormous three-foot-round homecoming mums hung from each point of the scallops, more streamers hanging from them. Through the glass windows spanning the width of the cafeteria, I could see the festive decorations continued with black, red, and

white balloons, tables laden with teenage-centric appe-
tizers and sweets, others with punch bowls and small
clear plastic cups, and more streamers hanging from the
ceiling.

I looked around. The coast was as clear as it was going
to get. "Come on," I said, crooking my finger and beckoning to Madelyn. I darted to the doors and slipped into
the cafeteria, Madelyn on my heels.

Inside, twinkle lights, a spinning reflective ball, and
ambient light kept the room darker than the hallway had
been. I blinked, waiting for my eyes to adjust. "Keep to
the wall," I said, hoping we wouldn't be spotted by an
on-duty administrator who'd be sure to kick us out. We
were trespassing, after all.

"Where's the cavalry?" Madelyn whispered.

"Maybe they can't get in," I said, but I forgot about
them the next second as I spotted the makeshift stage in
the front of the room. The DJ was set up on one side. A
teacher stepped up to the microphone and tapped it,
sending an echo through the speakers, and then cleared
her throat.

"Welcome, Bliss High School students!" she said, her
voice booming into the room.

A cheer went up from the students.

"It's time to welcome your homecoming court!" she
said. She held her arm to the side, the DJ played a drumroll, and the woman introduced the prince and princess
from the freshman class. They made their way to the
stage, arms linked.

My heart beat erratically. Carrie was homecoming
princess for the sophomores. Was she still here and in

danger, or had her mother come and whisked her away, and was she safe?

"And now, the homecoming prince and princess for the sophomore class," the teacher announced. "Jacob Walters and Carrie Levon!"

I held my breath. Carrie didn't appear.

"Jacob Walters and Carrie Levon!" the teacher repeated.

Jacob Walters broke through the crowd, looking around, presumably for his homecoming princess. He made his way to the front.

Still, Carrie didn't show.

The crowd had grown quiet, kids looking this way and that for the missing homecoming royalty. The teacher tapped the microphone as if the problem was that she hadn't been heard, not that the princess was MIA. "Carrie Levon?" she said for the third time.

Suddenly, a cheer went up and the crowd parted like the Red Sea. I could just see the very top of Carrie's blond bob glowing under the disco lights as she walked through the center of the throng. I heaved a sigh of relief. She was still here, and she was safe.

She wasn't smiling, but she accepted a bouquet of flowers, took Jacob's arm, and together they walked onto the stage. A small, flat purse lay against her side, the gold chain strap crossing over her front at the same angle as her homecoming sash. Maybe she'd been about to leave with her mother, but they'd called her name instead. Despite the trauma in her life at the moment, in her vibrant emerald dress and the shimmering tiara, she was beautiful. I wondered what her deepest desires were at the moment. Justice for her father? Wanting someone to pay for hurting him?

If I'd made her dress, they'd be coming true.

I knew the pain she was feeling had to be excruciating. She was putting on a brave face for the homecoming event, but inside was all her uncertainty about her father's recovery after his near-death experience.

But I hadn't made her dress, so she'd have to come to peace on her own terms, and in her own time.

"What do we do now?" Madelyn asked.

It was a great question. As I saw it, we had a few options:

1) Roam the crowd and look for Sue Blake;

2) Wait for Gavin and the rest of the intrepid Bliss law enforcement team to show up;

3) Go straight for Carrie to escort her out of here once the homecoming court presentation was over.

Number three seemed best. "Follow me," I said, my voice barely audible above the hundreds of teenage conversations going on. We kept close to the wall as we skirted the perimeter of the room, getting closer to the stage with every step.

The teacher on the stage had already brought up the prince and princess of the junior class, and now the DJ had a drumroll sounding as the homecoming king and queen were called out. The crowd applauded, the couple ascended the steps to the stage, and the Bliss High School royalty was complete.

I tried to catch Carrie's eye, but she stared straight into the crowd. She gripped her flowers with one hand, the chain strap of her purse with the other. She looked ready to bolt. I suspected that Jacob's hold around her waist was the only thing keeping her grounded.

Scanning the back of the room, I looked for Sally. She had to be here somewhere, had to have found her way into the school like Madelyn and I had, but so far, there was no sign of her.

I spotted Leslie, Gracie, Danica, Holly, and the rest of their group standing in front of the crowd and knocked Madelyn with the back of my hand, pointing. "There's—"

"Can I help you?" a man said from behind me.

I whirled around . . . and bumped smack into a portly man in a gray pinstripe suit. "Mmph, sorry!" I stepped back and started to turn back toward the stage, but he grabbed my wrist.

"Ma'am, you are not allowed in here. This is a school function and—"

I notched my head toward Gracie. "I'm here to see my . . . my . . . stepdaughter," I finally said, going with what would make the most sense to him. Better than saying my boyfriend's daughter or some girl I knew.

"I don't care if you're here to see Jesus Christ himself, you're not allowed in here."

For the first time, I noticed the walkie-talkie in his left hand. He raised it to his mouth, depressed a button with his finger, and started talking. "Officer Cole, we have two individuals who need to be escorted off campus. Would you please assist?"

I pulled my arm back, trying to loosen his grip. "No, but wait—"

"Ma'am, you need to stop now," the principal told me.

The walkie-talkie crackled and a tinny voice came back with, "Ten-four. What's your location?"

"South wall inside the cafeteria."

"Copy that."

"Sir, please, you don't understand," I said.

"Excuse me." Madelyn stepped forward, holding out a badge. I tried to get a better look at it, but the light was too dim. "I'm with the sheriff's department. I'm here to keep an eye on one of your students. She's the daughter of a man who was brutally attacked yesterday."

I gasped, staring. "Madelyn," I said with a hiss.

The principal didn't look to me like he'd just fallen off the turnip truck. He spoke into the walkie-talkie again. "Officer Cole, are there law enforcement personnel authorized to be on campus?"

I held my breath, waiting for Madelyn's exaggeration of the truth to come back and bite us. "Affirmative."

"I can explain—" I started to stay, but then the "affirmative" registered. "Wait. What?"

Law enforcement personnel authorized to be on campus. That couldn't include Madelyn, so that meant Gavin had to be here. Hallelujah!

"Who's on campus?" the principal asked, looking at Madelyn with a wary eye.

"Deputy sheriff," the tinny voice of Officer Cole said. "Almost at your location."

I pulled my arm again. This time, instead of holding tight, the man let go. "Thank you," I said.

"We're not done here. Let me see that badge." He held his hand out to Madelyn.

The jig was up. She started to hand it over, but I stepped in the way and spoke loud enough to be heard above the music. "Sir, one of your students is in danger. There's a murderer . . ."

I trailed off as the music stopped and the teacher who'd introduced the homecoming court onstage stepped back to the microphone. "Let's give our homecoming court another round of applause," she said.

The kids started clapping. From where I stood, it looked like Carrie's entire body was trembling. Her hands fidgeted in front of her, and then she caught sight of someone in the crowd and all the color drained from her face.

I followed her gaze and saw the girl I suspected was Sue Blake. "Oh no," I muttered, starting toward the stage, but the principal pulled me back.

"You need to stay put, ma'am."

Carrie's lips started moving but without a mic, there was no way to know what she was saying.

As if on cue, one of her classmates yelled, "We can't hear you!"

"Yeah, speak up!"

A roar went up, someone started clapping, and before long, the kids chanted, "Carrie! Carrie! Carrie!"

Support, I knew, because of the ordeal her family had just gone through. She was the new girl in Bliss, but she'd made an impression on people.

I couldn't be sure from this far away, but I thought her eyes looked glassy. The teacher onstage raised the mic to capture Carrie's voice, the sound system catching the tremors in it midsentence. ". . . and he almost died. Why?"

The room fell utterly silent, everyone's eyes glued to Carrie; then, as if they were all connected, they turned to look at who Carrie was addressing.

Sue Blake stood there, her hands twisting around the small purse slung over her shoulder, staring back at Carrie. She didn't speak, but her lips pressed together into a harsh, thin line.

"Leave me alone!" a woman screeched from the back of the room. "That's my daughter up there!"

All eyes turned in the direction of the ruckus. "Ma'am," another woman yelled. "You can't come in here!"

I recognized her instantly. Sally Levon.

A woman tried to stop Sally from barreling forward, but Sally was on a mission, determined to get to Carrie and protect her. She dodged another parent or teacher chaperone who'd stepped in her way, skirting around clusters of kids.

The silence that had fallen over the students had been replaced by the sound of chaos.

"Carrie!" her mother yelled.

At that moment, a loud clatter ripped through the PA system. Carrie's group of friends had all climbed onto the stage. It looked like a small riot, with Gracie and Shane in the center. Carrie's voice cracked with emotion. It sounded far away, the mic unable to capture it fully. "The first time I saw you, I *knew*," she said. Her voice cracked and I knew the emotion I heard was fear. And it was no wonder. She was confronting a killer.

"How could you kill Shane's dad? Why try to kill mine?"

It took a few seconds before her words seemed to sink in with her classmates. Shane stared at her, then searched the crowd. "What? Who are you talking to? That woman, that Barbara Ann Blake, she confessed."

Carrie shook her head. "She lied. She's protecting her daughter." Her voice still cracked with tension and fear, but grew louder.

Shane's jaw went slack. He grabbed Carrie by the shoulders, staring at her. "What are you talking about?"

Carrie wove her hands up in between Shane's arms. Abruptly, she pulled them apart, breaking Shane's hold on her. She raised her arm to point just as a girl pressed her way through the crowd on the stage. "That's your half sis—"

The words froze on her lips as Danica Edwards lunged.

Chapter 32

Danica came up short in front of Carrie. "You don't know what you're saying," she said. Then in a louder voice directed at the homecoming group watching, she said, "She's completely lost her mind."

Carrie backed away, but her voice carried as she said, "Tell them who you are."

Danica, bless her twisted heart, pressed her palm to her chest. "Danica Edwards," she said.

"Tell them who your father was," Carrie insisted.

"I don't *have* a father—"

"Because you killed him!"

Everyone in the room watched in silence, riveted.

"Carrie," Danica started, but Carrie interrupted her, raising her hand, palm out to Danica's chest.

"Don't," she said, her lower lip quivering. "You *had* a family. You ran away and left them."

"I live in Serendipity House," Danica said, referring to the transitional home for kids on their own. "I don't have a family. It's only thanks to Mrs. James and Helping Hands that I can even be here tonight."

The teacher with the mic managed to usher both Carrie and Danica off the stage, the rest of the group following closely, but the girls didn't stop. "No family?" Carrie asked when she made it to the bottom of the steps. "You've *never* had a family?"

Danica spun toward her. She hesitated before responding, and I knew she had at least a shred of feeling for her mother, even if she'd never admit it here. "That's what I said. No. Family."

Tears streamed down Carrie's face, her words barely audible through her sobs. "Because you killed your father when you learned what he'd done. But why my dad?" She spun to face Danica head-on. "Just tell me why."

"You'd better stop," Danica threatened. There was no more mic, but there wasn't a single sound in the cafeteria other than the two girls, and we heard every word, and the threat behind them.

"Are you gonna kill me, too?" Carrie said, but she shook her head, backing away as she lobbed the rest of what she wanted to say. "Did my dad figure it out? Is that why you . . . why you . . . ran him over?"

"You did that . . . ?" Gracie moved toward Danica. Instinctively, I took a step toward them, but once again the principal grabbed my arm and held me back. I flashed a scowl at him, but he nodded toward the side of the room. Gavin and another deputy hugged the wall as they made their way toward the girls, moving slowly enough that Carrie and Danica didn't notice.

I scanned the crowd looking for Will. I spotted him a few yards behind the deputies, a third deputy behind him. We locked eyes, understanding passing between us. We both had to be careful, protect Gracie, and hope that Danica didn't unleash the violence that had led her to kill her father and nearly kill Otis Levon.

"She set you up to take the fall," Carrie said to Shane, flinging her arm out to point at Danica. "Broke into your house, stole some of your things, planted stuff in your locker . . ."

Shane stared at Danica. "Is it true?"

The utter coldness on her face said it all. Shane stumbled backward, distancing himself from her.

But Danica schooled her expression and threw her shoulders back. "I don't have a family. You are not my brother."

I thought about the fact that Danica had chosen Edwards as a last name. Was that a snub to her lying father? And Danica . . . another nod to her dad and their race-car interests? She'd left Granbury, and she might have disowned her family, but they—especially her father— were still part of her.

Danica swung her head, her gaze scanning the crowd as if she were trying to gauge who people were believing— her or Carrie. I couldn't tell what she decided, but her shoulders stiffened and she turned back to Carrie. She was all-in at this point. She had no other choice. She clutched her purse, her hand sliding down the gold chain and gripping the main part of the bag. There was something about the way she moved, the look in her eyes, that unsettled me.

Shane stared her down. "Did you kill him?" he demanded. "Did you really kill my dad?"

And then I saw it. Danica's hand emerged from her purse gripping the handle of something, the light reflecting off the exposed shiny portion of whatever she held. A knife?

Her gaze was intent on Carrie, and she moved stealthily toward her. An alarm went off in my head, but too late. Danica lunged, her arm outstretch.

"Carrie!" I yelled at the top of my lungs, my voice reverberating in my ears. It did the trick. Carrie lurched to the side in the nick of time, moving with lightning speed, managing to dodge the flashing blade in Danica's hand.

I broke into a run, skirting around the people who were riveted by the drama unfolding before them.

"Is this for real?" someone asked.

Oh yes, it was for real. Danica had done exactly what Carrie had accused her of, and now she was a caged animal doing whatever it took to escape.

Danica drew her arm back, the knife in her hand clear as day. "He ruined my life!" she bellowed, and then she lunged, swinging her arm down in a stabbing motion.

Carrie sidestepped her, careening into Shane. He yanked her out of the way, but Danica slowly turned and fixated on Carrie again. "You're just like your dad, butting in where you don't belong. He knew about my dad's other life. He *knew*. He used to come to our house, and then one day on the square, I saw him talking to my dad's other . . . other . . . *wife*." She spit out the word as if she could hardly stand to say it.

"And that's why you tried to kill him?"

"He *knew*!" she said again, as if that explained everything, and then she drew her arm back, the knife clutched in her hand.

From the corner of my eye, I saw Will. He'd sprung into action, charging through the kids in their homecoming finery. At the same time, I barreled toward the two girls. "Danica, no!" I screamed.

She hesitated just long enough for Shane to wrench Carrie out of the way, for Will to grab Danica around the shoulders to disable her, and for me to snatch the knife from her hand before she did something else she'd regret forever.

"Carrie!" Sally yelled her daughter's name as she battled through the rest of the crowd. For a second, Carrie seemed disoriented; then she blinked, her eyes going wide, and she fell into her mother's embrace, sobbing.

Chapter 33

The homecoming dance was over, and the kids had all gone to their after parties. With the exception of Carrie, who'd gone home with her mother, Gracie's friends converged at Will's house, as planned. But instead of playing spoons and swimming, they sat on the sofas, still in shock.

"Will they charge Danica with attempted murder?" Shane asked.

That was a good question, although I didn't think it mattered. Yes, she'd attacked Carrie, but she'd actually killed her father, and she'd be charged with that crime.

"How'd Danica get the knife?" I asked.

"She must have taken it from the restaurant," Gracie said.

"She didn't get one at her place setting." Libby twirled a strand of her dark hair around her finger, creating a soft ringlet. "She asked the waiter for one."

Gracie snapped her fingers. "I bet she *did* get one, but she put it in her purse right away."

"So she planned on attacking Carrie the whole time?" someone asked.

The kids fell silent at that revelation, no doubt trying to reconcile the girl they thought they'd known with the murderer she turned out to be.

"She snapped," Will said. We sat side by side. He had his arm draped around me, his fingers absently tapping against my shoulder. "How'd she figure Carrie knew the truth?" he asked.

Shane looked at me, shaking his head slightly. "How did *you* figure it out?"

"I think Carrie recognized Danica as Sue Blake the first time she saw her here in Bliss. The day y'all were taking pictures with your mums in the park, she even told her she looked like someone she'd known. Someone said that everyone had a twin, and Carrie laughed it off, but I don't think she ever doubted who Danica really was."

"How'd Danica get into my locker to plant that stuff?" Shane asked.

"She was an office aide," Gracie said.

Everyone nodded, as if that simple fact explained how she might have gotten access to secure information.

"But why'd she do it?" Shane asked, half to himself.

I'd given that a lot of thought. "She killed her father, and I'm guessing she blamed your mother for making your father fall in love with her. Which means she probably blamed you, too. What better way to get back at you than to frame you for murder?"

"Twisted." He snapped his fingers, his eyes popping open. "My dad taught me and Teagen how to break into our house by picking the lock. He probably taught her how to pick locks, too."

Gracie nodded. "Yeah, and how'd she know what to do to the car?"

Shane sat forward, resting his forearms on his knees. "My dad taught her," he said, as if he were one hundred percent sure of it. "He was always talking cars, showing me and Teagen his car magazines, and explaining things under the hood. Anything mechanical, he messed with it and taught us. I bet he did it with her, too."

"I think you're right," I said, remembering the line of cars outside the Blake's home. She'd grown up with cars, learning just as Shane had. "She went to driving school, too. Her mom said she was really good. Believing that she tampered with the steering and then barreled down on him, forcing him off the road, isn't a stretch."

I thought about what Sue Blake had wanted deep down inside. She'd learned the truth about her father, plotted a way to make him pay for his betrayal, and had started a new life as Danica Edwards to put the ball in motion. But I'd made her a homecoming dress, so what deep desire had she realized? Was it revenge, pure and simple? I closed my eyes for a minute, reeling at the horrible way the Cassidy charm could manifest itself.

"Her poor mother." Gracie cast her gaze down. Her own mother had chosen to leave her behind, so the idea that a daughter would choose to turn her back on her mother was something she probably couldn't understand.

Now Danica couldn't go back. She'd made irreparable choices and she'd pay for them for the rest of her life.

Texas's Hill Country. No sewing. No dress designing. No murder. Only the rugged hills topped with limestone and granite, a tiny town outside of Austin, and a bed-and-breakfast with Will Flores.

"I heard that Otis is past the danger zone," Will said. He had one hand on the wheel of his truck, the other clasping my hand in my lap. He wore his cream, woven cowboy hat, jeans, and a T-shirt. With his goatee and swarthy skin, he was wickedly handsome. But with his compassion, his Southern sense of humor, and our shared passion for our crafts, he was everything I'd ever wanted in a man, and I melted inside.

And we were headed for three days and two nights of our own bliss in the Hill Country. "That's what Sally told me, too. Carrie's doing better. Still upset about everything, but better."

"Good deal," he said. "The girl was wound tighter than a tick, all that anger and fear up under her skin."

He got that right. Now that her dad was out of the woods, I hoped she'd be able to let it all go and move on. "I'm going to make her a dress."

He kept his attention on the road, but gave my hand a squeeze. "Good idea."

"So maybe her desire will be for her dad to make a full recovery—"

"Which means it'll happen," Will said.

"Right. Sometimes I love having a charm."

He flashed that wicked grin of his. "If you make your own dress, will *your* wishes come true?"

Good question, and one I'd thought about many times, but hadn't quite gotten around to testing. "I don't know," I said, honestly.

"And if you make something for me, will I get what I want?"

I gave him my own flirty grin. "Depends what you want."

He turned into the driveway of Biscuit Hill, pulled off the road, and leaned over to kiss me. "Darlin', I already have you, so I guess I'm good."

"Shucks," I said, laughing. I hadn't felt this light and happy, maybe ever. I'd helped Gracie and Shane, I had Buttons & Bows, and I was here with the man I loved. "Will Flores, I'm good, too."

Sewing Tips

1. Sewing is a process, so enjoy the act of craftsman-ship, not just the end result.

2. Fit your pattern to the body you have, not the body you wish you had. If a garment fits well, it will look good!

3. Ask for help if you need it.

4. Buy a seam ripper.

5. Prewash your fabric, unless it is dry-clean only.

Mahi Mahi Tacos with Strawberry-Mango Salsa

Serves 4

 2–3 pieces of mahi mahi, approximately 6–8 ounces
   each, cubed
 1 tsp cumin
 ½ tsp salt
 ½ tsp garlic powder
 2 tb olive oil
 4–6 soft corn tortillas

Strawberry-Mango Salsa

 1½ cups fresh strawberries, chopped
 1 cup frozen or fresh mango, chopped
 ½ cup frozen or fresh pineapple, chopped
 ½ red onion, minced
 ½ cup cilantro, minced
 ½ lime

Cilantro-Lime Rice

 1 tb canola or vegetable oil
 1 cup long grain white rice
 2 cups water
 ½ tsp salt

½ cup cilantro, chopped
Juice from one lime

Toss cubed mahi mahi with cumin, salt, and garlic powder. Adjust seasoning to taste. Heat 2 tablespoons of olive oil in a frying pan. Sauté cubed and seasoned mahi mahi until browned and cooked through, stirring occasionally.

For Salsa:

Mix chopped and minced ingredients together (strawberries, mango, pineapple, red onion, cilantro) and squeeze lime juice into the mixture.

For Cilantro-Lime Rice:

Heat oil in sauté pan. Add uncooked rice and cook until browned. Add salt and water, cover, and simmer until rice is cooked, approximately 15–20 minutes.
Stir in cilantro and lime juice.

To Serve:

Spoon mahi mahi into warmed soft corn tortillas and top with salsa. Serve with Cilantro-Lime Rice.

Enjoy!

Continue reading for
a special preview of

A SEAMLESS MURDER

Available from Obsidian in January 2015.

Aprons.

No, they aren't couture garments. They aren't even knockoff couture. But it was looking like they were going to be my next project. Seven individual, unique, stylized aprons for the women of Bliss's Red Hat Society chapter, to be exact.

I had to laugh. Last week I'd been creating a suit for a woman in Fort Worth who wanted a highly tailored linen ensemble, not an easy task. But as my great-grandmother Loretta Mae Cassidy always said, success is something you have to work for. Harder than you may want to most times. That linen suit pushed me to the edge of my ability, but I came out on the other side a better dressmaker and tailor. In the end, the outfit could have competed with any high-end handmade Italian affair—and come out on top. And I'd sewn it not in Florence, Rome, or Milan, but in little ol' Bliss, Texas.

Now it looked like I'd be making aprons, and I was good with that. Working in the fashion industry in New York taught me to expect surprises. Moving back to my hometown of Bliss taught me to embrace them. I'd come back home to live in my great-grandmother's old yellow farmhouse right off the town square. I'd opened up Buttons & Bows, a custom-dressmaking shop, and made two bridal gowns (one for my mother, which was more like a cowgirl dress than a fantasy gown), countless bridesmaid dresses and homecoming frocks, period dresses for the Margaret Moffette Lea Pageant and Ball, and holiday creations for a Christmas fashion show.

But at the moment, surrounded by a bevy of red-hatted, purple-attired women, I was being challenged with something completely different from anything I'd done before.

"Aprons," I said, contemplating the idea. I was ready for the challenge. Or lack thereof. I homed in on Delta Lea Mobley, my neighbor—and apparently the leader of Bliss's Red Hat ladies, all of whom currently stood in a half circle around me, looking expectant. Delta Lea was a robust, rosy-cheeked woman with lots of soft curves, but her personality didn't quite match. Although she looked like a middle-aged Mrs. Claus, there was no twinkle in her eye, no laughter in her voice, and no spring in her step.

Her sisters, Coco and Sherri, on the other hand, had the same huggable curves without the abrasive personality. Unfortunately, though, neither of them happened to be present under the big white tent in the church parking lot, so I was left with Delta. "Yes, aprons. I know you're a big-shot fashion designer and all, but I thought—" She broke off, then waved her hands at the other Red Hat ladies. "We thought you could probably make aprons, too. Since you come from simple stock, I'm not sure how creative you can get with them. We want something more than burlap coffee sacks, you know."

Sarcasm dripped from her voice, and I swallowed the anger that had quickly bubbled up. Delta Lea Mobley brought out the worst in me. We'd had a few run-ins since I'd moved back to Bliss, mostly because of Nana's goats. Delta; her husband, Richard; her daughter, Megan; and her mother, Jessie Pearl, all lived next door to me. Thelma Louise, the grand dam of Nana's Sundance Kids herd, had led the other goats straight into the Mobley yard on more than one occasion, and I was guilty of letting it happen by simple association. As if Thelma Louise listened to me. *Nana* was the goat whisperer. *My* Cassidy family charm worked through my dressmaking, allowing the deepest desires of the person I designed for to come true. The goats weren't my domain, not one little bit.

"I'm not a big shot, Delta," I said, knowing her abrasive attitude didn't spill over to the other women in her Red Hat group. I hoped they would back me up.

Cynthia Homer, her ginger hair shimmering in the diffused light of the morning, sucked in a bolstering breath. "We're *hoping* you'll be able to fit it into your schedule," she said. She was shooting daggers at Delta as she continued. "We'd be honored if you'll do our small project, in fact. Just tickled pink."

I ignored Delta and mustered up a healthy dollop of sweetness, dropping it into my voice. "I'd love to make y'all some aprons," I said, realizing the moment I spoke that it was absolutely true.

The tense expressions on the women's faces relaxed. Cynthia clasped her hands together. "Harlow Jane, that's wonderful." She extended her index finger and counted the Red Hat women surrounding me, her mouth moving but no words coming out. "With everyone, that'll be seven aprons. We need 'em finished by next Friday, in time for our first annual Red Hat progressive dinner. Can you do that?"

I barely stopped myself from sputtering. "Next Friday?"

They were just aprons, but still, with my other obligations, that was a tight deadline.

"That should be a piece of cake for you, Harlow," Delta said, stepping forward and shouldering Cynthia out of the way. "Especially for something as pedestrian as aprons. Why, I've seen you whip out homecoming dresses and those bridal gowns in a matter of days. Aprons have to be the easiest thing on the face of the earth for someone with your sewing finesse."

I couldn't decide if she was really trying to be nice, and I was just imagining the healthy doses of sarcasm I heard in her voice. Maybe she was trying to butter me up, but somehow I doubted it.

What I couldn't tell her was that my hesitation wasn't due to how easy or difficult the aprons themselves would be to make. She was right. I could pull off a complicated dress design in a day if I had to. My hesitation stemmed from my charm. I had to get a sense of a person before I knew what design and textiles to use, and a week and a half wasn't a lot of time to get a reading on seven women, volunteer at the church tag sale, which I'd already committed to, and execute the aprons with the finesse Delta was ascribing to me.

"Of course, if you *can't* do it . . ." she said, trailing off.

And instantly I knew that she was challenging me for some reason. She wanted me to fail. "Oh, I can do it," I said, realizing a second too late that I'd fallen smack into her trap. She'd baited me, and I'd fallen, hook, line and sinker.

She shook her head and directed her gaze toward the tent's ceiling, as if she didn't believe I could make seven individualized aprons. "I don't know . . ."

"Well, I do," I said, this time fully aware that I was being played. But I was all in. Delta Lea Mobley would not get the better of me.

Or maybe she already had.

"If you're sure," she said, still not sounding convinced.

"Enough, Delta, good Lord." Cynthia glared at my neighbor. She clenched her firm jaw, her mauve lips thinning with her aggravation. "They're aprons for a progressive dinner, for pity's sake, not *Project Runway* extravaganzas."

"And she said she can do it," Georgia Emmons said. Georgia looked like a former beauty queen with her thick eyelashes, even thicker auburn hair, and hourglass shape. She was like an ageless Mary Tyler Moore. I feared it would catch up to her all at once, she'd age forty years, and she would completely freak when the wrinkles hit full throttle.

They were talking about me as if I weren't front and center. I wanted to wave my hands and shout, "I'm right here! I can hear you!" But instead I kept my mouth shut. I got the distinct feeling that I wasn't the only one Delta Lea Mobley rubbed the wrong way, and the Red Hatters were sticking up for me. Sort of.

"Right," Bennie Cranford added. "We're not walking the runway; it's just dinner."

Randi Martin hung back, clearly uncomfortable at the direction of the conversation, her upper lip pulled down over her teeth. Her short, spiked blond hair made her long, narrow face look longer, and her tan skin accentuated the map of wrinkles that crossed the surface. She'd enjoyed too much sun during her youth, and now her skin was paying the price. "You all shouldn't argue about it," she finally said, her voice small and a trifle shaky. If someone yelled, "Boo!" I feared she'd clutch her heart and keel over.

"You know me," Delta said brusquely. "No-holds-barred. Life's too short not to say what you mean. If Harlow can't do the job, she just needs to say so."

"Just because you think you should say every thought you have doesn't make you right," Cynthia snapped. "And it doesn't mean you can't have some tact and decorum. I'm sure Harlow can manage a few measly aprons—"

"I'm sure I can," I said, finally butting in so they'd stop acting as if I wasn't present, but Cynthia continued as if I hadn't spoken at all.

"—and, Delta, you are the last person who should be giving advice to someone on how they do their job, given your recent—"

"You'd best hold your tongue, Cynthia Homer," Delta snarled, splotchy red spots appearing on her cheeks.

Randi Martin took a step backward, eyeing Delta's clenched fists as if she were afraid Delta might let loose and lay an uppercut on Cynthia's jaw.

"Why? You think people aren't going to find out? Things in this town have a way of coming out. You have something to hide, you'd best do your business in Granbury or Glen Rose or some such. There aren't any secrets in Bliss." Cynthia stepped closer, leaning in and lowering her voice a touch. "And surely you know that man can't keep a dang thing to himself."

Delta's jaw tightened, but she held her tongue, instead turning back to me. "I'll see you at Buffalo Bill's at nine tomorrow morning," Delta said with a jab of her finger in my direction.

I didn't have time to argue before she had turned on her sensible flats and marched off in the opposite direction.

And don't miss where it all
started for Harlow Cassidy in

PLEATING FOR MERCY

Available now from Obsidian!

Rumors about the Cassidy women and their magic had long swirled through Bliss, Texas, like a gathering tornado. For 150 years, my family had managed to dodge most of the rumors, brushing off the idea that magic infused their handwork, and chalking up any unusual goings-on to co-incidence.

But *we* all knew that the magic started the very day Butch Cassidy, my great-great-great-grandfather, turned his back to an ancient Argentinean fountain, dropped a gold coin into it, and made a wish. The Cassidy family legend says he asked for his firstborn child, and all who came after, to live a charmed life, the threads of good fortune, talent, and history flowing like magic from their fingertips.

That magic spilled through the female descendants of the Cassidy line into their handmade tapestries and home-spun wool, crewel embroidery and perfectly pieced and stitched quilts. And into my dressmaking. It connected us to our history, and to one another.

His wish also gifted some of his descendants with

their own special charms. Whatever Meemaw, my great-grandmother, wanted, she got. My grandmother Nana was a goat-whisperer. Mama's green thumb could make anything grow.

Yet no matter how hard we tried to keep our magic on the down-low—so we wouldn't wind up in our own contemporary Texas version of the Salem Witch Trials—people noticed. And they talked.

The townsfolk came to Mama when their crops wouldn't grow. They came to Nana when their goats wouldn't behave. And they came to Meemaw when they wanted something so badly, they couldn't see straight. I was seventeen when I finally realized that what Butch had really given the women in my family was a thread that connected them with others.

But Butch's wish had apparently exhausted itself before I was born. I had no special charm, and I'd always felt as if a part of me was missing because of it.

Moving back home to Bliss made the feeling stronger.

Meemaw had been gone five months now, but the old red farmhouse just off the square at 2112 Mockingbird Lane looked the same as it had when I was a girl. The steep pitch of the roof, the shuttered windows, the old pecan tree shading the left side of the house—it all sent me reeling back to my childhood and all the time I'd spent here with her.

I'd been back for five weeks and had worked nonstop, converting the downstairs of the house into my own designer dressmaking shop, calling it Buttons & Bows. The name of the shop was in honor of my great-grandmother and her collection of buttons.

What had been Loretta Mae's dining room was now

my cutting and work space. My five-year-old state-of-the-art digital Pfaff sewing machine and Meemaw's old Singer sat side by side on their respective sewing tables. An eight-foot-long white-topped cutting table stood in the center of the room, unused as of yet. Meemaw had one old dress form, which I'd dragged down from the attic. I'd splurged and bought two more, anticipating a brisk dressmaking business, which had yet to materialize.

I'd taken to talking to her during the dull spots in my days. "Meemaw," I said now, sitting in my workroom, hemming a pair of pants, "it's lonesome without you. I sure wish you were here."

A breeze suddenly blew in through the screen, fluttering the butter yellow sheers that hung on either side of the window as if Meemaw could hear me from the spirit world. It was no secret that she'd wanted me back in Bliss. Was it so far-fetched to think she'd be hanging around now that she'd finally gotten what she'd wanted?

I adjusted my square-framed glasses before pulling a needle through the pants leg. Gripping the thick synthetic fabric sent a shiver through me akin to fingernails scraping down a chalkboard. Bliss was not a mecca of fashion; so far I'd been asked to hem polyester pants, shorten the sleeves of polyester jackets, and repair countless other polyester garments. No one had hired me to design matching mother and daughter couture frocks, create a slinky dress for a night out on the town in Dallas, or anything else remotely challenging or interesting.

I kept the faith, though. Meemaw wouldn't have brought me back home just to watch me fail.

As I finished the last stitch and tied off the thread, a

flash of something outside caught my eye. I looked past the French doors that separated my work space from what had been Meemaw's gathering room and was now the boutique portion of Buttons & Bows. The window gave a clear view of the front yard, the wisteria climbing up the sturdy trellis archway, and the street beyond. Just as I was about to dismiss it as my imagination, the bells I'd hung from the doorknob on a ribbon danced in a jingling frenzy and the front door flew open. I jumped, startled, dropping the slacks but still clutching the needle.

A woman sidled into the boutique. Her dark hair was pulled up into a messy but trendy bun and I noticed that her eyes were red and tired-looking despite the heavy makeup she wore. She had on jean shorts, a snap-front top that she'd gathered and tied in a knot below her breastbone, and wedge-heeled shoes. With her thumbs crooked in her back pockets and the way she sashayed across the room, she reminded me of Daisy Duke—with a muffin top.

Except for the Gucci bag slung over her shoulder. That purse was the real deal and had cost more than two thousand dollars, or I wasn't Harlow Jane Cassidy.

A deep frown tugged at the corners of her shimmering pink lips as she scanned the room. "Huh—this isn't at all what I pictured."

Not knowing what she'd pictured, I said, "Can I help you?"

"Just browsing," she said with a dismissive wave. She sauntered over to the opposite side of the room, where a matching olive green–and–gold paisley damask sofa and love seat snuggled in one corner. They'd been the nicest pieces of furniture Loretta Mae had owned and some of the few pieces I'd kept. I'd added a plush red velvet settee and a coffee table to the grouping. It was the consultation area of the boutique—though I'd yet to use it.

The woman bypassed the sitting area and went straight for the one-of-a-kind Harlow Cassidy creations that hung on a portable garment rack. She gave a low whistle as she ran her hand from one side to the other, fanning the sleeves of the pieces. "Did you make all of these?"

"I sure did," I said, preening just a tad. Buttons & Bows was a custom boutique, but I had a handful of items leftover from my time in L.A. and New York to display and I'd scrambled to create samples to showcase.

She turned, peering over her shoulder and giving me a once-over. "You don't *look* like a fashion designer."

I pushed my glasses onto the top of my head so I could peer back at her, which served to hold my curls away from my face. Well, *she* didn't look like she could afford a real Gucci, I thought, but I didn't say it. Meemaw had always taught me not to judge a book by its cover. If this woman dragged around an expensive designer purse in little ol' Bliss, she very well might need a fancy gown for something, *and* be able to pay for it.

I balled my fists, jerking when I accidentally pricked my palm with the needle I still held. My smile tightened— from her attitude as well as from the lingering sting on my hand—as I caught a quick glimpse of myself in the freestanding oval mirror next to the garment rack. I looked comfortable and stylish, not an easy accomplishment. Designer jeans. White blouse and color-blocked black-and-white jacket—made by me. Sandals with two-inch heels that probably cost more than this woman's entire wardrobe. Not that I'd had to pay for them, mind you. Even a bottom-of-the-ladder fashion designer employed by Maximilian got to shop at the company's end-of-season sales, which meant fabulous clothes and accessories at a steal. It was a perk I was going to sorely miss.

I kept my voice pleasant despite the bristling sensation I felt creep up inside me. "Sorry to disappoint. What does a fashion designer look like?"

She shrugged, a new strand of hair falling from the clip at the back of her head and framing her face. "Guess I thought you'd look all done up, ya know? Or be a gay man." She tittered.

Huh. She had a point about the gay-man thing. "Are you looking for anything in particular? Buttons and Bows is a custom boutique. I design garments specifically for the customer. Other than those items," I said, gesturing to the dresses she was flipping through, "it's not an off-the-rack shop."

Before she could respond, the bells jingled again and the door banged open, hitting the wall. I made a mental note to get a spring or a doorstop. There were a million things to fix around the old farmhouse. The list was already as long as my arm.

A woman stood in the doorway, the bright light from outside sneaking in around her, creating her silhouette. "Harlow Cassidy!" she cried out. "I didn't believe it could really be true, but it is! Oh, thank God! I desperately need your help!"

Also available from

Melissa Bourbon

Pleating for Mercy

A Magical Dressmaking Mystery

When her great-grandmother passes away, Harlow leaves her
job as a Manhattan fashion designer and moves back to Bliss,
Texas. But soon after she opens Buttons & Bows, a custom
dressmaking boutique in the old farmhouse she inherited,
Harlow begins to feel an inexplicable presence...

One of her first clients is her old friend Josie, who needs a
gown for her upcoming wedding. But when Josie's boss turns
up dead, it starts to look as if the bride-to-be may be wearing
handcuffs instead of a veil. Suddenly, Josie needs a lot more
from Harlow than the perfect dress. Can Harlow find the
real killer—with a little help from beyond?

Available wherever books are sold or at
penguin.com

facebook.com/TheCrimeSceneBooks

OM0062

Also available from

Melissa Bourbon

Deadly Patterns

A Magical Dressmaking Mystery

Bliss, Texas, is gearing up for its annual Winter
Wonderland spectacular and Harlow is planning the main
event: a holiday fashion show being held at an old
Victorian mansion. But when someone is found dead on
the mansion's grounds, it's up to Harlow to catch the
killer—before she becomes a suspect herself.

**"Harlow Jane Cassidy is a
tailor-made amateur sleuth."
—Wendy Lyn Watson**

Available wherever books are sold or at
penguin.com

facebook.com/TheCrimeSceneBooks